trypophobia

/ˌtripə'fōbēə/

noun

noun: **trypophobia**

1. extreme or irrational aversion to or fear of clusters of small holes or bumps.

BOOKS BY A.G. SULLIVAN

THE KATZENSTEIN KIDS
AND THE EYE OF HORUS

THE KATZENSTEIN KIDS
AND THE 12 MINOTAURS

TRYPOPHOBIA
A NOVEL

TATTOOS & POETRY

TRYPO PHOBIA

A NOVEL

A.G. SULLIVAN

To my mother, **A**ngela and father, **G**erald.
For all the years of support and encouragement.
You will forever be the **A.G.** in A.G. Sullivan.

CONTENTS

PART I

"Man is not what he thinks he is, he is what he hides."
André Malraux

1

THE BEAST THAT LURCHES IN THE DARK

Brian Brennan sits outside the office of Dr. Susan Lew, a psychologist whose name he'd pulled from a directory of doctors in the area, one among many selected at random. When he booked the appointment, there were no significant details that stood out about this particular psychologist, nor about the perfectly lovely receptionist who took his details over the phone. There is no reason to think that coming here would bear any major weight on him, but now, sinking into the cushions of a sofa that threatens to engulf him whole, he finds that he's absolutely terrified of what she might find buried in the crevices of his mind.

And more than that… there is the fear that she might find nothing at all.

White noise fills the small waiting area, the sound is manufactured by an electronic device that isn't difficult to locate. The source of all the noise is plugged into the wall. Sitting atop an end table, it looks inconsequential but Brian, the sole occupant in the otherwise quiet room, takes notice of it. He sits upright and hears a low creak, the sofa complains as damaged springs threaten to burst through the frayed leather beneath him. The sound causes him to freeze for a moment, but nothing happens; the seat doesn't buckle beneath him or send pieces of metal flying through the air, and no one enters the room to glare at him disapprovingly. Still, he can't shake the feeling of unease that courses through him as it does in every waiting room. Perhaps the idea that they never change—whether full or empty, busy or quiet, adds to this. Perhaps it's that, unless there is a clock on the wall, a steady tick-tock adding to the hum coming from the machine on the end table across the room, time seems to stand still. Whatever the cause, it makes Brian wish he could be the sort of man who didn't care about being a few minutes late to an appointment, the sort of man who doesn't set ten alarms for fear of being anything less than punctual, for fear of the consequences.

A wry smile comes to Brian's mouth at the irony of wishing to be a different person while sitting on a shrink's sofa. Granted, it isn't the one in her office, but he'd never been one to argue over semantics. A cliché is a cliché in his eyes.

Though a lot smaller than the clamor it emits,

something about the whirring device adds to the unnerving atmosphere of the space, pulling his attention back to it. *Could such a device really work?* Brian wonders. *Are all my secrets hidden behind a thin veil of white noise, waiting for my newly found psychologist to unearth?*

The smirk only grows at this train of thought. He knows what he is about to share will probably seem unbelievable to anyone listening anyway. His imagination runs wild with her potential reactions, and he wonders if her experience in the field has taught her how to maintain a poker face for the patient's sake or if he would be able to read everything on her features before she could stop herself.

"Brian?" A woman's voice breaks through Brian's reverie and he stands expectantly to see her in the doorway of the waiting room, notepad in hand.

"Dr. Lew?"

The woman nods in confirmation, turning back to the hallway she'd entered from and gesturing for him to follow. Glancing over her shoulder with a warm smile, she says: "Please—you can just call me Susan."

Following Susan, it's hard not to notice how attractive she is. The long, silky legs under the navy pencil skirt and her bright eyes are nothing like the picture he'd had in his mind leading up to the appointment. Had it been her title that caused him to imagine spectacles sitting on the bridge of her nose and gray hair pulled into a stern bun on the top of her head? He doesn't know, but the thrum of his pulse heightens the smallest amount as he falls into step behind the woman who definitely does not match that description.

A brass plaque on the door reads "PsyD. Susan Lew."

Light shines through the open door at the end of the corridor and as they enter the room, Brian is greeted with sunshine filtering through the open curtains. One of the tall windows is open slightly, allowing the soft chirps of birds outside to drift inside. Taking the seat closest to him, he sees that there are plants in the room, cleansing the air and adding an unexpected burst of color against otherwise white walls. He doesn't have much experience with psychologists, though he is surprised to find that he appreciates the comfort the room exudes, especially since he'd been expecting the same sterile environment that he'd experienced in every doctor's office he'd ever been in before this one. Dr. Lew's office is different—it doesn't hold the same eeriness as the waiting room, instead, it invites him in the way his study at home does, maybe even more so.

A good first impression, he thinks.

The feeling doesn't last long. Only a few seconds of sitting in silence makes the air around him harden, cementing him in place, albeit on a much comfier chair than the battered leather sofa from the waiting room. The air grows thicker as the minutes pass. Time is impossible to miss in this room because Doctor Lew—Susan, he mentally corrects himself—actually does have a clock on the wall, reminding all her patients that their time with her is limited. It's during these first few moments as Susan takes a seat across from him in an armchair that he's certain is meant for patients, rather than behind the neatly decorated oak desk that dominates the room, that Brian comes to terms with the reality that there may not be anything wrong with this or the waiting room at all—and he knows he can't say the same for himself.

Offering the first words between them since they entered the small space, Susan speaks in her clear voice, calm and full of purpose: "So, Brian… What brings us here today?"

The question seems like an unchallenging one. On the surface. And yet, tension wears through Brian as he reasons with himself, trying to figure out the right words to explain to the woman before him what his problem was—is. In his late thirties, he'd had the gall to think that he had seen all the world had to offer, but now, leaning forward and resting his face in his open hands, he knows better. Deep lines of worry have begun to set in around his eyes, tainting an otherwise handsome appearance.

With a deep breath and a single stroke upward, Brian slides his hands back over his forehead, combing his fingers through his hair. It was now or never. He couldn't keep hiding forever. Raising his head, he begins to speak. His first words slip from his lips with an unintentional snicker, as if what he's about to say might be amusing. Only, he knows it's devoid of mirth; a moment of unsound humor if anything.

If there was ever a place to reveal a moment of madness, Brian thinks it could be this one.

"You know, I don't even know where to begin… I never considered myself a man with problems. You know what I mean, *real* problems. The stuff that someone would need to talk to a professional about."

He pauses, holding back the laughter that threatens to

spill forth as he looks around the room. What does he call this then? He isn't exactly here for pleasantries.

"Things were fine until this past week or so," Brian continues. "My life has been rather good overall. Yeah, I'm divorced and I'm a single dad, but I'm doing better than most. I mean, everyone has issues of some kind, don't they?"

Her voice as calm as ever, Susan interjects. "Let me start with a statement I like to share with people who come here for the first time. A British psychoanalyst named Nina Coltart once called it 'the beast that lurches in the dark.' She believed that when people understand the things that are negatively affecting them, it is relatively easy to make the changes necessary to improve the situation."

Brian watches her, waiting for her to continue. Things are never that simple. There's always a *but*.

"However, when we do not know what's causing those negative imbalances—be it depression, anxiety, and other mental illnesses—we become, in a way, victims of ourselves. We have no power to change the thing that is making us suffer. So, there's this unknown part of us that chooses to remain busy and distracted, hurrying us along, only to allow the things we suffer from to follow us. These things will be an invisible shadow from which we cannot escape, always in the background. After all, how can we escape from something if we haven't even admitted its presence?"

The tension in Brian's face falls away and his easy smile returns as he looks at the psychologist, beaming at her ability to offer him some clarity. Another thing he didn't expect. The woman is full of surprises.

Maybe coming here wasn't a bad idea. It's been nothing like I thought it would be so far. And maybe that's a good thing.

He can't quite put his finger on what it was about her words, perhaps an old memory reignited, offering him a place to begin after all.

"When I was a boy, I would play this game…" He begins again. "I called it the Scare Game."

2

NINE DAYS EARLIER

The dark doesn't stop Brian from making out the sensual curves of his girlfriend Rosa as her body grinds against his. On the contrary, seeing her naked silhouette is as sexy, if not sexier than ever while they make love in the shadows. His view of her is the best one he can ask for—one from beneath her, his own naked body flat against the bed. With his hands wrapped around her hips, fingers pressing into her silky soft flesh, all he can do is enjoy the pleasure of being inside her. Reaching down, Rosa presses her hands against his chest and as she rolls her head back with a gasp, Brian can tell she's close. The same sensations shudder through him, but he wants her to get there first, so he moves a little faster.

Sliding his hands up her body, he can feel the sheen of sweat that lingers on her skin and a trail of goosebumps rises in the wake of his fingertips. She arches back, pushing her chest forward when he cups her full breasts in his hands. The deep moan she gives is as exciting as the weight of her body on top of his. Rolling his thumbs over her hard nipples, she releases a breath and a shudder. The closer she gets, the more erratic the movement of her hips becomes and Brian's hips have a mind of their own as he presses deeper, knowing that she's going to reach her climax any second.

"Oh, baby," she whispers.

She's going to kill me, he thinks, watching her eyes roll back in pleasure. *Is it possible to die from pure ecstasy?*

He didn't think it could get any hotter until just then. With a slip of his hand from her breast, he reaches up behind her and wraps a handful of hair around his fist, tugging slightly. Even if it weren't for the whimper that escapes her full lips, he knows she likes that—he likes it too.

Proving to him how much she enjoys it, Rosa releases a low and breathy sigh, "Ahhh…"

Her body shakes above his and he can feel her core tightening as she trembles in his lap. With her hair in his hand, Brian is blessed with the sight of her face as her orgasm consumes her, the way she shuts her eyes and her mouth falls open. When she comes back down from her high, Brian releases her and she falls onto his chest moments later, her silky hair falling over him like a curtain.

He can't hold back any longer as the sounds of her pleasure roll through him like a tidal wave and he's intoxicated by the scent of coconut, which he knows to be her favorite type of shampoo, now that her head is buried in the curve of his neck and shoulder. Shutting his eyes and grinding gently against her, he groans his release deeply before finally coming to a stop.

Afterward, she gives that spot where her head is buried a gentle kiss and the sweet action brings a smile to Brian's mouth. In post-coital bliss, their climaxes dissipating, Rosa rolls off and onto the bed beside Brian, wrapping her legs around his.

"That was so good," Rosa whispers breathlessly. "You know just how to get me off!"

Brian kisses the curve of her neck in appreciation, whispering back, "I love the way you ride me, baby." Brian grins when she squirms against his side. He loves what he can do to her with his words alone.

The two barely have a chance to allow themselves the pleasure of lingering in this moment, their hearts still racing and their nerves still alight with sensation, when an ear-splitting scream sounds out through the house. His heart still pounding loudly in his chest, Brian is out of bed in seconds, whipping his arm out from under Rosa so quickly that she is sent rolling off the other side of the bed. Nimble, she springs to her feet rather than falling onto the floor, her eyes wide. With haste, Brian grabs his boxers off the ground and shoves his legs into them, urgency coursing through him as he heads toward the direction of the noise, every instinct on red alert.

The scream came from his son's bedroom.

Another scream rings out and Brian's feet stomp against the floor heavily as he races down the hall, trying to force his body to move faster, past the room they converted into Rosa's art studio, past the stairs that lead to the first-floor landing and all the frames hanging on the wall, past the faces within those frames that were all cast in shadows that make it look like their eyes are following him as he runs. There's no time to focus on that—he can see the doorway to his son's bedroom at the end of the hall, the slightest glimmer of moonlight across the wall because his boy believes himself too big for nightlights, though he never sleeps with the curtains fully closed. Apart from this, all the lights are out and Brian's breath catches with the thought that a stranger may be inside their house right now. For the first time, he worries that they may have a weapon and all he has is a pair of plain boxers. It's enough to make him freeze outside the last door before the end of the hall; one of the bathrooms. Staring at the shadows on the wall up ahead as if they might move at any second, Brian tries to slow his breathing and takes a careful step forward again as his eyes begin to adjust to the darkness. There were no items he could grab on the way, not without turning back, but the element of surprise could be on his side if he was quiet enough.

A chill whistles past Brian's chest as he steps past the bathroom door, doing his best to tread lightly, avoiding that one plank that creaks. He bristles at the cold breeze and from the corner of his eye, catches a movement. The hairs on the back of his neck stand up. With a gulp, Brian turns slowly to look into the dark room.

It's all he can do to hold back the yelp that threatens to bubble up his throat as his eyes make contact with a set of glowing red embers; a pair of crimson eyes are trained on him. The rest of the face is hard to make out, the profile hidden in a shadow, but a distinct rush of terror emanates from the other end of the room, as if blowing through the window on the icy breeze and clutching Brian by the throat. Without thinking, Brian flicks the bathroom light on hurriedly.

Brian's eyes shut reflexively as the brightness hits and his pupils take a moment to dilate. After he blinks away the spots of color that invade his retinas, the moment he can see clearly again comes with utter disbelief and overwhelming confusion. The gruesome face he saw outside the window is nothing more than a tree, its gnarled branches are devoid of leaves and reach through the blinds as if they were alive. His mind is playing tricks on him. *It has to be, right?*

Still, Brian can't shake the chill that runs through him at the sight of the window. Even now, standing in the doorway, he's certain there's someone—maybe something—watching him. A tingling at the base of his skull tells him so. It makes more sense for the face to be a figment of his imagination, for it to be a manifestation of his fear playing tricks on him, but Brian isn't so sure. He doesn't have long to dwell though. Another scream pierces through the house and he jumps, cursing himself for wasting precious milliseconds as he dashes out of the bathroom, leaving the window behind and the bathroom light on.

His mind gives him no respite for those last few steps, but the thoughts are fired through his brain with such speed that he knows if anyone were to ask him what was on his mind, he would not be able to tell them. The only thing he's aware of is the terrible, unwelcome fear that they bring. Fear that comes with an intensity that, as a grown man, he never thought himself capable of feeling.

Once he's finally through the door, Brian's eyes immediately fall upon his son, standing beside the single bed in the center of the room. Before moving toward his son, Brian takes in the rest of the room as best he can in the dark, quickly determining that there is no one else in sight. In the time he takes to do this, his 11-year-old starts to writhe frantically where he stands, his arms flailing and swatting in every direction like he's having some kind of fit. Brian can scarcely believe his eyes—he'd been certain he'd discover that there was either an attacker or that his son was having a bad dream.

Faced with neither of those things, he isn't sure what to do. *If it were a seizure, Ben would be on the floor, wouldn't he? What is going on?*

Another cry rings out as Ben's hand smacks down against his own face and Brian leaps forward, wrapping his arms around his son's, forcing the flailing motions to come to a stop. "Ben! It's okay! You're okay…"

Although he's lowered his voice, his words do nothing to calm his son down. On the contrary, Ben takes up wriggling around in his arms like a worm, reluctant to be restrained and doing his best to escape from his father's grip—he's making a surprisingly good effort too. Brian is shocked to find that the boy's body is freezing, his skin cold to the touch. He finally frees himself of Brian's hold, only to throw his hands out at his own skin once again, swatting and smacking down hard enough to leave small pink handprints behind.

"Something's crawling on me!" Ben shouts. "I can feel crawling all over me!"

The room is still dark, but Brian believes his eyes to be fully adjusted. At the sound of his son's shouts, they widen further, practically protruding from their sockets. *Surely there must be something crawling on Ben's skin. Why else would he be so upset?* But Brian sees nothing.

"Dad!" Ben screeches, his pitch heightening to the point that it hurts Brian's ears. "I feel spiders! Spiders are crawling all over me! Get them off!"

Perhaps it's shock that prevents him from moving but Brian can only watch, frozen, as his son finally rips free of any hold on him.

A boy in utter horror deconstructs in front of his father, screaming over and over.

"Get them off, get them off, they're all over me, get them off!"

The room is thrown into sudden brightness, blinding Brian, as Rosa arrives and hits the light switch. "Pobrecito," she mutters. Brian knows the statement to mean poor boy. "He is having a nightmare!"

Brian blinks, an argument on the tip of his tongue. This is no nightmare—at least, not for Ben. That much, he knows. Before he can say anything, goosebumps travel up the base of his spine all the way to his neck and his skin goes cold at the eerie, unpleasant feeling of something tiny creeping up the skin of his arm.

The crawling. Brian can feel it too.

Looking down, Brian sees the tiny creature; a small red ant makes its way up his arm, quickly put to a stop as Brian's hand flies down and connects with the skin. The smack is like a wake-up call and as he dusts away the insect, Brian looks back up at Ben. Sure enough, there he stands, covered from head to toe in small red ants. They dance and weave in frantic lines all over his skin.

The sight of the bugs sends Brian into overdrive. He grabs a hold of his son's pajama top and tugs it off his body, followed by his pajama pants. He moves as fast as he can, swatting gently at his son's skin to get those things off of him without causing the boy any pain. His face, hair, neck, arms, legs, his entire body...

Covered.

Brian's hands are trembling as he attempts to help Ben and, glancing beyond the shivering frame of his 11-year-old son, he is wholly shocked to see that they are everywhere. The ants are crawling within Ben's bedsheets, like minuscule dark granules of pepper dancing across and in between the creases of his child's bedding as far as the eye could see. A trail of them leads up the wall, around the edge of the ceiling.

Before he can find the start of the trail, Ben cries out again, his eyes scrunched up and his face red. "Hurry! Hurry, please, they're biting me!"

"Oh my God, he *is* covered in ants!" Rosa shouts as she,

too, realizes the source of Ben's panic.

Tearing his eyes away from the trail of ants climbing up the wall, Brian lifts his half-naked son off the ground, cradling him and hurrying toward the bathroom one door down.

The light is still on in the bathroom and Brian's eyes unconsciously flicker toward the open window, seeing nothing but the gnarled tree branches twisting in toward him from earlier. No glowing red eyes—those were plainly imprinted in his memory. He gently sets his son down in the bathtub where he can be sure he'll get rid of all of the ants and pauses only to close the window and the blinds. His paranoia is at an all-time high—the fear and adrenaline that came from hearing his son's scream still pulsing through him; the ants have been no less terrifying than an attacker being in the house would have been. Brian didn't know what to make of the current circumstances. He was pretty sure ants didn't do things like this all the time.

Still, it could have been worse. No armed robbers or anything like that.

An ache goes through his chest at the sight of his little boy shivering in the bathtub, knowing that this will still leave some kind of trauma behind. With the window closed, Brian opens up the faucets and adjusts the temperature of the water until it's warm before aiming the showerhead at his son's body and watching as the reddish spots fall off his body into the bath. They don't have time to climb anywhere else and Brian ensures that the flow follows them until they're gone, aiming the jets of water downward as they wash away, nowhere to go but down the drain with the current.

"What's going on?" Morgan, Brian's 13-year-old daughter, appears in the doorway, watching Brian rinse her little brother off with furrowed brows. She rubs one eye with a scrunched-up fist. "What happened to Ben?"

Brian doesn't take his gaze off the ants as they wash away. How is he supposed to explain this to his daughter? He isn't even able to understand it himself. Thankfully, Rosa spares him the trouble.

"Come on, honey, come with me." Brian turns back in time to see Rosa's olive hands on his daughter's shoulders, leading her away from the bathroom.

The water is running clear by this point, so Brian puts the showerhead down, lowering the water pressure slightly so it doesn't spray upward in every direction and drench everything. Carefully, he prods around Ben's body. The poor kid simply sits there, breathing heavily, as Brian searches for more ants.

There are none left, satisfied, Brian turns the water off before grabbing two towels from the cabinet beneath the sink. Setting one down on the floor, he kneels down and holds the other open in his outstretched arms. A shivering Ben climbs out of the bath and into it, allowing his father to dry him off. In another room, he hears the vacuum cleaner turn on. While drying him off, Brian sees that there are several red marks on Ben's skin where the ants bit him, but he notes it's nothing a little calamine lotion won't cure.

Ben seems content to look into the bathroom mirror while Brian dries him off, his eyes unfocused. As Brian watches, the 11-year-old picks at his nose and suddenly, his eyes go wide. From his left nostril, an ant crawls out and down the side of his face. Ben gasps for breath, his body going rigid under Brian's hands.

"Whoa," Brian murmurs. Grabbing a tissue from the box on the edge of the basin, he puts it up to Ben's nose. "It's okay. Blow."

Ben does as he's told and blows into the tissue, shutting his eyes with the effort of blowing as hard as he possibly can. The vacuum shuts off at this moment and the sound of Ben blowing his nose is like a trumpet. If it weren't for the seriousness of the situation, Brian might have laughed. Instead, he pulls out another tissue and has his son blow into it again, clearing his nose of any ants that may be taking refuge inside.

No sooner has he pulled the tissue away and tossed it into the bin does an ant crawl out of Ben's ear hole. Ben sees the movement in the mirror at the same time as he feels it, his eyes focused on the sight. He begins to tremble once more, a low whimper coming from his mouth.

"It's okay, buddy. I'll get it," Brian says, hoping to keep his son calm long enough for him to retrieve a Q-tip from the cabinet. With it, he cleans Ben's ears out, shushing him comfortingly. The sight of two ants on the cotton bud makes his stomach turn and he tosses it into the bin before his son can see. "It's okay, Ben, I got them all off. It's okay." Ben says nothing, but Brian spots the tremor in his hands. Grabbing a third clean towel, he wraps it around his son's shoulders and hugs him close, rubbing his hand up and down Ben's back in an attempt to warm him up again. "My brave boy."

A few moments later, Rosa enters the bathroom. "I put Morgan back to bed. I also replaced the sheets and cleaned up everything I could in there."

"Thank you, love. I appreciate your help." Brian stands. "Would you mind helping Ben dress?"

"Of course not," Rosa murmurs. Concern is written all over her face as Brian turns away, heading back to his son's bedroom while Rosa gets clothes out of the dresser.

Walking into the room is a surreal experience. Brian is hyper-aware of everything around him from the glowing multi-colored lights that glint off last year's science project to the slight movement of the curtains as the cold breeze blows through the cracks in the windowpane. What he's looking for, he doesn't exactly know. Glancing up at the ceiling where he had previously seen the trail of ants makes him feel foolish and he absently considers calling an exterminator to come and investigate for him. Who does he think he is? He has no experience dealing with this sort of thing, no idea of what he should be looking for.

Ben's bedroom feels completely different from before thanks to Rosa's handiwork; vacuum lines run along the carpet. The bed has been made with fresh linen, all Ben's toys have been packed into boxes and stored on shelves, and a soft vanilla scent lingers in the air. All but one of the ants seem to be gone and there are no obvious signs to justify the infestation—at least, none that Brian can see. Ignoring the insect, he begins to search the room, knowing that his girlfriend has probably ensured he won't find anything. Getting down on his hands and knees to check underneath the bed, he can't see any pieces of food or crumbs, nor the telltale stickiness of spilled soda, though that makes sense anyway since he and Rosa rarely let the kids take food out of the dining areas of the house. That's part of what's confusing him so much. There should be no reason to have such an infestation, let alone out of nowhere like this.

The odds of Rosa having gotten every single nook and cranny in the time he bathed Ben didn't seem high but maybe he shouldn't underestimate her. He's pretty certain there's nothing more to find and with that, he heads over to the most fascinating thing he's come across since he returned to the bedroom. An ant doing the most peculiar thing and for a few minutes, Brian simply watches it, wondering what on earth brought it and the rest of its friends to torment his son.

There's a hole in the wall. Not a small hole either, nothing that a thumbtack or nail would leave behind. No, this hole is a bit bigger.

If I had to compare it to anything...

Brian didn't want to compare it to anything just then but the thought did not leave when he wished it would. Now that it had reared its head, it wanted to linger. If Brian really had to compare the size to anything, he would hate to admit that it looked to be the diameter of a finger. A young boy's finger. A boy about Ben's age.

Odd, he thinks.

Ben slowly trudges into the room, wearing fresh, slightly creased, pajamas. Brian's hand swings out to quickly squash the last insect he's been eyeing before his son can see it. From afar, the ant looks like a mark on the wall.

Ben's arms and neck are spotted with calamine lotion and Brian can see that he's visibly shaken, reluctant to be in the room at all.

"They're all gone," Brian says, waving his arm around the room. "Rosa cleaned every single one up. And there are new sheets on the bed, too!"

Ben doesn't look comforted by this news.

"Perhaps you'd rather camp out on the sofa bed in the TV room?" Brian offers.

His son gives a weak half-smile before his eyes flick toward the hole in the wall.

"Did you make this hole?"

Ben shakes his head. "I've never noticed that hole before."

Glancing between his son and the hole in the wall, Brian finds it difficult to believe. It's the perfect size for Ben to have made and it couldn't have just appeared out of thin air. His son must have made it and didn't want to tell him the truth for fear of getting into trouble. The closer Brian looks at the hole, however, the stranger it seems. The edges of the hole fray outwards and, on the floor in front of it, there are drywall particles and dust sprinkled along the base board. It's almost as if—Brian cringes internally—the hole was pushed out from the inside.

Odd, he thinks yet again.

"Do you think that's how they got in?" Ben asks, interrupting his disturbing thoughts.

"I think so," Brian says honestly.

"Can we pull the sofa bed out now? The hole is scaring me."

In that moment, Brian realizes how traumatizing the evening must have been for his son and that it must be taking a toll on him. "I have an idea. Come with me."

They trek down toward the garage and, with Ben close by his side, Brian retrieves a roll of duct tape from his tool bench. He pauses momentarily, checking out the rest of the tools scattered on the bench to determine if there was anything else that could help them. Nothing catches his immediate attention, the only thing of note being that his cordless power drill is plugged into the charger on the wall. He'll need to unplug that later. Impossible as it was, he couldn't help but think the hole in Ben's room could easily have been created with a power drill. Only, he knows that's not possible.

Ben is staring at the drill too.

"This will do the trick!" Brian says, holding the duct tape up.

Together, the two return to Ben's bedroom and head straight for the wall. Pulling a piece of tape off the roll, Brian places it over the hole in a clean vertical line, pressing and smoothing it down with both hands. For good measure, he pulls off a second piece and covers the first horizontally.

"Gotta press it on real good," Brian says, giving his son a gentle pat on the head in the hopes that he feels less scared of the hole and the ants. "Now they won't be able to get in anymore."

Knowing that duct tape isn't enough of a comfort to keep Ben in his room, the two leave, switching the light off behind them. In the TV room, Ben watches as his father pulls out the sofa bed before he climbs in. Brian tucks his boy in and can't help but notice that his son is still trembling slightly. He makes sure the blankets are tight around his boy.

"Okay, buddy," he whispers. "Let's try and get some sleep. You have nothing to fear."

"Can you leave the hall light on?" Ben asks quietly.

"Of course," Brian nods, turning out the main light in the same breath. *Is it time to get Ben a night light?*

•••

Ben doesn't know how he's going to fall asleep. Almost as soon as his dad tucks him in, walking down the hall and leaving him in the dark, an awareness that he's alone settles in on him. Something about being alone feels dangerous, so he tries to stay as still as he possibly can, his mind racing with imagery from the night. The hole, the duct tape, the hole again, the ants everywhere and all over him, the biting, the appearance of his father in the doorway, and the panic that came when he stood there doing nothing while he screamed over and over again. Ben shuts his eyes, trying to block it all out, squeezing them as hard as he can.

Preoccupied as he is with his thoughts, Ben barely notices that he's twitching. He doesn't see or feel the scratches his own hands leave against his skin. The smallest of movements against the fibers of the blanket feels eerily like things crawling on him again.

Eventually, he pulls the blanket up and over his head, hiding away.

•••

Brian stands at the far end of the hallway, keenly aware

of every time his son twitches and moves, tossing and turning. As he is about to enter his bedroom, Brian hears the first subtle sound of his boy trying to get comfortable, the scratching of his boy's nails against what is now incredibly sensitive skin. His stomach turns and a painful pressure spreads throughout his gut. The knowledge that his son is suffering hurts him. His own thoughts are as rampant as Ben's.

Is he reliving the evening in his mind? Or is he just plain scared, traumatized? Can he feel the crawling sensations on his body, even though they aren't real?

A child's trauma is a parent's trauma, Brian knows. And all the things that trauma can bring to a young mind haunt Brian. The disturbing thought that this could be little more than the beginning enters his mind before he can stop it and slip away, filled with quiet dread.

3

BIG CRACKS

*M*onday.

The following morning is a rush of events as Brian, Rosa, Ben, and Morgan all wake up, shower, and get dressed before gathering downstairs in the dining room to eat and get ready for their days. Their morning ritual of attempting to do all the things that needed to be done before Brian and the kids left the house didn't change despite everything that had happened the previous evening, though everyone seemed groggier than usual. Rosa had taken an extra ten-minute snooze before getting out of bed with an exaggerated groan to prepare breakfasts and lunches for the household while Brian is fueled by the same thing he is every morning, a good old-fashioned fear of his boss. It's hard to tell how Morgan feels because, for the most part, she carries teenage angst and attitude with her everywhere she goes now, accompanied by earphones and a permanent disinterested expression meant to deter anyone from interacting with her. It's only when the three are in the kitchen, helping themselves to the morning's selection, that anyone says anything at all.

"How are you feeling, Ben?" Brian asks as his son walks into the room. Rosa and Morgan both look up from what they're doing.

Ben nods, but says nothing. It's unusual to see him so quiet and somber. Brian barely knows what to say; his son is hardly ready for school, sloppily dressed, and the deadened expression on his face is more than a little concerning. He looks as if he hasn't slept a wink. Every movement Ben makes is slow, measured, as if when he sits down and spoons cereal into his mouth, it's because he has to rather than wants to.

Turning his attention to Morgan, Brian catches onto what she's wearing. A T-shirt clings to her and a pair of short-shorts reveals more than three-quarters of her legs. He knew this age was coming, but he didn't expect it to arrive so soon. "Shorts, really? I know we live in Arizona, but it is March."

"I already asked Alexa what the weather is going to be like today and she said it's going to be seventy-six degrees," Morgan chirps with a confident smile.

Brian shakes his head and looks over at Rosa in disbelief. He's only faced with a smile, followed by a whisper, "She's your daughter."

"Am I going to mom's tonight?" Ben asks, his voice quiet and sluggish.

"No dummy, it's Monday," Morgan snaps. "You go to mom's house on Friday. Why can't you remember that?!"

"Shut up! I'm not a dummy!" In an instant, Ben is angry, and it's the most alive he's been all morning. "Do you want me to hit you?"

"Both of you, stop it immediately," Brian interrupts. "Morgan, don't you talk to your brother that way."

"I'm going to kill you," Ben says, ignoring his father and throwing himself toward his sister, his leg knocking into the table and sending his spoon flying out of his cereal bowl and onto the table with a splatter of milk on the tablecloth. "Stop looking at me!"

Brian stands at this point, stepping in front of Morgan. "Ben, stop it. You're making things worse than they need to be. You can't speak to your sister that way either."

"Yeah..." Morgan says, her voice is distant and less confident than before.

Rosa is in the middle of preparing lunches for both children to take to school. The expression on her face says everything Brian feels. She's as disturbed by Ben's outburst as he is.

"Mijo," she says softly. "You can't act that way with your sister. It's very disrespectful."

"Why am I always the one in trouble?" Ben mutters. "She's the one who started it."

Brian looks between his children. "You're both wrong. Morgan shouldn't call you a dummy and you can't try and hit her or ever say that you'll kill her. Do you understand me?"

Both kids, teeth gritted, nod their heads.

"All right, now both of you apologize to one another," he says, calming down.

"I'm sorry," they murmur in unison.

"Okay," Brian breathes. "Good. Now, Ben, do you understand what I'm saying?"

Ben nods again.

"Do you feel better?" Brian finally asks him, opening one of the kitchen cupboards and pulling out a bottle of capsules titled Methylphenidate. His son doesn't answer as he places the pill onto a teaspoon of applesauce. Guiding it toward the 11-year-old, he asks, "Will you take this please?"

Ben opens his mouth, swallows the pill, and storms out of the kitchen without another word.

"That should help," Brian says, looking over at Rosa, who says nothing as she packs sandwiches into lunchboxes and then lunchboxes into backpacks.

Not long after, it's time to leave for school. Morgan is already in the SUV by the time Brian calls Ben down, but his son doesn't come when he's called. Brian already knows Ben is still upset and, with a sigh, he heads up the stairs with a reluctant glance at the watch on his wrist.

The frames hanging along the wall are far less eerie in the light of day, but Brian doesn't feel any better walking past them and he knows his son doesn't feel any better today either.

Ben is sitting on the edge of his bed when Brian enters

the room, his face pulled into a grimace that must surely hurt to keep wearing for so long, and his small arms are crossed over his chest. There are tiny splotches of calamine on them and Brian softens as he goes to sit next to his son.

"You had a rough night, buddy," he says softly.

Ben nods, his frown ever-present. Brian thinks for a moment about being Ben's age and a story comes to mind, so he starts telling it.

"You know, when I was your age, my brother Paul had this huge terrarium. This thing was full of everything. It had a bowl of water in it and Paul added dirt, moss, leaves, and small logs… It looked like a rainforest in a glass box," Brian describes a long-forgotten memory. "And he filled it with everything too. He would catch stuff from all over the yard and from the pond near our house."

"I know what you're doing," Ben says, scrunching up his nose.

"Oh? What's that?"

"You're trying to make me laugh with some kind of funny story," the kid says skeptically. "It's not going to work. I'm still mad."

"Well, let's see about that, shall we?" Brian tries to hide the grin creeping in. "Okay, so, this thing was full, right? I mean, it had lizards, toads, spiders, worms, beetles, and ants. He put everything and anything he found in this thing."

"How big was it?"

Brian stretched his arms out, spreading his hands as far as he could. "It was pretty big. I wasn't bigger than you are right now and it seemed huge to me."

In spite of himself, Ben's eyes widen in interest.

"Now," Brian continues. "Unlike my brother, I hate bugs. Hate them. Spiders are the worst."

"Ants are my worst," Ben says, letting out a huff that was almost a laugh, but not quite.

The shift in his mood is a subtle one. An almost laugh is better than none at all in Brian's eyes. He nods understandingly and gently pats Ben's shoulder once.

"So, my brother and I shared a room..." Brian continues, seeing Ben's shoulders slump slightly, "...Which means that I, of course, had to live with this terrarium of terror. Well, one night I climbed into my bed and I looked over and I saw the terrarium..." He pauses for effect. "And it was cracked open. The whole side was totally broken. I was instantly freaked out."

"What happened to all the spiders and bugs and stuff?" Ben gasps.

"That's what I asked! I jumped up," Brian leaps off the edge of Ben's bed, spinning to face him, his legs in a wide stance and his arms above his head. "Then I stood on my bed to keep my feet off the floor and I cried out to my brother, 'the terrarium is broken open and all the spiders and bugs are going to get out!' Paul looked at me like he had no worries or cares in the world and simply told me that the glass box had broken that morning." Waving his arms in the air the same way his brother had all those years ago, Brian adds, "Paul shouted, 'everything inside got out and crawled everywhere!'"

Ben's mouth drops open.

"I know," Brian says, shaking his head with a face full

of wonder. "I couldn't sleep all night."

Ben stares at his father and then, giving Brian hope, lets out a big laugh. It was the kind that rumbled through the belly. Brian could only look on, smiling.

I knew I could get him to laugh again.

A few minutes later, they are all strapped into the SUV and on the road to school, but the clock on the dashboard is in his peripheral the whole way there—he, a man whose punctuality at times faltered, is running late.

•••

It's as if the moderately priced watch sitting on his wrist has its own pulse, thumping gently against the inside of his wrist. Brian knows that's not possible, that the subtle ticking couldn't actually be felt through the stainless-steel backing of the timepiece resting loosely against his skin, nor heard from where his arms swung back and forth at his sides. The traffic of the street is far louder than a watch. The ten-minute walk from the three-story parking garage to the office building is as brisk as it can be without making him sweat any more than he already is. His dress shirt already feels tight, beginning to stick to what was quickly moistening skin while he tries not to think about whether he had soaked through the fabric yet. He hopes not.

Anxiety fills Brian's body and the ticking and his heartbeat begin to blend into one another, getting faster and faster.

Hate walking into work late.

"It shouldn't even be that much of an issue," he snaps to himself, causing a woman walking past to glance sideways at him. He quickens his step.

31

The irritation hasn't eased. *I work hard*, his thoughts press in on him. *I'm a professional. Why can't my boss just have some flexibility, let me get to work, and do my job? Everything gets done.*

But of course, he doesn't. The company where Brian works is called Foster Merrick Engineering. Although the company's marketing and services are young and trendy, its principal is an old-school kind of guy, an older man who everyone from the highest of positions down to the grunts at the bottom of the corporate chain knew Martin would be working well into retirement, locked into the mentality that he would be running FME until they take him out on his back, cold and gray. It's a joke he makes regularly during quarterly meetings.

Brian knows how this part works, what the routine is. He has been late several times in the past, much to his chagrin, and he already knows that his stress is about to heighten and it's only when he slips into his seat only when he settles down at his desk and carries out the pretense of having been there since 8 a.m. sharp that he'll know if his tardiness was noticed. *Should it feel like a crime? No, probably not.* Nevertheless, the fear of getting caught doing something he shouldn't be rushes through him. There's no thrill in it. He wonders if his boss will be in today or if his door is closed, whether he'll be in a meeting or on a phone call. Is he worrying for no reason?

Entering the building on the ground-floor level, Brian turns left toward the elevator. He's on autopilot as he steps into it, noting that it's empty. The lobby is bustling with a combination of employees, new clients, and prospective clients. Brian thinks that he could be the only person from his department moving around at this time. Everyone else is probably knee-deep in a job they don't want to be doing. He keys in for the fourth floor and as the elevator travels up, his stomach goes down, sinking further into the pit of worry his insides are made of. With a gentle ding, the elevator comes to a halt and he steps out of it with a softness to his step, as if sneaking through the lobby is remotely possible.

With a low "good morning" to Christina, the receptionist, Brian hurries on through to his desk. She arches her brow, but Brian misses it because he's focused on the ground and the sight of one shoe stepping in front of the next along a clean, cheap maroon carpet. The clock hanging on the wall behind Christina served as a reminder of his lack of punctuality, displaying a digital 8:14 a.m. Before Christina can get a word in, he's off, maintaining the softness of his walk and acting casual.

He can't believe it when he finally arrives at his desk, seating himself in the cubicle and powering the computer up so that he can log in for the day. It's been too exciting a morning compared to the usual M.O. The operating system's log flashes across the screen as the machine whirs to life and Brian allows himself a long exhale of relief, some of the anxiety lifting from his shoulders.

Just then, before he can confirm the password that would see him past his login screen, his boss, none other than Martin Merrick, approaches. Regardless of his balding head and the liver spots on the backs of his hands, Martin is formidable. He wears a suit with thread work so fine

Brian knows it must cost more than his entire paycheck and carries himself with confidence——arrogance? On his face is a scowl, though that's nothing Brian isn't used to.

Martin pointedly checks his watch in front of Brian. "You're late!"

Brian has nothing to say, he *is* late. The prudent thing, it seems to him, is not to make excuses. It was bad enough that his hopes of slipping in and easing his anxiety had been dashed.

"Did you read the email from Scott at Hagstone?" Martin growls, frustration appearing in the form of creases at the corners of his mouth and eyes. He knows Brian hasn't had a chance to open up the email. Martin doesn't wait for a reply. "Well, it looks like we've got structural cracks at the crusher slab. You need to give him a call and get to the bottom of this! Sign out a car and drive up there if you have to, but let them know that we are working on it A.S.A.P!"

Martin walks away while speaking, the last instruction practically yelled at Brian as his boss goes back to his own office. Heat travels up Brian's face and neck and he knows without seeing a mirror that he must be red, flushing with pure embarrassment. The guilt of being late catches up to him again and he shakes himself off as Martin disappears. He needs to pull himself together and focus. Brian is relieved to find that it's a lot easier to push his family to the back of his mind when he's behind his desk. He opens all the programs necessary for doing his job and checks on a few catch-up items while waiting for other things to load up in the background. Remembering the way Ben had laughed that morning has stuck with him as he throws himself into his work and soon, the anxiety of being late starts to fade away.

After logging his details into the system, Brian signs out one of the company cars and, having hardly been in the office for 20 minutes, leaves to make the drive over to Hagstone Mining. The new crusher building is still currently under construction, so inspecting the structural cracks before they move beyond the foundation is of the highest importance. With Martin as frustrated as he is, Brian can only imagine how angry Scott must be. He'd avoided the email before signing out. Whatever it is, he'll find out about it when he's on the site. His boss made it pretty apparent that there was no time to waste.

When he arrives at the construction site, the drills are at a standstill but a persistent clank-clank-clank sounds out as someone or something hammers against metal in the nearby area. Brian can't see where it's coming from, but in the distance, he sees the crusher building. It will be a short drive there, once he's geared up and has met with Scott. The site coordinator is easier to spot than anything else— he stands out with his safety vest, and his helmet a darker color than everyone else's. Another vest in the same shade hangs over his arm and a second helmet is hooked to his waist.

Brian recognizes him and walks over, greeting him simply by name, "Manny."

"Hey, Brennan. I'll need you to get these on."

The coordinator's been expecting him. He hands Brian the spare vest and helmet and begins walking away while

Brian puts both on. It takes him a second to realize he's meant to be following and he hurries to catch up, gravel crunching noisily beneath his feet.

"Hop in. This is the truck we're taking over to the crusher," Manny wastes no time on small talk, leading Brian into another vehicle; this time, a service truck with dirt on its tires. "We're just waiting for Scott."

Manny and Brian hoists himself in and fasten their seatbelts. Static comes through the two-way radio sitting on the dashboard and Manny taps on the steering wheel, listening intently when a male voice crackles through the small speakers, speaking frantically in another language. The line is so scratchy that Brian doubts he would be able to make out what was being said even if he understood the language. The olive-toned man in the driver's seat has no such qualms on the other hand.

Manny grabs the radio and clicks the button on the side when the voice on the end of the line finally stops speaking. "Understood. Over and out," he says before setting the radio back down and, to Brian's surprise, turns the key and powers up the truck.

"What was that all about?" Brian asks.

"There's been an accident. Scott's gonna have to meet us at the site."

"What sort of an accident?"

Gravel crunches under the tires and Manny's mouth turns grim. He doesn't take his eyes off the path ahead. "One of the workers stopped to fix a barrier cone along the haul road. A haul truck just ran over him."

Brian nods and the rest of the drive is a quiet one. It's

unnerving how nonchalant Manny is about the accident. He thinks that must be a somber part of the job. Accidents happen all the time. It isn't exactly a low-risk position.

Their journey to the crusher site is slowed down when they come upon the scene of the accident. Morbid curiosity takes a hold of him and Brian glances out the window to see the huge mining haul truck stopped in the middle of the road. The longer he looks, the more details he becomes aware of. First, the truck itself, with a distinct splatter of blood across its massive wheel-well, a wet patch of crimson lining its wide tread. Parked near the wheel-well is another small service truck, its hazard lights flashing. A small group of men in safety vests and helmets is gathered at the side of the road. Brian recognizes Scott among them. The men huddle around the scene of the accident. Over the clear remains of an impacted body. Brian's heart races. On the ground are the crushed remains of a man who could almost be peeled away from the tarmac, several parts of his body flattened by the massive machine. The mix of flesh and bone on the ground, as well as the surrounding area darkened by a pool of blood, make Brian want to gag.

"That's the second one this month," Manny murmurs. "I keep telling those dumb bastards… Those trucks got a seventy-foot blind spot. You just can't go off and park on the side of a haul road and expect them to see you."

Brian doesn't answer. It's all he can do to take his eyes off the horrific scene before him but even when he eventually looks away, the images are burned into his eyes. Never before has he felt so mortal. Gulping, he nods absently at Manny.

You're here to do a job, he chides himself mentally. *Remain vigilant. Stay alert.*

Soon, they arrive at the crusher construction site. Manny leads him to the third floor under metal panels and slates that he knows must be far stronger than they look until finally, he's standing in front of the slab that brought him all this way. It's while he's inspecting it that Scott shows up.

"Sorry I'm late. We had a fatality on the haul road."

Brian looks up from the lines running through the floor. "Yeah, we saw it coming in. Very tragic."

"Yeah, tragic!" Scott waves his hands in the air while shaking his head and, as if only now noticing Brian in front of him, he races onto the next thing; the reason they're all there. "Listen, you got my email!" He walks over the floor area, pointing his fingers in the direction of what Brian had already been taking in. "We are putting a six hundred and fifty-thousand-pound Gyratory crusher right here! I need to know if these big cracks are going to be a problem."

Cracks are never a good sign, Brian knows. From his brief examination, they do indeed appear to be cracks rather than fissures, which can be normal. But these are far larger.

"I'll be honest, Scott. These cracks are not a good sign. I think we need to request an x-ray to determine how deep they go." Brian paces, getting a look at the cracks in the floor from a different angle. "We also need to go over the Geotech report again—make sure our boring samples aren't the issue. I don't think this is a compaction issue; most likely related to curing and moisture. An x-ray of the slab will help."

"We're over budget, behind schedule, and you think this could be a curing issue?" The frustration in his voice can't be replicated in an email.

"Yes," Brian reluctantly confirms. *Why is it that things always go wrong when I'm dealing with the least understanding person in the world?* "But," he goes on, "I'll take another look at the Geotech report as well…"

"You said that," Scott interrupts. "Look, we hired FME because your marketing material states that you're an industry leader in mining design and engineering. So, 'Industry Leader'" he uses air quotes around the title, "Will the floor slab support the fucking crusher or not?"

Brian holds back a sigh as frustration creeps in. He can feel the weight of the day piling on and a quick glimpse at his watch tells him it's not yet noon. Knowing his responsibility is to deescalate the situation, he lowers his voice. "Listen, Scott… I will back-check the numbers. But we definitely need to request an x-ray. The slab is two feet thick, so if the cracks are shallow, we can order a compressive strength test. If everything checks out, we'll be able to fill the cracks with structural resin. But let me run the numbers before anything else."

There's no mistaking the clenched jaw for happiness, but Scott nods and, with nothing else to do, the three awkwardly make their way back down to their respective vehicles. It feels like there's a rock in Brian's stomach as he watches Scott drive off and Manny says nothing the whole way back to the main site.

"See ya, man," is the farewell he receives when he

climbs out at the admin building, which is just as well because he finds he can only wave his hand in response. His tongue feels heavy.

Before he leaves, Brian removes the hard hat and safety vest, dropping them in a bucket filled with other vests and helmets at the entrance to the lobby. On his way out, he notices something he hasn't in the past. Beneath the company's wall-mounted logo reading "Hagstone Mining Company" is a glass display case. Inside, atop a velvet slip, is an assortment of rocks and stones of various shapes and sizes. They all have one thing in common—a hole goes right through each of them.

That hasn't always been there, has it? He meanders toward the glass case, unsure of why he's intrigued by its contents. One rock, in particular, has a hole that flares outward, similar to the one in Ben's bedroom, and Brian thinks perhaps the reminder is what drew him to the display all along.

"You're still here?"

Brian nods at Manny, who has removed his safety vest and helmet.

"They're called hag stones," Manny states. "Like the name of the company. I guess they're pretty rare, found naturally throughout the world. A few years ago, I bought one for my son at the annual Gem Show. He loved it. Did some research of his own. Told me they're sometimes called fairy stones."

"Fairy stones?" Brian inquires.

"Yeah. People once believed if you held one of them up to your eye and looked through the hole, you could see fairies, see into another world." The site coordinator snickers at the thought, a smile on his face.

Brian's thoughts return to his own son once more, *perhaps Ben would like such a gift.*

"That's interesting," he finally says, stepping back from the case. "Thanks for sharing that story with me!"

Manny's smile grows brighter. "You're welcome, man."

After shaking hands with the man, Brian turns away and heads back out of the building.

4

TINY HOLES

The family is seated around the dinner table. Rosa's hands are folded as she says grace, Morgan's in the middle of a bite, and Brian is simply taking in the mouthwatering aroma before he digs into the delicious meal.

"A boy at school went to the hospital today," Ben tells everyone, ladling gravy over the roast on his plate.

Ben is so busy with the gravy that he doesn't see the looks of confusion directed toward him.

"Who went to the hospital?" Brian asks his son.

"A kid named Jackson. He was full of tiny holes."

Rosa catches Brian's eye across the table, her brows

furrowed. "What do you mean he was full of holes, Ben?"

"He was playing football on the field with some other kids during recess and he wasn't paying attention, I guess. He fell onto a prickly pear cactus." Ben stares down at his plate as he tells the story. "Everybody saw him. His face... His cheek... All covered in tiny holes."

Rosa's alarm is evident as she looks to Brian again.

"That's gross, why are you talking about it?" Morgan snaps, setting her fork down.

Ben ignores her question, looking around the table without meeting anyone's eyes. It's as if he's looking slightly past them, over their shoulders, when he speaks. "You guys should look around. Have you ever noticed... there are holes everywhere?"

Brian's mind flits back to that afternoon, to the hag stones in the display case. "Yes," he whispers.

Rosa and Morgan both stare at Brian, bewildered by his unusual response.

BANG.

Rosa and Morgan jump in fright as the entire table shudders, the cutlery clinking against the crockery as Ben's fists slam down onto the table.

"Don't you see them?" Ben cries out, drawing everyone's attention back to him. "There are holes everywhere!" He stands from his seat and walks toward the kitchen sink, pointing at the yellow sponge sitting on the side. "Look! Tiny holes!"

Brian takes in the sponge, knowing that it's porous but not knowing what to do about his son's behavior at this moment. He can see that his daughter and his girlfriend are unnerved by Ben and, quietly, he stands and makes his way over to his son.

"Ben," he says softly. "Stop. You're just freaked out because of what happened with the ants last night."

Immediately, Brian knows that he's said the wrong thing. His son's face falls as if he's delivered the most terrible news.

"No... No," he murmurs, backing away slowly. He looks from his father to Rosa and Morgan sitting at the table, sadness in his eyes. Brian can see that he isn't sure why no one seems to understand him. "No, there are holes. There are. There are."

Ben's eyes search the room and quickly find the sink again. He reaches in and grabs a strainer hastily, knocking several other dishes over into the sink in the process. The dining room echoes with the cacophony of cutlery and crockery crashing onto itself and Brian flinches. He's thankful to see that nothing is broken.

"Holes! Look, holes!" Ben shouts, waving the strainer around in the air before throwing it back into the sink. "All I see are friggin' holes!"

Almost nothing, Brian thinks, looking at the frantic 11-year-old in front of him.

"Ben!" Brian raises his voice, shocked by the sudden outburst and language. "Stop it! Don't you dare speak like that."

Ben stops, stares at his father, and then gives a furious screech, the kind that hurts the throat and causes the face to turn red, and then runs out of the kitchen and up the stairs to his bedroom, stomping his feet as he goes. The family hears the door slam shut moments later. It's not until Ben's gone that Brian notices how heavily he's breathing. Rosa and Morgan are both freaked out. Morgan's hands are visibly shaking and Rosa is a shade paler.

"It's okay, mi hija," Rosa takes Morgan's hands. "It's okay."

"What the hell just happened?" Brian looks back at the two of them, but doesn't wait for an answer. "I'm going to go check on him."

Leaving the girls behind, he does his best to keep his mind blank. He focuses on the thud of his stride as he races up the stairs, counting the steps, too afraid to allow his mind to drift.

•••

Upstairs, Ben has locked his door behind him, guilt already beginning to stir inside his stomach. Almost as soon as he does, his eyes find the duct tape on the wall and he can picture the damage lurking beneath it clear as day. The look of the hole beneath will probably stay with him forever. That's what it feels like. He recalls how his father had asked him if he was the one who'd made the hole and he knew why, and what his dad had really been suggesting. Burying his face in his pillow doesn't help. The images are burned behind his eyes and there is nothing he can do to stop the memories from flooding his mind. Memories of the ants. The way they'd been everywhere, a small scurrying army. If he thinks about it too long, he can almost feel the way they'd crawled into his nose and ear holes and worse than that, how they crawled out of them all over again.

•••

Brian is surprised that the door doesn't give when he presses down on the handle and quietly, he grabs the spare key pin he keeps on the overhead trim above the door, unlocking it. Walking into the room, he's faced with the sight of his son face down on his bed, his body wracked with sobs. With a pang in his chest, he takes a seat in the open space beneath his son's feet.

"How did you get in my room?" Ben asks, muffled by the pillow.

Brian holds up the flat-headed piece of metal and says, "With the key pin."

Turning his head slightly to look at his father, Ben sees the key and sniffs. "I don't suppose you have a key to unlock what's going on in my head?"

Brian is not sure how successfully he is able to cover up how disturbed and shocked he is to hear something like this coming from his son, but he tries his best. "It's okay, Ben," he murmurs as comfortingly as he can. He leans over and strokes Ben's back.

His eyes red with tears, Ben turns and takes hold of Brian's arm. "I'm sorry, Dad... I don't know why I freaked out!"

The day keeps getting more and more surprising. His son never says sorry, not without being told that an apology is expected. It's a lesson that he and Rosa have been struggling with, one that got worse when Brian and Kim separated.

"It's okay, Ben, there's nothing wrong with your head," Brian answers immediately. "You've been traumatized. I mean, it had to be scary for you to wake up covered in ants, to find a hole in your wall that they climbed through. It's traumatizing. You know what that means?"

Ben shakes his head even as Brian tries to push down the anxiety bubbling in his stomach.

"It means that you have every right to be upset, but the ants are gone. You're okay now. They can't hurt you. The hole is covered."

"What about Jackson? He has holes in his face now."

"Jackson will be okay. He'll heal. Just like those little red bites on your arms and neck."

When he looks down at the splotches of calamine on his arms, the troubled expression remains on Ben's soft features, but he nods his head and uses the back of his arm to wipe the moisture off his face.

Brian ruffles his son's hair gently, standing from the bed. "Let's try to put this behind us, all right?"

"Sure," Ben says unconvincingly.

•••

Later that evening, after everything has wound down and his fingertips resemble prunes from being submerged in warm dishwater for the past half hour, Brian makes his way upstairs to check on the kids before bedtime. Naturally, he finds himself at the door to Ben's room first. Unlike before, it's unlocked and standing open. Before he enters, he already sees a sight that brings him more pleasure than he expected, one of normalcy; Ben is playing a video game, the persistent movement of his thumbs tapping at the buttons matches that of the quiet fight sounds coming from the device.

"Having fun?"

"Almost at the end of the level," Ben answers, as if that's an indication of whether he's enjoying it or not.

Brian smiles. "Last one, then, okay?"

"Sure, Dad," Ben doesn't take his eyes off the game, tap-tap-tapping away.

Brian leaves the door only slightly ajar and makes his way to Morgan's room next. When the door doesn't open, he raises his eyebrows. *Two times in one day.* Both his kids are doing things they don't usually do.

With a sigh, he raises his fist and taps his knuckles against the door.

"Who is it?" Morgan's voice rings out.

"Dad," Brian responds.

A few moments later, she unlocks the door and sits on her bed. Brian enters and takes the edge of the bed. "What's up? Why did you lock your door?"

"I just wanted to."

"Is everything okay?"

"Yep."

It doesn't take a genius to figure out that things aren't okay and Brian, knowing that getting a teenager to answer a direct question honestly is like pulling teeth, asks again in a firmer voice. "Are you sure everything is okay?"

"Yes, Dad," Morgan snaps with a huff. "I was just getting changed, okay?"

Brian presses his lips together, but the look on Morgan's face tells him not to push it. He wonders if she knows she's a terrible actress and, trying to find the silver lining, he decides that perhaps it's a good thing that he can tell when she's lying. It doesn't feel good right now though.

"All right," he claps his hand against his thigh and stands, leaning over her to kiss her on the forehead. "Goodnight, honey."

"Night, Dad."

On his way out, Brian heads back to Ben's room to make sure he's not still playing video games. The door is still ajar, but the light is out and his son is tucked in under his blankets. Brian can see the handheld sitting on the bedside table next to half a glass of water. His eyes spot the silver tape on the dresser and he considers taking it back down to the garage, but thinks better of it.

"Goodnight, Ben. Love you."

"Love you, Dad," Ben whispers, surprising his father, who didn't expect a response.

As he walks down the hall toward his and Rosa's bedroom, Brian hears the soft click of a door knob locking. He stops in his tracks and glances back to find that Morgan's door is closed. For a moment, he considers going back to speak to her, to find out what's really going on. Deciding better of it yet again, he keeps walking. The last thing he wants to do is make the week any worse than it already has been—for both of his kids.

In their bedroom, Rosa is applying moisturizer to her face, an integral part of her nightly routine. Brian goes to the bathroom to do his, which consists almost solely of brushing his teeth and changing into sweat shorts.

"Morgan is locking her door," he says from the other room.

"Can you blame her?" Rosa stands in the doorway,

folding her arms over her chest. "Ben got really scary tonight."

"He was just traumatized. The poor kid had ants all over him——I mean, *all* over him; they crawled out of his ears, Rosa. He freaked out between that and the hole in his room."

"I understand that, but what happened tonight was frightening. There's something wrong."

Brian starts brushing his teeth, meeting his girlfriend's eyes in the mirror. The expression on her face is a grave one and, at that moment, he isn't sure how to deal with it. As far as he is concerned, this isn't a run-of-the-mill incident. *How does anyone know how a child will respond to something like that?* Surely a momentary breakdown can't be considered an unrealistic result.

Eventually, he spits out a mouthful of toothpaste. "Can you ask your uncle to come by and pest control the house? Let him know about the ants."

Rosa sighs in exasperation. "Yeah, I'll let Reyes know, but you're being naïve. You need to wake up. There is something wrong and you can't keep changing the subject. I understand Ben has ADHD and I understand he is on meds. But this was—*is*—different."

"The whole situation is different," he repeats his thoughts. "Do you know anyone who's ever gone through something like Ben did? No. So how can we say for sure what is and isn't an appropriate reaction?"

This time, Rosa rolls her eyes, pursing her lips into a tight white line. Rather than argue with him any longer, she turns away from him and leaves the bathroom, going back to the bedroom. Brian rinses his mouth and makes his way back to find that she's lying on her side and facing away from his end of the bed, the light of her phone shines on her face as she scrolls through it.

Brian turns the lights off and climbs into bed. He gives up on speaking for the night too. It doesn't seem that there's much use in dragging it out any longer than they already have and he's tired after such an incredibly long day.

5

THERE WILL BE BLOOD

*T*uesday.

Yet again, the house is shaken awake by a loud scream. This time, it's distinctly feminine and comes from Morgan's bedroom. Rather than pitch darkness, light shines through the gap between the curtains in Brian and Rosa's room. The sun is already up and outside, birds are beginning to sing their morning songs. Brian takes no notice, leaping out of bed before his pupils have a chance to dilate while Rosa tries to follow in her half-asleep state.

Brian is amazed to find himself once again running down the hallway, bare feet slamming against the wood. *What the hell is going on around here lately?*

When he turns the corner before the kids' rooms, Brian's breath catches in his throat. The sight before him makes his heart race faster than the scream and run combined. Ben stands eerily still in front of Morgan's door, the small key pin necessary to unlock her room hangs from his fingertips.

"Ben," he breathes, filled with panic as he takes the last few steps toward his daughter's room. "What happened? What have you done?"

From Ben's other hand, a baseball bat falls to the floor with a thud and Ben begins to tremble.

"What have you done?!" Brian yells again.

Ben flinches, fear causing him to shut down as tears stream down his face. He lifts his hand slowly and points his index finger into Morgan's room. With a quivering voice, he cries out, "I didn't do anything!"

A second scream rings out and Brian's attention flits quickly from his son to Morgan's room and he opens the door hurriedly. Stepping into the room, Brian sees Morgan sitting upright on her bed, her hands red with blood. Looking down, Brian sees that not only is it all over her hands, but it's also all over her sheets. The expression on her face is one of horror.

Oh my god, what has he done? Brian thinks again. He's frozen in place, too shocked by what he sees and too afraid of what it might mean to move.

Rosa enters the room and rushes over to Morgan's side, shifting the sheets aside. "Mi hija, it's okay. You're fine." She wraps her arms around Morgan's shoulders, pulling her in for a hug, and whispers something in her ear that seems to take the look of horror off Morgan's face. After that, she walks over to Brian. "It's okay, Brian. You can go ahead and leave the room. I'll take care of this. It's Morgan's first period."

With the realization that she's okay, Brian takes a breath of relief. Part of him wants to go over and hug her, but he has a feeling she wouldn't respond well to that right now. He nods and backs out of the room and Rosa closes the door once he's back in the hallway.

Brian looks down at his son, feeling more than a little guilty for his earlier reaction. The moment they meet eyes, Ben shakes his head angrily, turns on his heel, and runs to his bedroom. Brian hears the metallic click of the lock shifting into place and it feels as if a stone has hit the hollow pit where his stomach ought to be. Never had he imagined that such a small sound could have such a heavy impact on him, but the regret is so sudden and heavy that the breath is knocked from his lungs and he brings a hand to his throat in the hopes that it might relieve the tightness he feels there. It doesn't. He has a feeling nothing will. There's no way to turn back time and stop himself—he can only move forward and accept whatever consequences his reactions might have.

Brian shuffles over to his son's door and rather than knock, he speaks to him from out in the hall. "I'm sorry, son. I didn't know what was happening. I saw you with the key and baseball bat and I didn't understand." He runs a hand through his hair nervously. "I made a mistake."

From inside the room, Ben doesn't respond, but Brian can hear him sobbing again. Grimacing, Brian walks back to his own room, knowing that nothing he can say or do right now will help. He simply hopes his son will be okay.

"Everything's okay," Rosa says matter-of-factly when she enters their room sometime later. "She started her period. It's very common for her age. I'm surprised that she didn't have it sooner."

"Will she be all right?" Brian asks.

To his surprise, Rosa giggles and then, seeing his face, wraps her arms around his shoulders and gives him a big hug. "Of course. Your daughter is growing up; she's becoming a young lady."

A young lady? Oh boy...

When she pulls away, she gives another giggle at the look on his face and he knows his thoughts are written all over it. "I think she should stay home from school today. I don't mind hanging out with her. I just think she needs a bit of time to adjust."

"I think you're right. A day off will be good for her," Brian nods, remembering the terror he'd seen in her eyes. "Ben is a mess. I feel so bad. I accused him of doing something to her."

Rosa's eyes soften and she pulls him in for another hug, stroking his back. "You've been through so much these past few days, my love. Don't beat yourself up." She kisses him on the cheek. "He's been acting very strange lately and you were just scared. Go talk to him."

"Okay," Brian murmurs.

The words Rosa used were the same things he'd thought to himself while he sat in their room doing nothing. They were the thoughts he used to justify his reaction. He felt no better having heard them from her lips than he did when they went through his mind.

"Good," Rosa says simply, unaware of the turmoil he's going through. "You're such a great dad. That's why I love you so much."

"Thank you, baby, I love you more," he gives her a weak smile.

"Oh, and don't forget to text Kim. You need to tell her about Morgan. She's her mom and she'll want to know."

"Sure."

•••

Before anything else that morning, Brian showers and gets ready for work. It's only 7:30 a.m. when he puts his shoes on and it already feels like the longest morning this week---—two days into it!

The next thing he does after getting dressed is visit Morgan in her bedroom. He's relieved to see that her door is open today. She's sitting on her bed, cell phone in hand.

"How are you doing, honey?"

"I'm okay. Mom's super mad at you by the way."

"Why?"

"I texted her. She's mad that you didn't tell her."

It takes a substantial amount of willpower not to laugh or roll his eyes. "Okay Morgs, don't you worry about that. I planned to call her once I got on the road."

"Sure," Morgan says dismissively.

"Rosa said you can skip school and stay home with her today. You can text your mom some more. She'll be able to answer all your questions and help you handle things."

Morgan raises her eyebrows. "Handle things? You mean

get me tampons?"

A fully grown adult he may be, but Brian can't help but cringe and he wonders momentarily if his daughter says things like this for no other reason than to rile him up or make him uncomfortable. "Yeah," he nods. "And whatever else you may need."

"Okay, Dad. Rosa told me she'll help me too."

"Okay, good. That's great."

At least I don't have to do anything in this department.

Brian heads over to kiss her on the forehead. "I love you. Take it easy today, okay? It's a big day!"

At this, Morgan rolls her eyes and quickly changes the topic. "Am I still going to Mom's on Friday?"

"Of course. When I call your mom in a bit, I can see if she wants to come by and pick you up later today, or maybe Rosa can drop you off. You can get some mom time in."

"Mom *hates* Rosa!"

Instinctively, Brian looks toward the door. He's not sure why. There isn't an indication of whether his girlfriend heard Morgan in the doorway, nor would there be since Rosa is downstairs. "Shhh, that's not nice," he says, looking back at his daughter. "I'll ask your mother what she wants to do as soon as I leave."

There's a hint of attitude about Morgan when he walks away; it's in the way she pouts her lips and raises her eyebrows disbelievingly, the way she almost imperceptibly gives a shake of her head. Brian doesn't know what he's going to do with her—she's too sassy for her own good and visibly so. He leaves the room with a roll of his own eyes.

His son's room is the next destination, but when Brian raises a hand to knock on the door, it swings open to reveal Ben on the other side. He's already fully dressed and ready for school. Without so much as a word, he storms off past his father and stomps down the stairs.

"Ben, wait!"

Hurrying down after him, Brian stops in front of his son, preventing him from going any further.

"I just want to leave and go to school!" Ben cries out.

"Listen, Ben... Sometimes dads make mistakes too. I told you; I'm sorry. I didn't know what was happening."

"What did you think? That I would beat my sister with a baseball bat?"

Brian can't help but flinch. With a sigh, he squats down so that he and Ben are eye-level. "No, I don't think you would ever do that," he says softly. "I heard a scream. I was afraid and I saw you standing there. Sometimes fear can play with your mind, make you see and even hear things that you don't want to."

A flicker of understanding seems to cross his son's features. "I heard the scream too and that's why I got my bat. The door was locked. I got the key so that I could unlock it."

"I know, son. And you know, actually, you're really brave for doing that, for coming to save your sister. I'm proud of you."

Brian can tell his son isn't ready to stop being angry, though the praise seems to calm him down. For a moment, he even thinks he sees Ben smirk a bit. The moment is quicker than he'd like. Part of him wants to hug his son and part of him knows that Ben will come to him when he's ready to be hugged. Now isn't the time.

At least he isn't angry with me anymore.

"Where's Morgan?" Ben asks.

Getting a distinct feeling that his son is trying to change the subject, Brian stands up. "She's gonna stay home today, so it's just us today. I'll let you control the playlist."

Ben beams. "Cool!"

They head into the kitchen, where Ben picks up the lunch Rosa has prepared for him and Brian gives his girlfriend a quick kiss before leaving, Rosa calls out to them to have a good day just as the door closes behind them.

•••

It's no surprise to Brian that Ben is late for school after the morning they've had. The road outside the property is quiet, unmanned by a crossing guard now that the drop-off rush is over. There are no other cars in sight, no straggling children, and no overbearing parents. It strikes him as eerie how quiet the grounds are at this hour; he knows the school is currently full of students and yet, the building and surrounding areas feel empty.

"They're going to mark me as tardy."

"We'll see about that," Brian turns the ignition off, the music going with it, and unbuckles his seatbelt. "C'mon, let's see what we can do about that tardy."

Being late means Brian can't simply drop Ben off and leave for work. He has to walk Ben into the school through the office, a separate smaller building not normally used by the students to enter the premises. Normally, when they're with him, the kids get to school on time. His ex-wife, on the other hand, has no concept of time. He had plenty of experience during their marriage of walking both Morgan and Ben through this particular entrance.

They walk down a small hallway until they reach the admissions area. Running along one wall are several seats, and on the other is a long laminated countertop. A receptionist sits behind the countertop with spectacles perched on her nose, separated from the waiting area and anyone in it by a glass screen. Her eyes follow Brian before falling onto Ben, at whom she smiles.

"Hey Ben," the woman says. "How are ya?"

"Okay," Ben mumbles.

"Hey Sylvia," Brian greets her. "Sorry about this."

She shrugs. "No need to apologize to me. It doesn't impact me if you're late. But you know you're gonna have to sign him in and we're going to track the tardy."

"Right, about that," he lowers his voice. "The reason why we were late is actually because Morgan had a rough morning. She's uh… turning into a young lady, if you know what I mean," Brian pauses to look over at Ben, who's sitting in one of the seats against the wall, his legs swinging back and forth beneath it. "Is there any chance we could make an exception this one time?"

Sylvia glances between the pair worriedly, eyes lingering on Ben, who is staring at the ground, and then, to Brian's immense relief, she gives a resigned sigh. "All right. But I can only do it this one time, Brian. I could get in trouble, you know."

"Thank you. Seriously, I appreciate it."

"Don't mention it," she sighs again. Telltale pink creeps

up her neck, a reaction he's not unfamiliar with receiving from women. "Ben, you can head on off to class. Let your teacher know you signed in with me."

•••

Back in his SUV, he pairs his phone and dials his ex-wife's number into the system, his nerves scattered. The ignition starts with a growl and he sets off down the road to the sound of the dial tone, wishing he could simply play music instead. She picks up on the second ring.

"Brian! Why didn't you call me as soon as our daughter woke up bleeding this morning?"

"I'm calling you now," Brian says defensively. The sweat on the back of his neck is all-too-familiar, his anxiety returns to him as if it had never left. Kim's voice is the key to bringing back years of a dysfunctional marriage. "As you may or may not know, it was a pretty chaotic morning."

"You always have an excuse for why you don't call me. She's my daughter and I don't need Rosa involved in her first period. That's my role." Brian opens his mouth to respond, but Kim continues. "I don't care who you decide to fuck, but I'm Morgan's mother and I want to be a part of this. I deserve to be respected."

Brian smirks at the irony and hits the hang-up button on the dashboard, effectively silencing the nasal voice coming from the car speakers. Over the years, this was a tactic that Brian had learned to use to reset the boundaries.

Kim wants to be respected? That's rich.

The phone rings and Brian hits the answer button.

"Brian," Kim starts calmly. "Don't hang up. I know I shouldn't have said that. I just want to be involved."

"First of all, let's clear one thing up—Rosa has nothing to do with this." He pauses only to let that statement settle before going on. He takes Kim's silence as confirmation. "Now, you're her mother, so of course you have every right to be involved. I kept Morgan home from school today. If you want, you can come get her any time."

"Okay, I will. I can get off early today and stop by around three p.m."

"Okay, just text her and I'm sure she'll be ready." The traffic light in front of him turns red and Brian returns to tapping on the steering wheel. "Listen, there's something else."

"There always is," Kim snaps.

It's tempting to hang up again, but Brian swallows the urge. "Ben has had a bad couple of days. He woke up covered in ants on Sunday night."

"Ants? Oh, my God!"

"Yeah, I cleaned him up and he was really upset about the whole thing. He's also been acting out since then, really angry and frustrated." The light turns green and Brian turns off to the right.

"Well, what do you expect? He's probably traumatized."

"I agree, I just wanted you to know in case things got any worse or he brings this up at your house on Friday."

"I hope you're not telling me this just to have his meds increased again. You keep telling his doctor that his scripts aren't working. I wouldn't put it past you to use this as a way to drug him up."

Brian's knuckles whiten where he grips the steering wheel a little tighter. He can hear the frustration in his voice when next he speaks. "I don't want to drug him up. We can both tell he's not as focused as he needs to be—he can barely do math cards! I don't think his methylphenidate is strong enough and his teachers agree too."

"You can't just keep drugging him up. It's probably a side effect that he can't focus properly. You're fucking him up every time you suggest increasing the dosage!" Brian's foot involuntarily presses down, accelerating the tiniest amount. "I'm not fucking him up. What good are ADHD meds if they don't help?"

"All you do is suggest more and more…"
A truck's horn blares on Brian's left side and when he looks over, the driver is flipping him off. He slows down slightly. "Kim, stop. I'm not a doctor. It could be side effects, but his last dosage increase was two months ago, so it makes no sense that he would start experiencing the behavior changes two whole months later."

"That's right, you're not a doctor," Kim agrees firmly. "How would you know? I mean, he just turned eleven last week. He's growing and his body keeps changing. What kind of behavior changes have you seen?"

He knows that the question is rhetorical, but Brian answers it anyway. "Well, the poor kid was really shaken up by the ant thing. Then he got super angry last night and said some pretty scary stuff at dinner. He told Morgan he would kill her and he freaked out, saying all he sees are tiny holes. There was this weird moment with a sponge and a strainer."

"Jesus, what the hell is going on at your house?"
Deciding to leave out that morning's events, Brian

continues. "Perhaps he's just traumatized. The ants were coming out of a hole in his bedroom wall. Who could blame him?" Remembering another detail, he grimaces. There's no avoiding telling Kim about Jackson. "Also, I guess I should tell you that a boy at his school fell into a cactus and he had tiny holes in his face after the fact. So, no wonder Ben freaked out. He was one of the kids who saw it happen."

"God, well, that would explain a lot. That would freak me out too." In his mind's eye, Brian can see her chewing on the tips of her painted nails like she did whenever she was anxious. "But don't forget; he had side effects before. Remember a few years ago on a different set of meds, he once felt like things were crawling on him."

Truthfully, Brian didn't remember that. "Maybe," he murmurs. "Anyway, I spoke with him and he's going to try not to let his anger get to him like that again. So, you'll need to reassure him that he has nothing to be afraid of."

"This is bullshit. Morgan starts her period and Ben is freaked out about ants and holes. This is how you're going to send them back to me?"

Brian sighs again, for what seems like the hundredth time that morning. "We both know you're not perfect, Kim. I need to decompress both of them every time I get them back. They tell me how you and Doug fight all the time and how you've changed since Andrew was born..."

"Please," Kim interrupts, her tone dripping with sarcasm. "We don't fight that much and they love their little half-brother."

Brian pulls off into the parking lot of the nearest

convenience store. He's uncertain if he'll enter, but he needs to get off the road and it seems as good a stop as any.

"I've gotta go," Kim says.

"Okay. Text Morgan when you're on your way."

Brian hangs up once more and releases a breath that feels as if it's been lodged in his chest since he left the school. While a coffee would be great, he simply sits in the driver's seat for a minute. *Silence has never sounded better.*

6

BODY PARTS

A human torso is laid out on a table at the front of the room. Its skin is peeled back, starting at the base of the forehead with only a hint of the yellowy white piece of skull visible. The skull isn't important, not for this; it's been sliced open to reveal the brain beneath. Just over 20 kids sit in the room facing the table, where they can see the sinewy muscles spreading through the open face's cheeks. They can examine the spot where the perfectly clean eyeballs—staring dead ahead—connect to their sockets. The torso's chest cavity is neatly opened and the stomach has no covering at all, no indication that there had ever been anything more than the open hole that now exposed the internal organs.

Standing over the desk, a man without gloves reaches into the stomach and pulls the organs out, one at a time. There's no slime on them and the man's arms don't come away covered in blood. The organs remain solid and without give when he passes them to the nearest person, an 11-year-old girl with blonde hair tied high into a ponytail. She shows the girl beside her and the two poke and prod at what looks like a liver, giggling. The man pulls out another organ and passes it to a different set of kids, a boy and a girl who don't look impressed. In fact, they appear to be bored.

"The lungs," the man calls out to the room. "Can anyone tell me what they do?"

There's no response.

"Anyone?"

While he speaks, he continues ripping body parts out of the torso, emptying and deconstructing it. In place of the organs, all that remains are dark voids and crannies of veins and arteries. Ben watches each part leave the fake body splayed out on the table, his mind wanders as he focuses on the torso—or what's left of it—more than the organs, more than the lecture. All he can think about are all the holes in the torso being created by his biology teacher.

Just then, the girl in front of him turns around and casually drops a lung on his desk, snapping him out of his thoughts. Ben stares at the organ for a moment before lifting it. He knows it's plastic, but he's still surprised by the smooth, cool feel against his fingertips. He's seen lungs before—in books and movies and once in real life during a lesson on lung cancer and the dangers of smoking, something that had been backed up by a floating black lung in a jar full of what was once clear liquid. This lung, although made to look realistic, is nothing like that one. The longer Ben stares at it, the more entranced he becomes by the spongy texture of it, the plastic molded to reflect realism. Dozens of tiny dark spaces dip into the plastic cavity and the hair on his neck starts to stand up as he runs his fingertip along the bumpy surface.

How long has he been holding this organ? He doesn't know and he can't bring himself to tear his eyes from it, slipping further and further into a dreamlike state, one where he can only see the blurred dark holes, getting bigger and smaller as his focus shifts. His eyes begin to burn and even then, he can't turn away, not as the holes start to sear into his eyes. It's like he's looking into the sun directly, fire burning into him, hot and painful.

"Ben! Ben," the teacher, standing at the front of the classroom, calls out to him. "Ben, please pass the lungs along, so everyone can get a turn."

Ben finally rips his eyes away from the lung in his hand to gaze up at his teacher and he shakes his head once to rid himself of the image. He must be seeing things; there's no other logical explanation. After shaking his head, however, the image doesn't disappear. His teacher's flesh, from his face down his neck and peeking out of the sleeves of his shirt, is as porous as the organ. Thousands of tiny holes, deep and black, stare back at him from his teacher's skin and Ben's throat constricts with fear as the scream he wants to release refuses to come out.

Dropping the lung onto the desk, Ben's hands go to his throat, trying to relieve the pressure he feels there, but his struggle for breath causes him to start gasping for air. He's hyperventilating. It gets louder the more he tries to suck in and somehow, it doesn't help.

I can't breathe, he thinks. *I'm going to die.* Again and again.

The teacher has taken notice of him. Ben knows only because he can hear the teacher's voice, but he doesn't want to look at him, and doesn't want to see his skin. It's exactly like the boy from the day before, the one who fell into the cactus, but so much worse.

Suddenly, Ben realizes the teacher isn't the only one calling his name; the other children in the class have noticed him too. They're all staring at him and Ben scans the room to find that each of them looks the same. Their skin is porous, the flesh made of deep and dark impressions, thousands of tiny black holes in their arms and faces. The faces move and the holes shift, growing bigger and smaller as they call his name, and Ben can't hold on any longer.

All the fight goes out of Ben like a light and he slips from his seat as his body finally gives in; he faints and falls to the cold linoleum floor.

"Ben! Ben…"

The voices of the other kids and the teacher fade away and so does his vision, which he's grateful for in the second it takes for his eyes to fall shut.

Somewhere in the distance, he hears a teacher shout, "Call Brian Brennan!"

•••

It's past lunchtime when Brian walks through the front door carrying Ben in his arms, with little memory of how he got there. The drive from his office was a blur of painted lines on tarmac, the trip into the school one of confusion and a mix of concerned and accusing expressions from the adults around him. All that mattered was getting to his son and then, getting his son home and out of there. It didn't matter that Mr. Merrick had scowled when Brian knocked on the door and informed his boss that he needed to pick up his son from school, didn't matter that he knew he was going to hear about his poor performance for the rest of the week—if not from his boss himself, then from his colleagues in the office. He imagined the gossip had already spread—no less infectious in a room full of men than it was women, though Brian knew all of them would deny it. There was no need to dwell on the young woman in a navy-blue sports car that honked and spun her wheels because of his recklessness on the freeway. None of that meant anything when he finally set Ben down on his bed, the gray duct tape along the wall stood out in his peripheral vision no matter how hard he tried to ignore it and no matter where he stood in the small bedroom.

"Brian?" Rosa walks into Ben's room behind him, toweling off her hands with a dish towel. She takes in the sight before her, perplexed.

"He fainted at school," Brian asks the unanswered question, not daring to take his eyes off Ben, who looks so small and pale on his bed. "The nurse says he's okay, but he needs rest."

"What happened?"

Brian searches his mind for what the school nurse had told him. "It was some kind of episode… He hyperventilated in his biology class." Then, in a softer voice, "He was mumbling about holes and holding a fake lung."

The biology teacher had been present when he arrived at school, holding the lung in question. It was fake and plastic and covered in holes, made to look as realistic as possible.

"Dios mio," Rosa murmurs. Out of the corner of his eye, Brian sees her raise her hand to draw the sign of the cross over her chest. Her lips move in silent prayer and then, louder, she says, "In the name of the Father, the Son, and the Holy Spirit—amen."

Brian turns to face Rosa as she raises the crucifix hanging around her neck to her lips, kissing it.

"I pray for you and the kids," she tells him. "I worry and pray for you."

"Thank you, Rosa," Brian nods.

He says nothing more. He was raised Catholic, but he no longer considers himself a religious man. He hasn't been one for a long time.

7

COME CLOSER

*W*ednesday.

Coming from somewhere in the distance is the gentle sound of wooden wind chimes. After a few moments, the chirping of birds joins in, creating a melody of sorts. Brian, sitting on a porch with a glass of iced tea in hand, looks around for the source of the sound and can't find it. It's not too noisy or disturbing, so he takes another sip and allows it to fade into the background because he's too comfortable to stand. The drink is sweet and cool, refreshing under the bright blue Tucson sky. He thinks it's the Tucson sky anyway. The day is hot and there's dust in the air. He doesn't quite remember how he got here or whose porch he's sitting on, but something about the gentle breeze and the garden full of flowers whose scents he's pretty sure he should be able to smell—but can't—sets him at ease.

Unfortunately for Brian, the sound of the birds is getting louder. He looks around for them and is frustrated that there isn't a tree or bird in sight. In fact, the landscape before him is remarkably still. Brian narrows his eyes at this. His suspicion grows by the second. The flowers didn't even move. How could they remain immobile? The wind chimes seem to grow more incessant by the second.

Beneath both the sound of the birds and the chimes, Brian recognizes another sound, an undertone to the song already lingering in the air around him. It resembles the crashing of the waves and Brian frowns. *Waves?*

That can't be possible.

No longer able to ignore the ruckus, it's with some annoyance that he sets his iced tea down on a table he hadn't noticed standing beside him and pulls himself up out of what could be the most comfortable armchair he's ever been in.

Brian is instantly thrown forward in bed, wide awake, back in his bedroom. The buzz of his phone vibrating against his bedside table is the first thing he hears, followed by his alarm tone; an ascending tone that features the sounds of waves, wind chimes, and birds, all of which grow louder the longer the alarm is left unanswered. With a sigh, he shuts it off, wishing that hitting snooze would put him back in an armchair with iced tea in his hand. Knowing it won't, he climbs out of bed and gets ready for the day, starting in the shower. Rosa, a deep sleeper usually, is unbothered by both the alarm and his disappearance. She rolls over and gives a sleepy hum when he leaves.

Checking the time only once he's ready, Brian is surprised to find that he's actually on time for the first time in almost a week. It makes him grin and by the time he's headed toward his son's room to wake him up for school, he's in a chipper mood.

That is—until he catches sight of Ben's bedroom door. His step falters slightly.

What havoc is this kid going to put us through today?

Brian shakes his head. What a horrible thing to think. This is his son, for goodness' sake. He shakes his head again and glances down at his watch; he's not late yet. Walking quicker than before, as if approaching confidently might make up for his thoughts, he continues down the hallway. The door is ajar and, despite how much he wishes he wasn't afraid, Brian enters the room cautiously. Only a few steps in, he involuntarily scrunches his nose up at the stench of ammonia. *Urine?*

A glance at the boy's bed confirms his suspicion; the blue covers are soaked. His son wet the bed. That's not the only thing Brian notices. There are several pieces of tape stuck on the wall, longer and shorter pieces spread out in different directions. On the dresser, he spots the roll of duct tape.

Did Ben do this?

Gulping nervously, Brian shakes his son's shoulder gently. Ben wakes with a start, no sign of fatigue in his wide eyes. The corners of his eyes are slightly red, making Brian wonder if he got any sleep at all. He sees Brian and says nothing, his eyes flitting to the lengths of tape on the wall before falling onto the sodden duvet covering his legs.

"What happened, Ben?" Brian asks. "Why did you wet the bed?"

"I don't know," Ben answers quietly.

"It's okay," Brian tells him. Ben's cheeks had taken on a pinker hue than before. "I'm not mad. I just want to know why you wet the bed. You never wet the bed…"

"I got scared," Ben continues speaking to his legs. "I didn't want to get up to go, so I just… stayed here and…"

"Scared? Of what? The ants again?"

Ben nods.

"Is that why you put tape all over the wall?"

Ben nods again.

With a sigh, Brian gets down on his haunches beside Ben's bed and rubs a gentle hand up and down his back. "It's all right, kiddo. I understand. I'd never judge you for something like this and you're not in trouble." Ben doesn't answer and Brian, uncertain of what to do, stands. "Let's get you cleaned up, huh?"

Ben nods for the third time and Brian gives him a hand out of his bed, which he reluctantly accepts as the wet sheets stick to him. Once he's out of bed, Brian removes the sheets, grateful that Rosa is the type of woman to insist on using mattress covers. He then silently helps Ben peel his wet pajamas off and picks up the pile of washing with both arms, gesturing for Ben to follow him through to the laundry room. There, he puts the washer on and grabs the nearest clean cloth to wash Ben off. The warm water seems to help relax his son and for that, Brian is relieved. Neither of them speaks—not because they wouldn't be able to hear one another over the sound of the washer, which they wouldn't, but because Ben doesn't appear to be in the mood to talk and Brian doesn't want to push that boundary. With the heavy noise of the cycle switching to the next setting behind them, Brian is satisfied that his son is clean. He pulls one of the towels out of a basket of clean laundry and wraps it around Ben before leading him back to the bedroom to help him get ready for school, something he hasn't felt compelled to do for several years.

A sense of foreboding comes with entering Ben's bedroom. It's been present ever since Sunday night, when the incident occurred that set all the strange happenings of the week into motion. Brian can't quite figure out if it's all in his head or if there's something more going on, but he can't deny the chill that rolls through him each time he crosses the threshold into the small room. One thing he is certain of is that he needs to pull himself together. He could practically hear the ticking of the watch on his wrist.

While Ben opens up his dresser and starts tugging clothes out, Brian decides to start removing the tape from the walls. The moment he gets a grip on the edge of the first piece, however, he's stopped by Ben yelling at him.

"Leave it! Don't take it off!"

"Why? I told you, there's nothing to worry about. The ants are gone."

"No, they're not. I saw more ants coming out of the wall again."

Brian draws his brows together. "Ben, I taped up the

hole. I'm telling you; the ants are not going to come out of it. It's duct tape—they can't get through duct tape." He grips the edge of one strip and tugs, peeling it back.

"You're wrong, Dad! I heard them…"

Heard them?

The longest strip of tape comes away and his eyes widen at the sight. There are two new holes. Beneath the long strip of tape Brian pulls off, the smaller pieces he'd crisscrossed over the original hole earlier that week are still there, untouched. Right beside it are the two new channels. Brian looks between Ben and the wall, stunned into silence yet again.

"See, I told you…" Ben whispers, pulling the towel tightly around his shoulders. "The ants made more holes."

"It doesn't make any sense," Brian mutters to himself, examining the wall.

The new holes are the same as the first one in appearance. It looks as though someone has burrowed their fingers through the walls from the inside out. Someone with fingers as small as those of a boy Ben's age. The floor and baseboard beneath the holes are covered in drywall dust.

"I could hear them making holes, so I used your tape and covered them up."

Brian's heart is beating wildly. "Ben…" He faces his son, kneeling in front of Ben and taking him gently by the shoulders. "Why didn't you wake me?"

"I could hear them inside the walls and I got scared. Everyone was sleeping, so I stayed in bed."

"I'm sorry, buddy," Brian pulls his son into his arms for

a hug. "I wish you had woken me. I will get Rosa's uncle over here to pest control the house, okay? No more ants."

Ben nods into Brian's shoulder and Brian is thankful that his son can't see his face. He knows better than to think an exterminator will help. Something just doesn't seem right about the situation.

How could ants burrow holes through a wall, especially at this scale? I've never seen anything like this, he ponders.

But he doesn't want to scare Ben so he keeps his face neutral. The poor kid is already traumatized.

"Go on and get dressed for school while I fix this up," Brian releases Ben.

It's official; they're running late again. While Ben turns back to his dresser, Brian grabs the duct tape and places a fresh piece neatly over the three holes. By the time he's done, Ben is already getting his socks and shoes. He still needs to brush his teeth and pack his bag, so Brian heads downstairs to grab a bite in the meantime. The smell of eggs is wafting up the stairs, a clear indicator that Rosa has woken up.

"Hey baby," she greets him with a hug. "How's Ben today?"

Brian glances back toward the stairs to make sure his son is out of earshot before he answers. "Things still aren't... quite right," he says, unsure of how else to respond.

"Be strong," she says, standing on her tiptoes to press a kiss to his lips.

It's impossible not to be comforted by her presence. She smells sweeter than any flower and her body is soft, molding perfectly to his. When she pulls away, he notices a blue smear of paint along her cheek and he wipes it away gently. Rosa rewards him with a radiant smile.

"How's the painting going?" He asks with a grin.

"It's going well! I'm about done with my final piece."

"Excited about the art show?"

Rosa nods, offering a happy grin and turning away from him to rescue his eggs with a spatula, she places them neatly on two slices of buttered toast.

Wishing he could stay and savor the food and her presence, Brian scarfs his meal down as quickly as he possibly can, washing it down with a glass of freshly squeezed orange juice before he heads out with the kids.

•••

Well after midnight, the house is as quiet as it can be. There is no such thing as true silence neither within its walls nor out in the neighborhood. Outside, the whirr and gentle flicker of streetlights and the rustle of leaves and crickets all create their own cacophony while inside, the wood creaks, the pipes groan, and the appliances all breathe mechanically. The house's sounds settle in and press down on its occupants. They never question why some noises are acceptable and others are not. They deem suburbia peaceful. It's only when something new and unfamiliar creeps through the neighborhood's veins with icy hands and sends every instinct into alarm that suburbia allows itself to be disturbed. The Brennan family feel this threat now, they hear each sound a little louder than they did before, and are suddenly less comfortable in their cushioned space than they have been since they moved in.

There's one person in the house who has been sleeping lighter than he's used to and as a strange grinding rumbles through the drywall of his room, Ben wakes, eyes snapping open so quickly that one might assume he's been awake the entire time. This is not the first time the grinding sound has pulled him from sleep. He didn't hear the ants on the first night but he's certain they must have made noise. The holes are covered with duct tape even now—he'd watched his dad cover them with neater strips than the ones he'd applied himself the evening before. The roll is still atop his dresser, alongside the flashlight he'd borrowed from his father's toolbox before bed. Grabbing it, he flicks the switch and shines it on the wall.

The silver tape flashes briefly back at him and Ben is only marginally relieved to see the holes are still covered. The grinding continues to burrow through the wall and he pictures an army of ants running toward the tape and sticking to it until there's no room to run and a wall of ants prevents them from pushing through the tape, a thousand red dots clustered on top of each other. *Is that when they would begin digging the next hole into the walls of my room?* The thought terrifies him.

Ben can hear his dad's voice in his head: *"I wish you'd woken me..."*

Glancing between the wall and the door, Ben wonders if he can make it to the door. Does he want to risk running past the wall or being between it and the exit? His heart is racing where he sits just imagining himself getting out of bed and making a run for it. Maybe if he pictures it, believes in himself doing it, he'll actually move. The noise is getting louder and louder and he feels like he's running out of time and yet, he can't stop staring between the wall and the door.

Then, as he watches, the drywall begins to give way in one particular spot. A hole begins to appear as something pushes through it, showering the floor in dust. Ben's jaw drops and he breathes heavier than before, but he can't bring himself to rip his eyes away from the sight of whatever it is that's making the hole. The burrowing seems to be all around him, so much louder and more insistent than the slow, creeping movements he can see in front of him. Suddenly, a small, dark object pushes through the hole and out of the wall, shooting forward and flexing. Every hair on the back of Ben's neck stands up straight. A chill travels up his spine as the dark object slowly withdraws back into the wall and Ben, practically hyperventilating, pulls the covers over his head and hides away, flicking the flashlight off.

Like the night before, he knows he has no choice but to remain hidden, unable to escape his bed or use the bathroom. The room still smells of urine and he winces at the thought of his father finding him in a wet bed again. After a while, his breathing begins to slow and Ben notices that the grinding noise has stopped. His room is significantly quieter. He considers getting out of bed to cover the new hole before the ants can make their way back in, trying to summon all the bravery he can. It's there, somewhere deep down inside—the same bravery that made him go to his sister's room when he heard her screaming.

With a deep breath, he readies the flashlight and pops his head up over the covers, shining it back toward the wall. The new hole is visible further away from the others, with no object piercing through it. Squinting into the spot of light, he sees a tiny red ant wander out of the hole.

Then another. And another.

I knew it, he thinks. *My dad was wrong. The ants are burrowing through my wall.*

Ben hurriedly leaps out of bed, grabbing the roll of silver tape from the dresser on his way. Then, taking slow, steady steps, he begins walking toward the wall. Balancing his flashlight under his armpit, he rips off a piece of tape as quietly as he can. He expects it, but he's still startled when it gives its unavoidable screech. His heart is already racing when upon his approach, the small, dark object pops out of the hole. This time, he's close enough to identify what it is and his breath catches in his throat, all the air is pulled from his lungs leaving him spluttering in shock.

A finger!

The finger flexes and Ben jumps back in fright, slipping on the rug and falling on the floor. His flashlight lands on the crumpled fabric, facing behind him, in the wrong direction. Ben can hardly breathe. He's blind; the direct sight he'd had of the hole had been completely extinguished and he can't shake the feeling that something is watching him. He didn't dare to move and soon, his eyes begin to adjust to the light. But all that does is present him with shadows twisted by what little indirect light the flashlight gives off as it shines on the wall behind him.

In the shadows, Ben can see the boy's finger, a Black

boy's finger, wiggling through the hole in the wall. With shaking hands, Ben reaches around blindly for the flashlight, mesmerized by the movement of the fingertip. The moment he moves, the finger stops. It points straight out, right at him, and then turns and bends inward, gesturing for him to come toward it.

Something about this sends Ben into action and he pushes himself back as far as he can, using his hands to slide along the wood away from the wall. He reaches the side of his bed and instinctively grabs his comforter and sheets, tugging them off his bed and down over his head and body, desperate to escape. He hopes he might find comfort in hiding.

It's dark beneath his bedding and he closes his eyes. He's trembling. From outside the blanket, he hears a soft hissing.

No, not hissing. Whispering. The faint words of a young boy drift to him, seeming to come from within the walls themselves.

"Come closer," the voice says.

Ben freezes, unable to escape the voice.

"Come closer… Come closer so you can see…"

But Ben doesn't want to see. His skin feels frosty, colder than it should be beneath the heap of linen atop his body. He doesn't know if this is shock setting into his bones or if this is how he responds to fear. He has nothing to compare to because he's never been so scared before.

Perhaps, it's because his body doesn't know how to deal with being so exhausted, cowering for what felt like hours. Ben can't help when his eyes flutter shut and he gives in.

Before he knows it, the room fades away and everything goes dark.

The voice continues to hiss long after Ben can hear it.

Waking comes with a painful twinge in his neck, after-effects of the uncomfortable position he'd fallen asleep in against the wooden frame of his bed. Consciousness returns slowly this time, coming with a sense of confusion. *Why is it so dark and quiet?* Almost as soon as he wonders, he remembers the voice, the whispers, and the strange grinding sound. He's not sure how much time has passed, but he knows he's going to have to leave the bundle eventually.

With sluggish movements, Ben opens the comforter to take a look. The first thing he sees is the flashlight lying on the floor, dimmer than before. The batteries are dying. He stretches his arm out, the comforter still wrapped around the bottom half of his body, and grabs it, boldly shining it on the wall with the holes before he has a chance to second-guess himself.

The coast is clear.

Ben inhales in surprise and relief and something else that wakes with the revelation that he's alone in his room. For now. Determined to cover the hole, he climbs out of his sheets and retrieves the duct tape. Each movement is quick but careful. He tiptoes across the floor, heart racing. The dim flashlight is once again tucked under his armpit. This time, he's prepared for whatever comes out of the wall and he's not going to let it stop him.

I'm not, he thinks, as if trying to convince himself. *I won't let you stop me.*

Under the dim light of his flashlight, he sees nothing. He shines it inside the newest hole hesitantly and sees that it's the same as the others. His father had asked him if he was the creator and Ben had secretly known why. The holes are all finger-shaped. He glances between his own index finger and the wall in front of him. They are almost the size of his, of a boy's. Curious, Ben lifts his finger toward the hole and compares the size closer, edging nearer and nearer to the wall.

Scarcely able to breathe, Ben brushes his fingertip along the outer edge of the ring and then, mesmerized, presses it into the hole. At first, he doesn't go further than the entrance, turning his finger around and around. Slowly, he slips the rest of his finger into the hole, until his knuckle touches the wall.

"Ahhh!" Ben yelps.

Something inside the hole grabs a hold of him by the tip of his finger and in a panic, Ben tries to pull it back out of the hole. The harder he pulls, the stronger the grip on his finger becomes. It pulls at him with an unusual amount of strength and he drops both the tape and the flashlight in his effort to rip himself free. His opposite hand flies out and smacks against the wall. He uses it as leverage to try and break away but he isn't strong enough and the next thing he knows, his shoulder hits the wall, too weak to continue fighting against whatever has taken hold of him.

Terrified, Ben releases a scream. It's one of fear and pain. He feels as if he's being pulled *into* the wall, his body bending in a way it shouldn't, not unless he was made of foam. His eyes widen and he screams again.

At some point, the room around him disappears and he is shrouded in darkness, blinded. The next scream he utters is swallowed by the wall around him as he sinks into it and quickly becomes aware that all the air has disappeared too. Lungs burning with the effort of trying to suck in another breath, Ben's throat closes up and he begins sputtering and choking when nothing comes. The darkness and the wood press in on him from all sides, claustrophobia sends shudders through him until, impossibly, his eyes adjust to the darkness and he can make out a shadow.

The silhouette of a young Black boy comes into sight, his body peppered with a thousand moving dots. Red ants crawl along every inch of his ebony skin, dancing inward and outward in a way that makes it look like the boy is made of them.

"Come closer," the boy whispers, staring down at Ben.

"Come closer so you can see the holes inside of me..." Ben follows the boy's gaze, eyes falling to the end of his finger. It's still in a hole, but the hole isn't in the wall—it's in the center of the Black boy's chest. Screaming again, Ben's lungs fill with a breath and he shuts his eyes as tightly as he can so he doesn't need to see the boy anymore. He feels his body go free, the grip on his finger and the pressure of the wall enclosed around him are gone.

Opening his eyes, Ben discovers that it's morning and he's crumpled on the floor, a pain in his neck and the comforter on top of him.

"Ben, wake up! Ben... you're having a bad dream," his father stands over him.

His eyes burn from the lack of sleep as he takes a look

around the room. The tape and flashlight are on the floor. His father takes notice of them too and shortly after that, Ben watches his father's face change at the sight of the wall and the fourth strip of tape covering the newest hole.

"I had to cover another one," Ben murmurs when his father looks back over at him. He's not sure what to do when his father walks back out of the room, muttering about how nothing makes sense anymore.

8

DENMAN ROSS

T hursday.

It takes Ben a few minutes to abandon the comforter after his father leaves his room. The only thing that gets him up is the desperate pressure in his bladder. Somehow, the sunshine makes things less scary, but not so scary that he doesn't look down when he walks past the wall with all the holes. He can see the duct tape out of his peripheral.

In the bathroom, when Ben goes to wash his hands, he notices a brown spot on the tip of his finger and brings it up to his face to further examine it. This close, he can tell the spot isn't brown and furrows his brows in confusion; it's more like a reddish-brown, like some kind of dirt or mud. With his thumb, he scrapes away and watches as it moves, crumbling to dust between the fine lines of his fingertip.

Strange.

It's only as the faucet is turned and the water turns slightly red that he understands the dirt on the tip of his finger wasn't dirt at all; it was blood. Waking up in the comforter made him think it had all been a dream and the possibility that it might have been real weighs heavy. He simply washes his hands in silence, wishing it was as easy to quiet his thoughts as it is to keep his mouth closed. His dad's right. Nothing makes sense anymore.

•••

Back in their bedroom, Brian is doing all he can not to pace lines into the rug on his and Rosa's floor. He had to undo the top button of his shirt for how tight it seemed to get the moment he left his son's room. Now, he wants to roll up his sleeves for how hot it seems to be.

"I just found Ben sleeping on the floor in his comforter," he finally says to Rosa. "His room had this weird smell."

"Smell? Did he wet his bed again?"

"No, no," Brian recalls the scent in his son's room. The only frame of reference he can think of is that it smells like a bar downtown. "It smelled like weed or sweet tobacco or something."

"You think he is smoking weed?" Rosa's eyes widen, lashes already black and voluminous from her mascara.

"Hell no. He's only eleven."

Rosa gives a half-shrug. "Well, he *has* been acting

strange."

"Don't be silly," Brian shakes his head. "It was smokey and could have been incense for all I know. Plus, just because his room smelled odd doesn't mean that he had anything to do with it." As he speaks, he watches Rosa put her hair into a ponytail and tries to identify the odor in Ben's room from memory. Weed doesn't quite fit the description. There were definite hints of tobacco and something else—something with a sweetness to it.

"Brian, baby," Rosa turns to him once her hair is up. "You are a good father. I love that you work to get your son help with his ADHD and learning. You've always been his advocate and I love that about you."

"Thank you, baby—"

"But please," she continues, speaking over him. It's then that he sees the lines of worry on her forehead. "There is something wrong with Ben. His behavior this week has been terrible. It's not just the ants… and the hole…" She looks down, taking in a breath. "I'm scared, okay? I mean, I seriously worry about sleeping without the door locked and even Morgan is locking her door."

It's not like Rosa to look as small as she does at this moment and Brian is compelled to pull her into his arms for a hug. Instead, he moves nearer to her and taps her chin, making her look up at him. "I understand, love, but Ben isn't going to hurt anyone. He was really messed up by the ants—this all started with them and with the holes in his wall—and we'll overcome this."

Rosa bites her lip.

"By the way, did you call your uncle? I want him to take

a look, see if he can find the root of this ant problem and treat it."

"I haven't yet, I..." She stops mid-sentence. "Wait, you said *holes*. There was only one hole on Sunday."

"Oh yeah," Brian murmurs. He forgot he hadn't told Rosa about the previous morning's incident further than Ben having wet the bed. It was a bit hard to avoid that topic when she was the one who put his washing out. "I didn't have a chance to tell you. There are four holes now."

The expression on Rosa's face says what Brian's been thinking all week, *what the hell is going on?*

"I'll call Reyes today," she says.

•••

The day is a long one. The office is a collection of cubicles ringing endlessly and the frustrated voices of the people answering, the same people who mutter beneath their breaths at those who allow their phones to ring, never intending to pick them up. Brian is among the former and his boss is among the latter—usually. Today, he's more than a little distracted. He's gone out to the smoking area several times throughout the day already, not because he smokes, but because it's the only place to get a little sunshine without leaving the building and he can't help feeling trapped inside, unable to focus on any tasks he sets out to do. The house had been in too much of a flurry that morning to eat breakfast, so he'd taken his lunch hour earlier than usual, eating a tuna salad sandwich on a bench that smelled mildly of nicotine.

It's on his way back from one such trip, smelling like smoke himself, that he hears the phone in his cubicle ringing.

"Hello?" Brian picks the phone up from the outside, having speed-walked the rest of the way here.

"Hi Mr. Brennan, this is Ms. Ramirez. I'm Ben's Language Arts teacher."

"Oh, hello Ms. Ramirez," Ben settles in at his desk. "Is everything okay?"

"Well, yes," Ramirez says unconvincingly. "I mean, Ben is okay. But I'm calling you with some serious concerns." Brian nervously looks around to see if anyone is within earshot or paying any extra attention to him, which they aren't. "Ben told me he's at your house this week. Is that correct?"

"Yes."

"Well, I have Ben for fourth period, right before lunch. We just finished this class and something quite disturbing came up. I asked the students to write a paragraph about their favorite TV shows. At first, Ben didn't want to participate. He told me he only likes YouTube."

It's not like Ben not to participate. He usually tries harder than the other kids, overcompensating in an attempt to blend in a little more.

As if reading his mind, Ben's teacher says, "I have found at times that his ADHD requires me to redirect him or allow him to use different methods to motivate him to learn with the class. Well, in this case, he suggested he could do the assignment if he could draw a picture with the paragraph. As we both know, he loves drawing pictures, so I was happy to accommodate."

"Yes…" Brian isn't sure he wants to find out where this

is going.

"Well, I think it would be best if I just read you his paragraph," Ms. Ramirez says with a sigh, "Ben wrote: 'I do not like TV no more. I have no favorite shows. I just watch my wall because it is full of holes. If I look inside the holes, I can see a boy looking back at me.'"

A boy looking at him? "Oh my god," Brian says in a hushed tone. "He actually wrote that?"

"Yes, he did," Ms. Ramirez says. Even before he continues, Brian senses foreboding in the teacher's voice and knows something more is coming. "He also drew that picture I mentioned earlier and well, it's more disturbing than the paragraph. It looks like a picture of a bedroom. There are holes in one of the walls and, in front of that wall, Ben drew what appears to be a little Black boy. The boy has several red circles drawn into him, as if he is made of bloody holes." The sigh Ms. Ramirez releases sends static into Brian's ear. "I'm sure I don't need to tell you that this is unorthodox and worrisome."

"I don't know what to say," Brian murmurs into the phone line, worried someone in the office will overhear the conversation. "Things at home have been very challenging this week. There was a bit of an incident involving ants in his room. They came out of a hole in his wall and they were crawling all over him." He glances around again. How can he judge Ben when his own paranoia has worsened over the week? The only person who seems to be paying any attention to him is the receptionist, but she simply nods his way when they meet eyes. Brian dips his head low, knowing she's not the reason he feels like he's being watched. "He's been shaken, talking about the ants and the holes. Probably trauma. But he's never mentioned anything about a boy inside the wall."

"I understand. Well, that does seem like a possible trigger for such strange behavior," the teacher says on the other end of the line. "I sent him to Mrs. Atwell's office. He got very upset when I tried speaking to him about the whole assignment. I can transfer you to her now. I just thought you needed to know what the situation is so that you can address it."

"Thank you for sharing. I appreciate your concern and I'll speak to Ben's mother as well."

"You're welcome. Let me transfer you."

Ms. Ramirez presses a button, a click sounds in Brian's ear, and then there's a long beep before he hears a dial tone. The phone rings twice.

"Mrs. Atwell," the school nurse responds.

"Hi Mrs. Atwell, it's Brian Brennan, Ben's father."

"Ah, hello Mr. Brennan. Ben is here now. He doesn't want to go back out to interact with the other kids and although he seems fine physically, I think it would be detrimental if we tried to force him to work when his mental state doesn't seem to be quite so stable."

Brian runs a frustrated hand over his face. Yet another day of asking his boss to let him take care of his personal life. *How much longer until my position is in jeopardy, if it isn't already?*

"Has he been sleeping?" The nurse asks when he doesn't respond.

"It's been a bit of a rough week. When I woke him up

for school this morning, he'd been in the middle of a bad dream."

"I see. That would explain a lot. I can suggest you try some Melatonin, it's a natural relaxant that will help him sleep. It's not a prescribed medication, so nothing too strong."

"Okay, that sounds fine," Brian nods. Ben could use the sleep. "I'll be there soon to pick him up and take him home. Do I need to sign him out?"

"I'll have the note ready for you when you arrive," Mrs. Atwell says. "We'll see you soon."

The call ends with another click and the line goes dead. Brian holds the phone to his ear in silence, glancing at the digital clock on his desktop. He regrets taking his lunch hour early. Right now, it's around the time his boss normally takes his lunch break at some upscale restaurant. Sure enough, when Brian stands to look over the rim of his cubicle into his boss' office, he finds that it's empty. A day where his boss leaves the office without calling him out is an unusual one, but Brian gets an idea.

The school is near enough that, traffic willing, he'll be able to pick Ben up, drop him off at the house, and get back before his boss. Not only does his boss leave for lunch early, but he tends to take a few extra minutes to get back to his office too.

Out in the SUV, Brian pairs his phone and dials Rosa.

"Hey baby," he says as she answers, speaking quickly because he knows his girlfriend loves chatting and neither of them has the time right now. "Listen, I'm on my way to pick Ben up from school. I'll tell you more later tonight. I have to leave as soon as I've dropped him off at home—my boss is getting sick and tired of all the coming and going and personal issues."

"Of course," Rosa answers. "I'm running a few errands right now, but I'll wrap things up and head home as soon as I can."

"Thanks, love you!"

Brian ends the call and, with a sideways peep at the time, presses his foot down on the accelerator.

•••

As evening falls, gravel crunches beneath the wheels of the SUV and the headlights against their garage door shine brighter than the house itself. Brian never misses the action of the evening, always arriving a second past dusk, which is arguably the quietest part of the day. No, the times he arrives home tend to be filled with several moments all at once; the preparation of dinner, a strange occurrence in which every light suddenly turns and remains on, reluctant requests to look over the kids' homework assignments for them, the chore of making sure they're ready for bath time, dinner, and the following day simultaneously, and his favorite of them all—the moment he gets to see everyone he loves at the end of a long day, gets to experience the briefest seconds of smiles and hugs and sometimes kisses that come with his return home, something that feels unique to this singular event in his life. This week has been different and, even driving up, Brian catches sight of the windows and a heaviness settles on him. Tonight, as far as he can tell, there are only three lights on in the house and none of them are in the kitchen. He already knows that inside, the hustle and bustle of the night is missing.

"I'm home," he calls into the house.

No sound returns to him, no movement, and no response. He finds himself switching lights on as he walks through the house. The only one he doesn't need to flick is the downstairs bathroom, but no one occupies it. Whoever switched it on left it that way when they vacated the area. There's no one downstairs at all. Hoping this is a temporary state and that things will get back to normal soon, he climbs the steps two at a time. He would be happy to greet *anyone* at this rate. It feels as if he's in someone else's house.

At the top of the stairs, a low whimper can be heard. It's high-pitched and distressed so Brian gravitates toward it with an ache in his chest. He's sure he knows what the noise is but he denies the sniffing and heavy, shaky sound of her breathing, not wanting it to be true.

The sound leads Brian into a room with high windows and walls covered in pieces of art, clippings of art theory, pieces of fabric and paper, and a variation of things Brian can't name by sight. Bright colors greet him from almost every angle of the room, the faces of children smile at him from frames with Rosa's signature on them, all compositions of Mexican folk art. Their mood doesn't match the energy of the room. In the corner, beneath a floor lamp that offers the only source of light, where moonlight and sunlight filter onto it, Rosa is curled up on a small, light brown love seat, her olive shoulders heaving with each sob. Her face is hidden in the crook of her arm and she doesn't notice him until his shadow falls over her.

Looking at him brings a fresh wave of tears crashing over the lined brims of her eyes.

Brian takes a gentle hold of her shoulder and rubs her arm. "What happened?"

"I'm so upset," she cries, sniffing loudly. "I'm so hurt…"

She then points behind him and Brian, turning, sees her easel. He can barely make it out, so he walks closer, until he can see the details of the acrylic painting up close. It depicts a young Mexican boy, his eyes open and gleaming. He looks refreshed and happy, pressing a classic glass Coca-Cola bottle against his cheek. Brian finds that the smile on the boy's face is contagious but when he steps to the side to look at the piece from a new angle, the lamp of the light hits it and more detail than Brian wants to see becomes visible. The artwork is almost complete.

Almost.

A long exhale falls from his lips, audible across the room where Rosa simply sits and watches him discover the source of her sorrow. His face sinks and his shoulders slump. He hadn't seen it at first, not without the light. The painting is completely ruined. It was destroyed by someone. Light now shines through parts of the canvas, made possible by over a dozen holes that had been pierced into it. Brian's eyes take it all in from the top of the canvas and when his eyes fall to the bottom, he sees the tool that was used to puncture Rosa's artwork; a paintbrush, its wooden handle snapped into a sharp, pointed edge.

Brian doesn't need to ask. He knows.

Ben did this. Deliberately.

The dull ache Brian felt when he walked up the stairs shifts into a steady pang that fills his chest, part of it strengthened by how sorry he feels for his girlfriend and a larger part of it disappointed that his son could do something like this. He sits back on a nearby painter's stool, shifting his weight and absorbing the damage before him. A tin can lies on its side on the work table beside the stool, paintbrushes spilling out of it and across the surface. The wall beside the canvas is Rosa's workstation, filled with a collage of inspirational sketches of bits and pieces of the facial expressions Rosa would have used to forge her final portrait. Within them are the color wheel and a second color chart used for referencing the grayscale color scale. The chart bears a bold label above it: "The Denman Ross Value Scale."

Brian finds himself zoning in on the scale. It's a nine-step value scale, lines of color going vertically in direction, starting from the top with lighter shades and getting darker down toward the blackest shade on the scale, moving from white into a light gray and continuing into the darkest of them all. They fan out before him and the longer he stares at the shades, the more the colors spread outward until he's seeing more shades than are actually in front of him, and the lines that separate them become blurry. He sits this way for a minute until the room fades away and his eyes start to water from staring into the color void.

When he blinks, the scale comes back into focus and the lines separate once more. The white is so clean against the background that it's almost invisible and the shift into the next color is less than subtle.

Kinda like Ben's shift in behavior. Quick, sudden, and incomprehensible.

Looking into the lines and taking in the descent from light into darkness, Brian fears that his son is going in the same direction. Things have been getting darker and darker by the day.

"I'm so sorry, baby," he whispers, sure that Rosa won't hear him.

"I know you don't want to hear it again, but something is *wrong*," Rosa whispers back. "Things are getting worse."

The voice he hears is different from the expression on her face. When Brian looks at her, he catches the tightness of her mouth and the way she narrows her eyes. Every muscle seems rigid and taut. He knows this stance well enough, though he's lucky to not often find himself on the receiving end of it. Rosa is angry.

And yet, despite the anger, her concern and disappointment shine through, showing him just how much she cares.

A glance back at the painting fills Brian's mind with the image of his son, angrily snapping the paintbrush in half and repeatedly stabbing it through Rosa's work of art. He imagines his arm pulling back and slamming down again and again, hard and fast. There is nothing precise or calculated about the holes and that leads Brian to believe there was some kind of negative emotion behind the action. As quickly as it's there, the image is gone and he shuts his eyes to rid himself of it.

"You're right, I know," he sighs and steps off the stool, going back to the love seat. "Tomorrow after work, Kim will be here to pick him up. You'll get to work on your art in peace and you won't have anything to worry about for a week. It'll give you—us—a little bit of a break from all the crazy that's been going on lately."

Rosa nods, her shoulders relaxing slightly. "I guess you're right."

When he opens his arms, Rosa shifts her weight into him without uncrossing her own arms, her way of saying she's still angry, but not angry enough to reject his embrace. He gives a fleeting smile against her hair and gives her a gentle squeeze.

"Will the painting affect your upcoming show?"

He feels Rosa's sigh more than he hears it, every inch of her seeming to sink into him as the disappointment rolls through her once more and he regrets asking. "I'll have to use another piece," she says with defeat.

Brian holds Rosa until her arms are no longer crossed, the white line around her mouth disappears, and, albeit a more reserved one than he was used to, he gets a giggle out of her. When she's feeling a bit better, she leaves to make dinner—by way of phoning the pizza place. He sits on the love seat for a while after she leaves and only when he hears her speaking on the phone does he leave the room, pointedly avoiding gazing directly at the painting on his way out, lest images of his son thrashing and brandishing a broken paintbrush as a weapon invade his mind again. The path to his son's bedroom is filled with anxiety.

The door isn't fully closed, nor is it ajar. It's almost as if someone closed it in passing and didn't want to bother going back when they didn't hear it click shut. Brian had been in that type of headspace before. He couldn't judge. Approaching, he's hit with a whiff of sweetness, floating atop a cloud of smoke. Distinct.

It's that tobacco smell again.

Hesitantly, he pushes open the door. His son is curled up on the bed, in much the same position that Brian found Rosa. The only difference is that Ben doesn't look sad, instead, he's staring dead ahead at the wall covered in strips of duct tape.

"Hey bud," Brian says.

Ben's head snaps toward his father and his eyes widen as if surprised to see him standing there. Brian could have sworn that wasn't possible, given that the door was uncovered and there was a direct line of sight from the bed. He pushes the thought away.

"I didn't mean to do it, Dad," Ben whispers. "I swear, I really didn't. But the boy in the painting wouldn't stop looking back at me."

It's only now, when his son's small eyes are looking up at him pleading, that Brian can see Ben isn't as unaffected as he first believed. His eyes are red from crying and his voice is hoarse. He's as upset, if not more upset, than Rosa was... *is.*

"Rosa's really upset, bud," Brian responds. "That piece of art meant a lot to her. It was really important for her upcoming show too. You know how hard she's been working on that."

"I know, Dad! That's why I would never do something like this on purpose!"

"Okay, okay. I believe you."

Truthfully, Brian isn't sure what to believe anymore. How could something like that have been an accident? It doesn't make any sense, but he doesn't want Ben to get louder, doesn't want to upset Rosa or Morgan any more than they have been, and certainly doesn't want to make Ben feel any worse. It's difficult not to feel like he's being pulled in different directions.

The two stare at one another, Brian standing across the room near the door and Ben sitting cross-legged on his bed. Something about Ben doesn't invite Brian to want to go near him. Perhaps it's that he can sense that Ben doesn't want him to come near or perhaps it's that the image of Ben's violent behavior in Rosa's art room won't leave his mind. The latter creeps through him coldly, leaving him hollow with guilt but still, he doesn't approach the bed.

"Do you wanna fill me in on what happened at school today?"

Ben winces. "I don't want to talk about it."

"All right," Brian says. "All right."

Ben doesn't answer, turning away from his father. The moment his eyes land on the wall, his face goes as blank as it was when his father entered the bedroom. Brian can't shake the feeling that he's been dismissed and finds himself turning to leave the room, glancing back at the wall on his way. It's a strange sight with all the tape strips covering it.

Wish I could fix Rosa's painting as easily.

In the back of his mind, he knows he hasn't fixed anything. His memory of his sons words, the paragraph his son wrote for his school assignment that morning is fresh in his mind: *If I look inside the walls, I can see a boy looking back at me.'*

Brian's relieved when he's back in the hallway, though every hair on the back of his neck stands on end.

•••

A low hissing echoes through the house, like the sound of rustling leaves. It seems near and far at the same time and, as much as he wants to ignore it, Brian can feel himself being pulled toward it. Everything is black and nothing exists except for him. The moment the sound started, it was as if his world started to fade away and he grew more aware that living in a dark void that seemed stable enough to hold him wasn't how he normally spent his days. The peace that had been present for so many precious seconds had been vacuumed up by the noise, the rustling, and now, Brian can feel it sucking him away too.

Whispers, he thinks, when his eyelids flutter open.

Brian shifts in bed and swallows, his tongue heavy in his mouth. The clock on the bedside table tells him he's been pulled out of sleep, dehydrated and confused, at three in the morning. He takes a sip from a water bottle on the table and sighs, settling back in beside Rosa. It's just as he closes his eyes that he hears the sound again, a gentle hissing.

What is that?

Not leaves. Voices. Whispers.

At three in the morning?

Carefully unwrapping his arms from Rosa, Brian steps out of bed and walks down the hall toward the source of the commotion. His feet lead him toward Morgan and Ben's rooms without his guidance. The voices have stopped but he's certain they came from this direction. A draft whips through the hallway and when his skin turns to gooseflesh, he regrets leaving the warmth of his bed and girlfriend's body.

Stopping at Morgan's room first, Brian reaches for the handle and finds that it's quiet. He starts to lean in to press his ear to the wood when he hears the whispers pick up again, far more recognizable now that he's closer to them. They're coming from Ben's room.

I shouldn't be surprised, Brian creeps further down the hall. Tonight, Ben has shut his door and, rather than open it, Brian decides to listen in on the conversation. The whispers are quick and insistent before he presses his ear to the door.

All at once, the sound stops. Brian spends a paranoid moment wondering if his son somehow knows he's on the other side of the door and then Ben speaks and it vanishes. He listens intently.

"I drew a picture of you at school and that got me in trouble."

Brian waits for the response, but none comes.

"I know," Ben says, as if answering someone. "It was stupid. Now everyone thinks I'm crazy."

There's another pause and, unwilling to believe his son is having a conversation with himself, Ben presses his ear to the door so tightly that it hurts. Still, he hears nothing.

"I don't mind. I'm not afraid anymore."

That makes one of us, bud...

"I told them, but nobody believes me. I am going to my mom's house tomorrow, so you won't see me for a while."

This time, when Ben stops speaking, he doesn't start

again. The silence lasts. At some point, he thinks he hears the shift of Ben's covers and imagines that his son has finally gone to sleep, but he's not so sure. Part of him wonders if Ben knows he's standing behind the door and that's the reason he's gone quiet. It seems impossible and yet, it's not a feeling that leaves him.

Brian is full of feelings, the biggest one being fear. More than that, as he stands there and absorbs everything he heard his son say, he can scarcely breathe. The ache in his chest resurfaces as Brian heads back to his bedroom. When he climbs back into bed, Brian can only think one sad thought: *What is happening to my son?*

9

MY SON

Friday.

"I have a favor to ask," Brian wraps his arms around Rosa from behind and presses his lips to the back of her head.

"Sí?" She passes him a fresh cup of coffee. He takes a heavenly sip.

"Ben's still sound asleep. It's the first time all week that I've gone into his room to find him… just, well, sleeping." He hasn't told Rosa that he heard Ben talking to himself in the middle of the night. He doesn't plan to. They've had enough drama for one week. "I was thinking it might be best if we kept him home from school for the day."

"And it's a favor because I'll be here," she turns to face him, one brow arched.

Brian's heart races as he nods his head. "I'll plant that rose bush you keep talking about, before the summer?"

Rosa gives him a small smile and he tries to ignore that it doesn't touch her eyes. "It's okay. This is probably for the best. He's had a tough week and a break from everything might be good for him. It was for Morgan."

"You have no idea how much of a sweetheart you are," he whispers, leaning in and pressing his lips to hers. He means it, especially considering everything she'd been through the previous day. She tastes like coffee and a hint of spearmint. "I wish I could spend all day with you too."

Desire flashes through Rosa's eyes and Brian knows that if Morgan had not been sitting at the table eating her breakfast in the next room, they might have had a very different morning. As it is, with Ben asleep, he might make it to work on time. A first this week. So, resisting the urge to take her upstairs, he turns away from Rosa with a wink and pokes his head into the dining room. His girlfriend gives him a playful pout.

"Ready to go, Morgs?"

"Yeah," Morgan stands from the table without raising her eyes from the smartphone in her right hand. With the opposite, she swings her backpack over one shoulder. "Bye, Rosa."

She's gone before Rosa can answer and Brian follows her to the SUV, giving Rosa a small shrug on his way out and leaving a half-finished cup on the countertop.

"Rosa's going through a hard time, you know," Brian

tells Morgan as they buckle up.

"Well, she's not the only one, I'm literally bleeding all day" his daughter replies. He's not quite sure what to say to that; he supposes she's right. "What's going on with Ben anyway?"

"He's going through a hard time too… What happened to him was very traumatizing and he hasn't been taking it well."

"Sooo, what does that mean?"

Good question. "It means that your mom and I have to take him to the doctor next week. He'll be able to tell us how to improve things or give your brother medicine. Hopefully everything will go back to normal after that."

Out of the corner of his eye, he sees Morgan look up from her phone for the first time since climbing into the SUV. "How do you know that?"

They pull into the school grounds and Brian turns to face his daughter, surprised to find she's still looking at him. Her voice has none of its usual bravado and even now, there's an inkling of fear in her expression.

"It's my job to know these things and I'm gonna make sure that they are. I promise."

Morgan chews on the inside of her cheek.

"Hey," Brian says, reaching out to tuck a strand of loose hair behind her ear. "You know I never break a promise. To prove it, I'll text your mom right now."

Tugging his phone out of its holder, Brian keys in Kim's number and types out a text message.

Brian 7:57 AM

Hey Kim, Ben is staying home from school today. Had to pick him up from school early yesterday and figured he could use the rest. We need to schedule an appointment with his pediatrician ASAP.

"There, see?" He locks his phone and puts it away, hoping his message is vague enough that Kim doesn't decide to call him back immediately after seeing it. "One step closer to things being better, okay?"

"Okay," she nods.

"I mean it."

"Yeah." She nods again, a little more vigorously than before and, like Rosa, none of that vigor touches her eyes. "I heard the bell for the first period. See you later, Dad."

"Love you!" He calls—right in time for the door to slam shut in his face.

Brian sits and watches until Morgan enters the school building, and then drives off. The conversation with his daughter plays on his mind throughout the drive to the office, as does her question. What is happening with his son? As much as he wants to put on a brave face for the girls, he doesn't know the answer to that question and it scares him more than he cares to admit. Worse than that, he promised Morgan that everything will be okay, that a visit to the doctor's office could—no, did he say *would?*—

fix Ben right up, but he has no idea if that's true. He tries to rationalize that he only lied to bring her some comfort and reassurance, but he feels heavy with the fear that what's happening to his family might be his fault. *What if Kim is right about all the medicine Ben has been taking?* He's afraid he made a promise he can't keep. *What if things don't turn out okay in the end?* There are too many unknowns and his stomach grows tighter with each second and each failed attempt to look on the bright side. *What if Rosa is right and there really is something wrong with Ben, something that medicine can't and won't fix?*

Kim sure would love that, wouldn't she?

Recalling the events of the week thus far, images of Ben flash through Brian's mind—Ben thrashing around his bedroom floor, Ben snapping a paintbrush and driving it through his girlfriend's art repeatedly, and Ben showing his class a picture of a boy in his room covered with bloody holes the way his teacher had described. Brian's arms tremble, knuckles whitening where his fingers grip the steering wheel. They're beginning to ache. As much as he wants to deny that there is anything to be afraid of, Morgan's expression seems to have struck a nerve and it's made him question everything he's been defending. He's finally on the same page as everyone else—Ben might not be right in the head.

And Brian feels like there's nothing he can do to help him.

Before he knows it, his face is hot and wet as tears pour down his face. A gasp bursts free from his chest. He swings a palm up to brush them away but they don't stop. The façade of strength he's been maintaining is finally caving in. He'd known this moment was bound to come. It's been inevitable. Mind racing with the fear of the unknown, Brian pulls off to the right of the freeway. He's far too emotional to be driving in the thick morning traffic. Someone blares their horn at him before he can come to a halt with a grunt from the engine. The fear and emotion send pain through his body and, wracked with sobs, he takes deep and shuddering breaths in an attempt to calm himself down. Traffic continues to whirr past the SUV but he's blind to it—everything is a blur of colors and lights until his tears eventually subside and his breathing evens out.

Brian blinks away what remains of the moisture on his face and in the distance, a daycare center comes into sight. It's one he's driven past many times before on his way to work. It's early enough that children flock around the playground equipment in the yard, innocent and free. They're too small to understand the kind of pain he's going through, blissfully ignorant, and Brian wishes that he could say the same for his son, wishes that children never have to eventually feel this way. The image of his son smiling at him comes to mind with the memory of the two of them laughing at his story about his brother's terrarium. It looks like there's a lone tire swing in the playground and Brian watches as a small boy climbs onto it. The sight causes his heart to flutter and he draws a long breath in as he watches the child sway back and forth. Raw emotion threatens to return at the sight of the innocent boy, his eyes prickling, but Brian feels something else beneath that. He feels a keen determination, a quiet strength emerging from somewhere deep down. Other children run around the tree with the tire swing and from where he sat, Brian imagines they are singing made-up songs. Ben used to have that kind of energy, he would run around and sing songs only he knew the lyrics to.

I have to help him. I will help him.

Sleeping at home right now is his own child, unable to experience the freedom that the children at the daycare do, and Brian knows that it's up to him to do something. If he's feeling this way, he can only imagine how helpless and scared Ben must be. They are all going through something, but Ben's the one who has the biggest fear of the holes and the ants; it's not his fault. There are things to work through and Brian doesn't think Ben can do it without his help. Eleven is too young. His son needs to know that he's not alone.

"I won't let you down," Brian whispers, choking out the sound. His voice is unfamiliar, husky with emotion. "I promise you, Ben… I will find a way to help you… Because I love you my son."

•••

Rosa's days are never quiet. Once Brian leaves with the kids, it's cleaning up the kitchen followed by a wander through the house in search of dirty laundry to put into the machine. After that, she normally does a store run for any groceries they might need—a list that grows longer on the weeks where the kids stay with them. She likes to think she has a good handle on the house and general affairs considering she does most of it alone. She has no children of her own, but she likes to think that three years with

Brian has taught her how to mother. Her heart swells at the thought of a child with Brian, a half-brother or half-sister to Ben and Morgan.

Alas, there are too many things happening right now. A child with her is probably the last thing on Brian's mind.

This morning, there are only two rooms she doesn't enter; one is at the end of the hall with the door slightly ajar, presumably from Brian having left it open when he checked on Ben earlier that day, and the other is a room that smells of paint at all times.

The shadows of canvases on the walls in her art room mock Rosa as she walks by, her heart beating a little faster with the memory of what happened yesterday. The curtains are drawn for what could be the first time since Rosa moved in, making the room appear dark and ominous with various shapes, pieces of art, standing tall and threatening. Before they'd gone to bed the previous evening, Brian offered to get rid of the damaged artwork for her and Rosa told him to leave it. She's not sure why. Now, passing the room, she wishes she hadn't. The last thing she wants is to be reminded of the piece, to look at Ben's destruction of something she'd been working on for weeks. Her art room once brought her so much peace but walking past it brings a tightness to her chest that she can only hope will go away soon. *None of this craziness can last long, can it?* Perhaps she'll ask Brian to get rid of the painting for her after all. That will fix things. She'll have no problem going in there after that thing is gone.

The sun is high when Ben finally wakes up. He wanders down the stairs and into the kitchen rubbing sleep out of his eyes. The gesture makes him appear smaller than usual, innocent.

"Hey Ben," Rosa greets him.

"Where is everyone? No one woke me up for school."

"Don't worry, you don't have to go. We thought you could stay home for the day."

"Really?" Ben moves slowly and carefully into the room. He doesn't look at Rosa, not once. His eyes are locked on the floor.

In spite of herself, Rosa's heart goes out to him. Many tears were shed over her art the previous evening and Ben hadn't joined them for pizza when it arrived, refusing to come out of his bedroom even after Brian had spoken to him. After it had happened, Ben had screamed he was sorry and she'd simply told him to get out.

It's a new day, Rosa thinks. *Maybe we can turn a new page. He clearly feels remorse—guilt—for what he's done. No use holding it against him.*

"Really," Rosa nods. "Do you want some breakfast? I can make pancakes."

Ben glances up, his eyes are brighter than she's seen them in days. Pancakes are his favorite and she knows it. "Yes, please!"

"Okay, go get dressed and tidy your room while I get started on those," she says, softening at his reaction.

In no time, she's got a bowl of batter sitting on the countertop with the handle of the ladle sticking out of it. The skillet top is steaming, sending the smell of butter through the house. The recipe is a family one. If Morgan were home, Rosa would have added chocolate chips to the mix. Soon, three perfect circles of pancake batter sit atop the skillet and Rosa watches with a spatula in one hand and her hip on the other. The sticky surface of the pancake batter gets hotter and bubbles slowly spread and pop across them.

"When you pay attention," a disembodied voice says from beside her. "Tiny holes seem to be everywhere."

Rosa jumps slightly, startled by Ben's sudden appearance at her side. He gestures at the pancake's surface, covered with an increasing number of shallow circular holes where bubbles had burst. Taken aback by the comment, Rosa hurriedly flips the pancake to reveal its golden side instead. Ben gives her a strange look and then sits at the table.

It's with his eyes on her back that his sudden appearance at her side when she hadn't heard him come back down the stairs finally registers and the realization sends a shiver up her spine. The fact that Ben is here had already occurred to her. What hadn't yet hit her until that moment was the fact that she was alone with him—and the hint of fear that comes with it.

The only sounds between the two are the sizzling of batter against steel and the occasional plop as Rosa flips pancakes. When she serves them, they come with butter melting over the top and maple syrup dripping down the sides of the stack. There's nothing ominous about Ben when he says thank you, nor when he smiles at her.

Rosa tells herself that things are returning to normal again and, deciding to take a break from all the stressful events of late, she grabs her gardening gloves and takes a walk outside. There, she tends to her garden, trimming leaves and watering the soil with bean water that she made the day before to feed the plants. The smells of sage, rosemary, and mint float around her and there are brightly colored peppers dangling invitingly. Working in the herb garden is the perfect way to recharge herself and already, she's feeling much better than when she woke up this morning. Her skin glistens under the sun and sweat drips down the tip of her nose. After a while, it turns out the ground is harder than expected and she's going to need more than her hands if she wants to make progress.

Rosa pulls the gloves off and leaves them on the grass beside the mint and then walks around to the back of the house, where there's a shed full of miscellaneous items that have no other home among Brian's overcrowded man cave in the garage, the most important of which at this moment are their gardening tools. It's a trowel that she seeks. The chain and lock on the door are rusty and take a bit of maneuvering after she's grabbed the key from a flower pot beside it. As she does, she takes note of a nail resting on the ground and takes a moment to check where it came from. It doesn't take long to find its source; it's come out of the wooden shed door. The rusty hinge is slightly loose because of its missing counterpart.

Another hole, she thinks. As soon as she does, she rolls her eyes. *Great. Now I'm thinking about holes and seeing the stupid things everywhere.*

Even so, Rosa's eyes remain on the hole that was once occupied by a nail when she swings the door open. She's almost mesmerized by it. That's when she notices movement. The tiniest flutter. She squints into the hole, unsure if she's imagining things, and sees it again. With a gulp, she looks closer and, as she watches, something forces its way through the small gap. A fuzzy black and yellow form crawls out—a bee. Her heart beats a little faster at the sight. She's always hated bees. They are quite possibly her biggest fear. The bee squeezes through, shakes itself out, and flies away. In its place, another bee comes crawling out of the hole. And another after that. As each bee flies away, Rosa cautiously pulls the door toward her again with shaking hands and pokes her head around it to find out where the bees may be coming from.

"Dios mio," she breathes, her throat suddenly tight. She takes an involuntary step back.

A beehive, the size of a pineapple, is molded into the line of the ceiling. Goosebumps rise and travel down every inch of Rosa's body. Sweat lingers on her skin, but she's cold with fear as she stares on. The honeycomb formation is constructed of holes, hundreds and hundreds of tiny holes, and she can't take her eyes away from it. The holes are everywhere, just like Ben said.

The coincidence is unwelcome and, barely able to steady her breathing, Rosa takes another step back out of the shed with care. How had she not noticed the bees? The entire shed seems to be radiating a distinctive hum as the hive buzzes with activity. There could be thousands of bees and, too afraid to look at the hole, to find out if they're still flying out of it, Rosa runs for the house as if there's fire on her heels. She doesn't close the door. Her mind is racing with the thought that her appearance has upset the bees, that there's a swarm of them behind her right now. She hears their incessant buzzing and it takes everything in her not to scream with terror she isn't sure is real.

It's no secret that she has a phobia of bees.

•••

Inside, Ben is unaware of the chaos unfolding out in the yard. Rather, he's preoccupied with his own fears, the fear that he's losing his mind being at the top of the list. Rosa thinks he doesn't know that he had frightened her but she didn't even notice that he wasn't dressed when she served the pancakes. She refused to look at him at all, nothing like she'd been when she offered to make them in the first place. Maybe she thought he wouldn't notice because he was young and naïve or maybe she simply didn't care but he did notice. He'd been worried he'd be in trouble because he hadn't gotten out of his pajamas. When Rosa told Ben to get ready for the day, he'd come to his room and, faced with the wall full of holes, stared at it motionlessly instead. The sound of the hand mixer had gone off, a telltale sound that the batter was almost ready and the smell of melting butter followed it up the stairs to where he sat and looked on. At some point, no longer wanting to be in the presence of the wall, he went back downstairs to Rosa and found more holes there, in his pancakes of all things. There'd been goosebumps on Rosa's skin when he pointed them out and he vowed internally not to say anything to her about holes again.

When he's done eating his pancakes, leaving more than half on the plate, he goes back upstairs. He wishes he were at school where there were other people around and enough noise to quiet his thoughts for a while.

"They think I don't see the way they're looking at me," he says to no one in particular. "That they're afraid. But they're wrong."

The terror of the past week feels as if it's more than any 11-year-old should have to handle—yet here he is, trying. Trying so hard.

"This is probably harder than I've ever tried before, not that anyone actually cares."

Normally, he would be happy that he didn't need to go to school. He gets a day off and he loves hanging out with Rosa. At least, he used to. Some days, she would make milkshakes. Today, she made pancakes for him. So why does he feel so empty? His teeth aren't brushed yet either and he runs his tongue along the plaque while he walks in and out of the rooms upstairs. His routines are eroding, like that of a tidal cliff. Each new wave that smashes against what was once rock breaks it down until there's nothing but sand drifting off the edge and falling away. It's only a matter of time before what's left of the cliffside is undermined and collapses into the dark waters below, leaving nothing behind and taking him with it.

Still malleable at his young age, Ben finds himself unable to contend with the darkness that seems to have extinguished everything inside him. The only way he's found to cope so far is to give in. Accepting that he's broken and helpless has removed some of the fear that he used to feel when he was around the wall, around holes. "This is simply the way things are," he tells himself.

It might not be the healthiest coping method, but what

does that matter when it's the only thing that's made him feel remotely better since Monday?

Talking to himself has brought him some comfort, albeit in small increments. Being alone is too much to bear and hearing his voice can be distracting. He regrets having taken every second before the ants and the holes for granted. Even when he's around his family, he feels alone. His dad is the only one who tries to act like everything's normal and Ben can't decide if that's better or worse than Rosa and his sister, who have no issue making their distaste for his behavior known.

"Better than being alone," he ponders. "At least Dad tries."

That one stair creaks under his foot.

Instead of making the left at the top of the stairs toward his own room, he takes the right toward Morgan's room. She left it unlocked today.

The room is clean and feminine. It's also neat, thanks to Rosa's DIY organization skills. Ben's room is the same, everything in its proper place. This room has an overarching purple theme; almost every poster has the color featured. If it didn't come that way, Morgan had placed stickers here and there to make it so. There are picture frames with images of her and her friends on her bedside table. Next to them sits a small glass aquarium. Ben makes his way over and taps on the glass.

"Lady!" He calls.

Sitting atop a perch within the tank is a western painted turtle. Lady isn't usually at the front of his mind, nor, is it unlike Ben to have entered his sister's room at all.

Normally, he's quiet and reserved, glued to the screen of his handheld game, unperturbed by the goings-on around him. He would never pet the turtle if he didn't have permission. Morgan would probably provide him with permission long before he ever asked for it. However, this week has changed things and he's devoid of his traditional emotions and quirks.

Perhaps it's for that reason that he dips his hand into the top of the aquarium, reaching in and petting Lady's head. After that, he hunches down in front of the tank and stares intently into the eyes of the turtle. They're dark green circles with a black stripe through them, her pupils bear a slight resemblance to those of a snake. Her skin bears the same resemblance, striking stripes of lime against a seaweed background. Ben thinks the wrinkles on her skin are the only thing that set her apart from a snake; the turtle's version of scales. Lady's shell has the same coloring, lime against seaweed, striped and separated by a deeper green so dark it's almost black. The name of the turtle comes from the colorful lines that run along its body. When they'd gone to the pet store a few years earlier, the man showing Lady to Morgan had told her that turtles don't hear sound but those two circular patches are the turtle's ears indeed. Ben remembers wondering how something with no ability to hear could have ears and the man told them that the ears register frequencies and vibrations rather than noises themselves.

"It probably feels like an earthquake to you when someone bangs on the glass," he whispers.

Ben's face is so close to the glass that his breath makes

it fog up and as the white cloud dissipates, the turtle is staring back at him. She lazily blinks her eyes. There's a stiffness to Ben as he stares at the turtle. He's entranced and unblinking. When Ben stands back up and turns to leave, the stiffness remains in his steps. Each one feels precise. Robotic.

In his room, Ben returns to what seems to be the only way to pass time; staring at the wall. He stands directly in front of it, close enough that if another finger were to pop out, it would probably be able to touch him. There are six holes now, each with strips of duct tape over them. He doesn't think anyone has noticed the two new holes. Minutes go by and he simply stares. Then, inexplicably, he reaches forward and peels back the tape covering the holes.

A chill seems to emanate from the wall and a soft hissing fills Ben's ears once the holes are uncovered, coming from nowhere and everywhere all at once. He gulps down the lump that has formed in his throat. The wall has begun to distort because of how fixated he is on it, blurring around the edges and pulsating in and out. Forcing himself to refocus, Ben concentrates on the first hole that ever appeared and squints deep inside it. It's deep brown, almost black, inside there. Under his gaze, the darkness shifts almost imperceptibly, something behind the wall moves the slightest amount, and his breath quickens.

An eye suddenly appears, the darkness shifting again to open. He'd been staring at a shut eyelid all along. Now the eye stares back at him and although he feels a shudder run through his body, he remains still. Curiously, he tilts his head to the side and, seemingly unmoved by the frightening sight before him, moves closer—until his eye is pressed to the hole, staring directly into the other boy's eye.

From behind the wall, the whisper gets louder. It's different this time. Rather than an incessant hissing, the voices have come together, sounding like one unit and whispering the same sinister intention at once.

The voice tells him something and Ben nods his head slowly.

10

THE LAST STRAW

Later that afternoon, Morgan arrives home from school and heads up the stairs as she always does. Rosa is nowhere in sight and Morgan assumes that she's in her art room, which is where she can be found most days at this time. She's been doing her best to distract herself from the madhouse that has become her home, so much so that she was barely aware of any tension at the dinner table the previous day. If she had, she might know that Rosa is avoiding her art room. Instead, all she's focused on is that it's finally Friday and she'll be going to her mother's house for the next week. She has to pack and feed her pet turtle, Lady, before she leaves.

On the first landing, the mechanical screech of a drill buzzes through the walls. It's coming from Ben's room. The door is shut. Morgan furrows her brows but decides to ignore her brother and head toward her bedroom. If he's doing something he shouldn't be, she doubts Rosa wouldn't have done anything about it by now. The drill gets louder as it punctures something, possibly wood. It's a bit difficult to miss.

I wonder if he's drilling more holes into the wall, she thinks.

In her room, she drops her backpack on the ground and goes over to the aquarium. She taps on the glass, hoping to draw Lady out from her hiding place beneath the mossy bridge in the water at the bottom of the tank. The turtle doesn't appear and Morgan taps again, this time harder. When Lady doesn't surface, she reaches in and lifts the bridge from its spot, revealing only murky water, algae forming in the corners.

No turtle.

From outside her bedroom, the drilling starts up again. Morgan hadn't realized it stopped at all. Once again, it sounds like Ben is drilling into something possibly wooden, something hard.

Morgan's stomach feels hollow and she can scarcely breathe walking out of her room. Her feet move toward Ben's room thoughtlessly. Her hand finds the handle of Ben's door first; she doesn't knock, pressing down and pushing her shoulder against the door. It doesn't give and her heart begins racing faster, panic starts to set in.

The drill stops.

"Ben?" She knocks her fist against the door. "Do you...

Do you have Lady?"

There's no reply.

"Ben?"

Zzzzzzzzzzzz...

Morgan takes a small step backward, frightened by the sudden sound of the drill coming back to life. When the regular sound turns into another mechanic scream as it punches into a solid surface, Morgan hears herself scream too. She throws herself against the door with fervor, banging her fists against it.

"Ben... Open the door! Ben! Please... Open the door," Morgan cries, panicking more than ever.

The drill stops and the sound of footsteps comes from behind Morgan. Rosa takes one look at Morgan, whose face is wet with tears, and shouts through the door. "Ben, open the door. Open it right now!"

Rosa, uncertain of whether Brian returned the key to its spot, reached for the trim above the door. She feels the cold metal beneath her fingertips and rips it off, shoving the tip into the lock. Morgan shoves the door open at the click and the two practically fall over the threshold in their hurry to enter.

Morgan and Rosa are shocked to see Ben standing in front of his wall, covered in drywall dust, holding up Brian's electric drill in his right hand. He's facing the wall with his back to them. It's covered in holes, so many more than there were before. Ben has been drilling tiny holes all along the surface, creating a contrast of minuscule dark circles in an otherwise pale background. If they look too long, the holes appear to move, almost pulsing in and out.

They force themselves to look away from the sight just as Ben stiffly turns around to face them. They don't see him though. Their eyes are drawn to color on the floor near his feet, a few paces away from the dust. A deep red. To their horror, they see what happened behind the door, what Ben had done, the damage he had caused to more than the drywall. The sunken green lump on the floor doesn't look anything like the beauty it had in its aquarium in Morgan's room. Its skin is sunken, darker, and worse than that, the ears that once stood out against green are practically indistinguishable among the other lime green marks on its shell and skin.

Ben drilled holes into Lady's shell, into Lady herself, with his father's electric drill. She's covered in red spots now, dark holes turned bloody. Too many to count. The turtle is covered in blood and its shell is full of holes. It's cracked in several places, dark lines breaking through in every direction. By all appearances, Lady is dead.

A tunnel closes in around Morgan and Rosa as they take in the disgusting sight of Ben's murderous act upon the turtle. Ben looks up at them, the drill dangling loosely. Although he's looking at them, neither is sure he really sees them. There's a distant stare in his eyes. For Morgan, everything seems to have grown darker.

"Come closer!" He screams. "Come closer… so you can see the holes inside of Lady!"

Morgan chokes out another hopeless sob, her face pale with shock and Rosa pulls her into her arms, whispering comfortingly in Spanish. It's hard when she's shocked and beside herself, but she somehow manages to pull Morgan away from the scene. Her only thought is to call Brian.

•••

"Brian Brennan, hello."

He has to strain his ears to hear the person on the other end of the line. All around him are the sounds of drills and construction. He's on another visit to the mine site.

He quickly realizes it's Rosa, shouting hysterically. She's freaking out so badly that he can barely hear what she's saying, with or without the cacophony around him. He catches Ben and Morgan's names but before he can say anything, before he can ask her to calm down, he's whipped around and pulled off the haul road by someone. A massive haul truck cruises past him, blowing hot air and exhaust fumes in his direction. Manny's hand releases the back of his shirt when it's gone and Brian breathes out a thank you. His heart is racing like a jackhammer, slamming against his ribs with such intensity that his chest hurts. It hits him immediately that he was inches away from being hit by the haul truck, by being flattened like the worker they'd seen crushed and bloody all over the road on their way to the site earlier that week.

"I have to go," he breathes.

Manny, annoyance evident on his face and in his voice says, "Yeah, I think you should."

They pack up and climb into the truck, leaving the other workers shaking their heads in disapproval. There's no remorse or pity on their faces. They see this kind of thing all the time and they, like Manny, are irritated by Brian's lack of care.

They've lost people who actually follow the rules. I can hardly blame them for being angry with this office guy who answers calls on the road.

Phones are dangerous distractions in a business like theirs. He knows that.

Manny drives him back to the main building, where Brian leaves without a word. There's no way he can go home in the company vehicle and it's all he wants to do. Every fiber of his being is telling him to steer in a different direction, to get off the freeway and go home to Rosa. He can still hear her panic and hysteria and his mind is running wild with the many reasons for why she could have called him in such a state. He ignores the urge, his muscles stiff with the impact of the decision.

Back at the Foster Merrick Engineering office, Brian finds himself greeted with a sight that heightens his anxiety. His boss, Martin, is standing beside his cubicle. He looks anything but happy.

"My office, Brennan."

Brian follows Martin into the office. He's still shaken up by what happened on the road, obsessing over the knowledge that his family issues could have gotten him killed. Taking a seat in Martin's office, he's surprised to see Julia, the Human Resource officer for the company. She's a severe-looking woman with light hair pulled back into a bun and she nods in greeting.

"Brian, I'm sorry to say but you're not here under positive circumstances. There's been an increasing decline in your performance this past week and it's hard not to question what's going on with you." Martin shakes his head, glancing over at Julia and it occurs to Brian that this conversation might be different if she wasn't here. He isn't sure he's ever heard Martin quite so calm. Scott probably called and informed his boss of the incident on the haul road the moment Brian left, so he's surprised he's not being sworn at. "Now, I tend to overlook the tardiness. But that ultimately depends on you and how you handle things around here. We're not in an easy business and we have to be able to handle the heat."

"Of course, sir, I—"

Martin puts his hand up to stop Brian from saying anything else. "The Hagstone project is a major client and I thought I could trust you with it but I'm not so sure you're up to the challenge anymore."

"Sir," Brian starts, waiting for Martin to nod before continuing. "This week is by no means an accurate measure of my performance. I've always been dedicated to the company. It's been a horrible week at home. Things with my son have been challenging..." He runs a hand through his hair. While he speaks, Julia takes notes on a pad. "He's gone through a traumatic event and things have kind of spiraled. I think it has to do with the meds that we give him for his ADHD. I'm taking him to the doctor next week and I've already arranged it all with my ex-wife. From there, things should return to normal."

The father rambles on until Martin holds up a hand to silence him once again. He gestures for Julia to take over, waving his hand in her direction. He's irritated.

"FME understands that you are going through a personally challenging time right now, Brian," Julia steps in on Martin's cue. "I have here with me a packet that outlines the FME Mental Health coverage we provide to all employees, as well as our Family Friendly Leave Act." She lowers the notepad, lifting a form with illegible scrawls along dotted lines. From beneath it, she tugs several booklets and hands them over to him.

"These will explain everything you need to know regarding the circumstances of your leave and the related compensation you can expect to receive during this period."

"My... leave?"

Martin nods. "We'd like for you to take four weeks of leave. We hope that this will be sufficient time to allow you to get all of your personal matters resolved. Thereafter, we will reconsider your return to employment."

Brian looks between Julia and Martin, considering his options. *Is this something worth fighting? Martin may be calmer than ever with his breathing level and... is that a tone of concern in his voice?* The vein in his forehead tells Brian a different story.

"Right," he eventually mutters, nodding slowly and telling himself it's not worth the fight. "I understand."

"The company cares about your well-being," Julia says, softer than before. "We don't want you to harbor any negative feelings toward us. We mean the best and if things improve after that, we have no doubt you'll return with a thirst for success, which means you'll put in the kind of performance we expect."

The statement instills no comfort in Brian. In fact, he feels like the last line has an edge to it. He knows Julia's speaking from a script. Interactions such as this one come with the territory of her position in the company. It's not his area of expertise, but he knows a line when he hears one. That doesn't take the sting off her words and Brian leaves the office devastated, fingers clasping the pamphlets so tight that he rips the edge of one before he tosses them into the box on his desk. He hadn't seen it behind Martin upon his arrival, but now he packs the few personal items he keeps at the office into it. There's a finality looking down at it and he can't help feeling as though everything in his life is falling apart and he's losing everything that he cares about. The insistent desire to get home, to do anything, has been almost entirely wiped out by the brief meeting.

That is, until he checks his phone.

> Kim 4:07 PM
>
> What the hell is going on at your house, Brian? Are you kidding me?

> Kim 4:09 PM
>
> WTF Brian! Call me...call me immediately. Do you really think this co-parenting?

> Kim 4:12 PM
>
> I'm on my way right now! I left work early to get the kids!

Checking the time, he notices that it's currently 4:45 p.m. His ex-wife works twenty minutes from his house. There's no way he'll be home first, she's had a head start. In addition to the flood of texts he's received from Kim, there's a voicemail from Rosa. He presses his phone to his ear to listen to it, wondering what on earth happened. Kim's messages have his heart racing for the second time that day.

"Brian, baby," she says into the line. Her voice is soft, as if she's trying not to be heard. He has to strain to hear her, pressing the phone closer, because it sounds as if someone is crying in the background. "You have to come home. Ben, he's... he's done something terrible."

The crying grows louder and Rosa's voice grows softer. Brian recognizes the sobbing before Rosa continues.

"Lady, Morgan's turtle, is dead. Ben drilled holes into the turtle with your electric drill. She's..." There's a sniffling and Rosa comforts Morgan in Spanish. "Please just come home. Kim has already called Morgan to say she's on her way."

The call goes dead. His daughter was inconsolable.

Brian grabs the box and rushes out of the office and down to his SUV too shocked to think. The drive is automatic and when he gets home, Rosa is sitting on the steps of the porch, her head in her hands. She looks the way he feels.

The face that looks up at him as he approaches is worn. Brian can tell she's been crying. Her face has been washed, but the mascara lingers beneath her red-rimmed eyes.

"I don't know what to do anymore, Brian," she says.

"I'm at my wit's end."

Brian misses his nightly routine, misses coming home to hugs and love. "I know," he takes a seat beside her on the top step. "I'm sorry things have been so rough lately…"

"No, I'm sorry, this is just… It's crazy. Shit like this is not normal. I can't and I shouldn't have to deal with it." She runs her hands through her dark, silky hair, brushing the strands back. Some fall forward, framing her face, and Brian thinks, *even at her wit's end, she's beautiful.* "And then I have to deal with Kim on top of everything else. Look, I know I'm not their real mother, but I'm doing my best! I don't deserve to be told that I'm not family. That woman is so mean and vulgar." She purses her lips. "You should have heard the things she said to me when she picked Ben and Morgan up today."

"I—"

"I'm not done," Rosa says flatly. "If you don't get help, if you, Ben, and Morgan, all of you, don't get help… I'm sorry, but I think I'll need to move out. I've already spoken to Uncle Reyes and I'm considering moving in with him. It may be for the best."

"What… What do you mean?" Brian snaps his head up. "No, baby. No. I… I'm losing so much already; I can't lose you too. First Ben, now my job, not you…"

"What do you mean? Your job?" Rosa turns to face him, brows furrowed. "You lost your job?"

"I… I was on the haul road when you called. We're not supposed to have phones out there because it's dangerous. I guess that's why they called Martin in the first place." He shrugs. "When I got to the office, he was with Julia from

HR. I've been put on leave temporarily due to performance issues. They gave me a pamphlet, so it's for a few weeks and then I go back for reassessment, I guess to decide whether or not they want me to come back permanently."

Rosa's eyes soften and she sighs. "I'm sorry, baby. That's devastating."

"You're telling me. It's my fault. I can't keep work and home separate."

"What you're going through is an exceptional situation."

Brian reaches out to brush one of those dark strands of hair out of her eye and Rosa sighs again. There's only disappointment in her eyes. "I'm sorry that you had such a terrible day," he whispers. "I'm sorry Kim said those things to you. You're right. You don't deserve to be treated that way."

"Sorry doesn't change things, Brian."

"I know. I'm working on things, okay? I promise. I'm setting an appointment with the pediatrician next week, so Ben will see someone. And, I know you're right that he's not the only one who needs help."

She arches a perfectly shaped brow. "Really?"

"Really," he nods. He hasn't moved his hand from where his fingers linger on her cheek. "I'll make some calls today to get in with a psychologist. Turns out FME covers that too. They gave me a pamphlet for that."

"How many pamphlets did these people give you?" Rosa asks with a weak laugh.

"There's that laugh I love so much. And that smile."

For this, he receives an eye roll. "I'm just tired."

"I know. We have a break now, remember? A full week

without the kids."

"Yeah, I guess so," Rosa looks away.

There's nothing more to say after that. Brian takes her hand and she squeezes it reassuringly. The two sit outside in silence until the sun goes down, before heading inside for an unusually quiet dinner, the majority of which remains uneaten on their plates.

11

APIS MELLIFERA

Saturday.

Without the incessant prompt of an alarm to drag them out of the warm confines of their king-sized bed, Brian and Rosa remain snuggled up until noon, when the sun is high in the sky. Rays shine through the gap in the curtains, momentarily blinding Brian as he blinks the sleep away. Rosa is curled up against his side, her head resting on his chest, and he gives her a gentle kiss on the forehead. They hadn't cuddled the previous evening before sleep and must somehow have gravitated toward one another in the night. The peace on her face is the most he's seen in days and he wishes he could keep it there forever. It takes him a second to register how late it feels and a moment of horror passes through him as he glances at his phone.

Noon?! How can that be?

A jolt of anxiety passes through him and he's ready to leap out of bed------as he has so many times this week—but all at once, two things hit him. The first is that it's Saturday and he and Rosa have absolutely no reason to get out of bed before noon. There are no responsibilities, no children, and no errands to get to. The second is that even if it weren't Saturday, he has no job to go to. He deflates at the thought, setting his phone back down on the bedside table and rests against the headboard. His movement causes Rosa to shift and stir, yawning.

"What's wrong?" She asks, catching sight of his face. Then, she shakes her head. "Silly question, I guess."

Brian laughs. He's not sure why. "Maybe I should focus on what's right instead, like you being in my arms right now."

He's rewarded with a smile and Rosa sits up, kissing him. She stretches out her body languidly, like a cat. Another yawn.

"Wait, what's the time?" Like Brian, Rosa has seen the light shining through the curtains.

"Late. It's already noon."

"Dios mio! That's crazy!" She leaps out of bed. "We never sleep this late!"

"If you think about it, it's not that crazy. We've had quite an eventful week. I'd say that calls for a longer-than-normal siesta." Brian watches as she gets changed into a pair of jeans and a tank top before ramming a brush through the knots in her hair. "Besides, it's not like we have anything planned for the day."

Rosa stops, raising her eyebrows. "That's true. The kids are with Kim."

As much as he adores Morgan and Ben, it's equally as nice to get a break from them and the chaos.

"Mm-hmm," he murmurs, reaching for her and pulling at the hem of her shirt to bring her closer. "So, you know, we could technically stay in bed all day if we wanted to…"

"Brian! Wanna have a quickie?" she grins. Assuming so, she starts lifting the top to reveal a hint of golden skin.

Just then, they're interrupted by the sound of the doorbell ringing. They pause, looking toward the sound of the door. For his part, Brian hopes that it's a fluke and whoever is out there doesn't stick around, but the doorbell rings again only moments later.

"Are we expecting anyone?" Brian asks.

Rather than respond, Rosa goes over to the window and opens the curtain slightly. "Ah," she says, opening them up fully. "Uncle Reyes is here to look at the infestation problem."

Brian sighs and slumps. "Of course he is."

"We had to return to reality sooner or later, you know," Rosa says. She's a lot more serious now and Brian recalls what she said the day before—that she's considered moving out because of all the craziness.

Better be damn sure I do everything I can to stop that from happening. Rosa is one of the best things in his life and he's not going to let this thing that's hanging over his family's head, whatever it is, take her away from him.

Pointedly glancing at the lump under the covers, Rosa asks with a tiny bit of humor returning, "Do you need to do something about that?"

"The mention of Uncle Reyes changes things a little," Brian snorts. "Not to mention that sexy word *'infestation.'*"

"I'll go let him in," Rosa leaves, trying not to laugh at his situation.

At least we can still laugh together after everything.

The bell rings again and Brian wonders if that's what woke him up in the first place. How long has Rosa's uncle been out there? He climbs out of bed and grabs something comfortable from the dresser, thinking he should probably get used to wearing comfortable clothes. The idea of taking a break from work weighs heavily on him—it's not something he's ever done before. It's not something he's ever needed or wanted to do.

"Mi hija! I was about ready to break down the door." Brian hears Reyes' heavy accent, followed by his boisterous laughter, booming up the stairs.

He finds Rosa and her uncle in the dining room together, both holding cups of coffee. Brian knows without asking that there's a third cup in the kitchen for him. "Hey Uncle Reyes," he smiles. "How's it going?"

"Brian! Finally decided to join us. Not like you two to sleep so late," he winks. Reyes has always been good-natured, a Hispanic man with a belly that hangs over his pants and rumbles when he laughs, which happens to be a lot. "Even on a Saturday."

"Oh, Rosa told you about that?"

"I rang the doorbell a few times. She had to tell me

something, huh?" He chuckles and it's contagious. Rosa's cheeks are rosy and her uncle doesn't miss it. "I'm just messing with you. Brian's still got sleep dust in his eyes."

Brian grins, wiping his eyes. "Thanks. It's good to see you, Reyes."

"And you. Seems like you've had a busy week. Rosa was telling me about the holes in Ben's room."

"Right down to business, eh?"

"Ah, you know it's not business for me. I love being there for my family," Reyes watches Rosa out of the corner of his eye and Brian gets the feeling there's more to this than Reyes' usual visits.

Is Reyes concerned? How much has Rosa told him? Are they going to talk about her moving out while I'm here?

"Besides, the sooner we get this whole ant thing under control, the sooner we can bring out that old barbecue. Grill us up some Sonoran dogs. What do you say?"

Brian hesitates, but after one look at Rosa's face with her eyes full of hope, he nods. "We'd love to have you over for Sonoran dogs, Uncle."

"How about we go check it out then? I've got my tools here. We can hang out and deal with the pleasantries afterward."

The smile on Reyes' chubby face is hard not to reciprocate. As messed up as things are right now, Brian knows that he can still turn everything around. He has time and he's always had a good relationship with Rosa's uncle. One week couldn't possibly turn that around. He's being paranoid and reading into things that probably aren't there.

Still, the way Reyes squeezes Rosa's hand when he

stands from the table bothers Brian more than he would like to admit. On the floor beside Reyes' chair is a black and yellow toolbox covered in random stickers, marking lines, and dirt collected over decades of Reyes' work as a handyman. He runs his own business which specializes in handyman and maintenance work, but never charges full price for family. Brian does his best not to think about the amount of money he's been saved as he follows Reyes up the stairs.

Reyes takes the steps slowly, carrying the box in one hand and using the banister as support with the other. Brian doesn't offer to help since he already knows from experience that Reyes won't accept it. It's simply a slower trip than he's used to.

Once on the landing, Brian leads the way to Ben's room, growing colder with each step there. He realizes that he hasn't entered the room since he brought Ben home early from school two days ago. Rosa had been left with the gory task of cleaning up after the death of his daughter's turtle, Lady. Guilt rumbles through his belly and he feels ill as he grabs the key from the top of the trim. Rosa had blessed the room and locked it the previous night, hoping to keep evil at bay. Inside, the first thing Brian sees is a cross hanging on the wall over Ben's bed. It's a new addition. Reyes, on the other hand, is focused on something completely different.

"What on earth?" He drops his toolbox in front of the door and walks toward the wall covered in holes.

From what Morgan and Rosa told him, Brian expected way more holes in the wall. There are small clusters here and there from where Ben took the drill to the drywall and amongst those, six holes stand out. They're the only ones that are finger-sized. Last Brian knew, there were only four. He's puzzled by the two new additions and follows Reyes to the wall.

"This is not like anything I have seen before," Reyes says.

"Do you smell that?" Brian asks. Nearing the wall, he's hit with a whiff of that sweet tobacco smell.

Reyes sniffs the air, breathing in deeply. "No, I smell nothing."

"That tobacco smell," Brian whispers. Reyes gives him a shifty questioning look. "Uh, sorry," Brian continues. "I'll leave you alone."

Wordlessly, Uncle Reyes waddles back toward his toolbox and begins rummaging through its contents noisily. Gulping, Brian pulls his phone out of his pocket and opens the camera, aiming it at the wall. There's a niggling fear that no one will believe him if he tries to explain this and he's afraid that once the holes are fixed up, any credibility he has will go out the window. A photo of holes in the wall doesn't explain the strange happenings of the week but that doesn't stop him from clicking the capture button. Turning away, the scent of smoke lingers in his nostrils as he leaves the room, getting fainter the further away he gets.

•••

In an attempt to distract themselves from all the patching and troweling coming from Ben's room, Rosa and Brian clean the house and then lose themselves in a cooking show on TV. They find themselves laughing and having a good time despite everything.

Eventually, around the time that they're beginning to get bored, Reyes comes booming back down the stairs with his toolbox. They turn the TV off and go to join him at the bottom, looks of apprehension on their faces.

"Well," the Hispanic man sighs. "There's no evidence of ants up there."

"What?" The couple gasps in unison.

"There were a few dead ones, but no sign of an infestation," Reyes reaches the end of the staircase. It's plain to see that he's bewildered. "There's no pathway or entry point either. Nothing. I patched up the wall, just need some touch up paint once it dry's. Those holes, the finger-sized ones, they're not normal for this kind of infestation, if there was one."

"That makes no sense." Brian shakes his head. *What does it all mean? If it isn't ants, what is it?*

Ants seemed like an easy problem to resolve; bring in the exterminator. There are so many things that have happened this week that make no sense and he only wishes he knew what it all meant. He feels like he's losing his mind. *Is Ben losing his mind too?* There are too many things that simply do not add up.

Rosa rubs Brian's arm while he mentally spirals. "Uhm, speaking of holes, there was something else I wanted you to take a look at, Uncle."

"Of course, mi hija," Uncle Reyes doesn't take his eyes off Brian, whose panic is becoming more evident as he runs his hands through his hair. "What is it?"

"Well, there are some bees out in the shed. When I was gardening yesterday, I came across an entire beehive."

Reyes is shocked by this new information, his eyes wide. "I think you probably should have told me about that one first," he says with a nervous laugh. Bending down, he opens up his toolbox once more, this time pulling out a big spray can of bee killer and shaking it back and forth noisily. They hear the contents swish around inside satisfactorily. "I'll go check that out. You guys stay here."

"Oh, you couldn't get me to go out there if you tried," Rosa says when her uncle walks off to the shed. Brian doesn't respond and Rosa strokes his arm again. "Hey, is anybody home in there? Are you okay?"

"Nothing makes sense. Am I the only one who feels this way?" Brian stares at his girlfriend. "Earlier, I smelled the smoke again and your uncle was standing right there with me and he didn't smell the same thing. The other night, Ben was covered in ants, but apparently, there's no infestation? What the hell is going on?"

Before Rosa can answer, the two are startled by a gut-wrenching scream coming from outside. Rosa hurries out before Brian has a chance to register what's happening and then he follows close after. She reaches the backyard first, running around the back of the house. There, a new nightmare unfolds before her eyes. Rolling around on the ground is Uncle Reyes, screaming in agony as a swarm of bees covers his skin. The sound of his voice can barely be heard over the angry buzzing of the hive.

The door to the shed is open and Rosa begins breathing heavily as fear rushes through her veins. Clusters of insects collect on his body, moving like one solid form.

There's a small table and two chairs in front of the shed, and Rosa, trying to find something to help her uncle, grabs a cushion off one of them. She begins swatting wildly at the rolling body in the dirt, hoping to get rid of the bees surrounding Reyes but there are too many. It's a half measure that has no real effect. The swarm continues to attack her uncle as he fights and rolls around. When she begins swatting them harder and faster, they start changing course, flying toward her. She gives a screech as two sharp pains ring out through her arm, the bees start attacking and stinging her instead of her uncle. Afraid that her uncle is in grave danger, she continues to swat, making them angrier.

When she feels the bee stings on her neck, Rosa slaps at them involuntarily. Too afraid to stay in the vicinity of the bees, she retreats, turning and running back to the house. She tosses the cushion down toward Reyes and the bees spread out and split apart, flying in different directions. That doesn't last long. They immediately swoop back in on their prey, but by then, Rosa is long gone, running past Brian with tears in her eyes. He grabs her arm to stop her and she screams.

"What happened?" Brian shouts, to no response. Rosa is hysterical and simply points him in the direction of the shed before continuing back to the house as if something is on her heels, chasing her. "Rosa!"

The temptation to follow her disappears as another cry of anguish comes from Reyes. Brian bursts into a sprint toward the shed and he's equally horrified to find Reyes on the ground. Uncle Reyes manages to roll over onto his large belly and crawls toward Brian, digging his hands into the dirt to leverage and drag himself forward. From where he stands, Brian can see that Reyes' hands and fingernails are caked in soil. Thinking fast, Brian rushes to the outside faucet, where their garden hose hasn't been unplugged for months, and turns the knob. He grabs the end and lurches forward, opening the end and spraying water out at the bees around Reyes. Much like when Rosa attempted to get rid of the swarm, it has little effect and the bees separate— only to return to continue attacking Reyes.

Upping the force of the water, Brian sprays harder and then leans down, reaching for Reyes. The overweight man grabs a hold of Brian's hand and with a big tug, Brian helps him up off the ground, keeping the hose trained on the swarm, offering them a moment to retreat into the house.

Brian is in such a hurry to close the door, he doesn't even shut the hose off and it flies back and forth on the ground, spraying water in every direction as they get back inside. The bees buzz angrily, in a way no one inside the house has ever seen before. Reyes, for his part, collapses on the floor, weakly slapping at his skin. Seeing why, Brian rushes over to swat and kill the remaining bees that have clung to Reyes' swollen, red skin. He's covered in stings.

"Please," Rosa's voice begs. "Send someone as quickly as you can!"

"I haven't even sprayed them yet..." Reyes mumbles, shivering. It's plain to see that he is in severe pain where he lies. "They just attacked me!"

"I called nine-one-one, Uncle," Rosa gets down on her knees beside her uncle. When she takes his hand, he groans. "They'll be here soon, okay?"

Brian, looking down at the scene, isn't sure that soon will be soon enough, but he says nothing as Rosa cries and Uncle Reyes tiredly closes his eyes.

•••

After the ambulance drives to the hospital with Rosa and Reyes inside it, Brian braves the yard once more. The bees have all but disappeared, only one or two linger on the flowers in Rosa's small garden bed. He keeps a lookout for more, but they've all disappeared. Switching the tap off, the hose spits and sputters before falling back down lifelessly. Brian grabs it and begins rolling it up, walking it back to its home on the shed wall carefully. The shed door is still open and he knows this is where Rosa said the hive was but when he enters, it's silent. There's no buzzing and no movement. In fact, there's no sign that the bees had ever been there at all. Utterly confused, he locks the shed door.

In the same moment, Brian sees two things: an unused can of bee killer sitting on the patio table and one lone bee, squeezing itself out of a hole in the door where a nail once held the hinge in place. The bee flies away and Brian's left staring at the black hole. He's itching to grab his tools from the garage and fix it, to get rid of yet another of the minuscule tunnels that are making his life hell, but there's no point and no time. Fixing the hole now won't magically repair the trauma he and his family, which now includes Rosa, have experienced recently. Besides, he promised Rosa he would join her at the hospital after shutting the hose off and locking up the house.

One of those things is done. It's been minutes since the ambulance left his range of hearing and he needs to get on the road after it.

•••

"The doctor is on his way there now actually, I just handed him a report," the nurse has short blonde hair and green scrubs on. Before he walked up to her, she'd been wearing a mask, which now hung around her chin. "C'mon, I'll take you there."

Brian knows it's unorthodox for a nurse to guide a visitor to a particular ward and his hands feel clammy with anxiety as he prepares for the worst. *Why else would I be accompanied?* It couldn't possibly be due to the haste in his voice—that must be a commonality in these hallways. No, the way the nurse keeps glancing furtively over her shoulder at him, as if he might stop following her any moment—why would he? This tells him something must be wrong. As much as he tries to push the thought away, to settle it down with positivity, it rears its head back at him with each step they take.

"Doctor," the nurse says suddenly.

Brian realizes that the woman up ahead, the brunette standing in front of a doctor in a clean, white lab coat a head taller than she is, seeming small and sad, is Rosa.

"Sorry to interrupt. This is Miss Degardo's boyfriend, Brian Brennan."

"Ah," the doctor says, exchanging a look with the nurse that Brian tries not to read into. *Is that surprise? Sympathy? Relief?* "Of course. Thank you, Sandra."

The nurse nods and, with another sideways glance in

Brian's direction, she walks back down the hallway whence they came, back to whatever she'd been doing before. The doctor addresses Rosa and she slips a freezing hand into his, which he squeezes tightly.

"Miss Degardo, Mr. Brennan, I'm Dr. Manning," he holds his hand out and Brian shakes it, but Rosa gives a curt nod when he offers it to her, leaving him to awkwardly withdraw it and take a deep breath. "I wish I had better news for both of you."

Rosa falters slightly and Brian finds his fingers grasping hers tighter, preventing her from pulling away from him. He knows he can't hold her together with one hand but he sure as hell is going to try. Water is already beginning to shimmer in her red-rimmed eyes.

"Your uncle didn't make it. I'm very sorry. Typically, a grown man can tolerate hundreds of stings, but Reyes had an anaphylactic reaction. We tried, but we were unable to reduce his blood pressure to a more controllable level." The doctor looks like he wants to say something more. However, one look at Rosa, who is sobbing quietly, keeps his mouth locked tight.

"Is there anything else you can tell us? Was there something on him to have made the bees act that way? They were so aggressive."

The doctor hesitates, seemingly disturbed by how distraught Brian's girlfriend is.

"They were close," Brian says. "Makes it that much more important to know what happened."

"I've been informed that he was attempting to exterminate a hive. Is that correct?"

"No," Rosa snaps, her voice raw.

"Well," Brian wraps an arm around Rosa's shoulder, stroking it. "Technically, she's right. He was going to, but he never got the chance. Before he got there, the bees started attacking him."

"I see," Dr. Manning winces.

"Do you know if they were maybe those killer bees? Africanized honey bees?"

"You see, we're quite familiar with killer bees because they're sometimes found in this region. Naturally, we've had to treat a few patients, though rarely ever to this degree. Part of ensuring that your uncle received the right treatment was examining one of the dead bees we found in his clothing." Dr. Manning shakes his head. "We determined it to be *Apis mellifera*. Not an Africanized hybrid. Just your common western honey bee."

"That makes no sense. That's total bullshit."

"Rosa," Brian breathes, taken aback by Rosa's sudden outburst.

"I... I'm sorry," the doctor says. "Something must have been done to anger the hive." Eager to change the subject, he gestures toward Rosa's arms and neck. "We should get you patched up. Those could get quite nasty if untreated."

Brian knows that she wants to fight it but Rosa sighs. It can't be fun for her to be covered in bee stings. As much as she hates the news from Dr. Manning right now, rejecting the care isn't something she's willing to do. She follows him quietly into one of the wards. It isn't long before she comes back out, a few band-aids covering areas of her soft skin.

"Can we go home? He said that I don't need to fill out papers or anything and they'll call regarding Uncle Reyes' funeral plans."

Rosa seems to have aged since that morning—*afternoon*. She's worn, shoulders slumping and eyes dim. Her voice has lost life too. Brian scarcely recalls how happy he was to have made her smile, to have heard her laugh. It feels like that was a lifetime ago, though he knows it's only been a few hours. A few twisted hours. Again.

"Of course," he says. She leans on his arm as they make their way out to the SUV and it occurs to him that he's probably in shock because all he can focus on is Rosa.

This is something 1 know I'm going to have to deal with too. Eventually.

Unbidden, Brian's thoughts drift to the old belief that deaths come in threes on the drive home.

Bad things come in threes...

"I'm so sorry, Rosa," he whispers, keeping his eyes on the road. "I can't imagine how awful this must be for you. I just want you to know that I'm here for you."

"I think there is an evil upon us, Brian. Evil forces are behind this."

Looking at her out of the corner of his eye, Rosa isn't looking at him. She's staring out the window, her lips moving wildly fast. The movement causes him to glance twice, taking his eyes off the road for a split second. *Is she saying something to me?* He hears hissing come from her mouth as she whispers and he's about to ask what's going on when she ends the prayer.

"Amen."

Eyes back on the road, Brian releases a breath, hoping to alleviate the tightness constricting his heart. *It was only a prayer. Nothing crazy.*

An image of Ben whispering to himself late at night comes to mind, an image of his son being possessed. For a moment, he was certain Rosa was possessed. He shakes his head.

What the hell is going on?

The phone on the dashboard vibrates against the surface loudly, startling Brian. He jumps in his seat but doesn't pick it up. Rosa doesn't take her eyes off the window, ignoring the phone. It continues to vibrate and he can see on the flashing screen, slipping and sliding along the hard surface that he's getting a call from a private number.

It's only when the SUV finally comes to a halt in their driveway that Brian picks his phone up. Rosa climbs out of the SUV without a word, walking lifelessly toward the front door. Brian watches her open the front door and look back at him before walking in and closing it behind her. There's a voicemail.

"Hi," a friendly female voice starts the message. "This is Ashley. We spoke briefly last night. I'm Dr. Susan Lew's receptionist. After passing your message on, Dr. Lew has agreed to meet with you on Tuesday. It's short notice, but we're willing to make an exception, given the urgency of your situation. Please call us back to book a specific time as soon as you can."

Brian lowers the phone and hits the dial button on a number saved as "Dr. Susan Lew," calling the office back.

PART II

"The soul that has conceived one wickedness
can nurse no good thereafter."
Sophocles

12

WHEN I WAS A BOY

"**B**rian, you were saying?"

Susan's voice breaks into Brian's reverie, deep in memories that keep playing over in his head, and the room comes back into focus. The birds are still chirping outside.

"I was saying… When I was a boy, I would play this game in the dark. I called it the Scare Game," Brian pauses. "It wasn't even my idea. My older brother made it up."

As the only witness in the room, a professional in the field of understanding human behavior and the human mind, Susan is captivated by Brian. Already, the first words out of Brian's mouth, the fact that he chose to start with a time when he was only a boy as the root of everything, gives her an understanding of the possible early origins of Brian's trauma, of what brought him here to her today. Her pen dances across the notepad she rests on her thigh. In all her years, she has never come across a case like this one.

He's easy on the eyes too.

"And what is your brother's name?"

"Paul… Junior," he adds as an afterthought. It's been a while since he thought about Paul at all and now, he's come to mind twice in a matter of days. "Actually, we called him Little Paul back then, named after my father."

Susan's pen can be heard scrawling along the page.

"So, as I recall, Paul and I would play the Scare Game at night, long after everyone else had gone to bed. Our bedroom was dark; the smallest bits of moonlight would form shadows in the darkest corners of it. The curtains we had on the windows were the worst. I could almost see through them, see the movements of trees rocking back and forth in the wind. At night, as a kid, well, the imagination can run wild."

The image of the tree outside the bathroom window the night Ben was attacked comes to mind. He can remember the face he'd seen—no, imagined. He ponders how similar the two occurrences are.

"We would talk about how scary it all seemed," Brian continues. "And one day, my brother asked me if I wanted to play a game."

"What was the game?"

Brian furrows his brows, thinking back. Remembering. The air is thick with tension.

"What was the game, Brian?" Susan repeats. Scrawl

scrawl, her pen scratches the paper.

"We would... We would both pretend that something was coming and we had to hide from it. We would cover ourselves underneath the sheet and blanket. My brother would help me make sure I was tucked in on all sides, that no light got in. No gaps. No nothing. Then, we had to be as still as possible." It's been a long time since he thought about any of these things. "My brother would whisper that something was coming to get us and we needed to remain hidden.

"I'd let my imagination take over and start thinking of some terrible, scary beast about to enter our room. I would psych myself out so much though, going into a full-blown panic, my heart practically beating out of my chest. My brother made it scarier by telling me that if I left one gap open in the blanket, the beast would be able to get me."

"How did the game end?" Susan asks. She's no longer writing anything down, focused entirely on Brian.

"The one who stayed hidden the longest would win the game. I remember getting so tired and hot, sweating profusely, that I would eventually want to give up and throw off the covers. I would be ready to accept defeat. But for some reason, my brother always gave up first." Brian shakes his head, recalling the short spats they'd had. "I always wondered if he did that so I could win."

"It's not unusual for children to imagine monsters hiding in their rooms; in closets, under beds, or in dark corners." She doesn't look at her patient when she says this.

"Sometimes, it felt like an hour had passed with me

curled up under the covers, creating images in my head of the beast entering my room in search of me. Sometimes, I would even think that I heard it enter the room and look around… Sometimes it breathed heavily, grunted."

"And no monsters or beasts were ever waiting for you?"

"No. My room was empty, except for my brother and me."

Susan has heard stories like this one, of adults traumatized by seemingly inconsequential things found deep within their childhood memories. She'd been helpless to prevent these moments, but has always been on call to pick up the pieces of shattered minds with confidence that her male peers lacked. Yet that knowledge in no way halted the chill that ran up her spine when Brian first injected the word "beast" into his story. The Nina Coltart reference referred to a lurching beast, yes, but why did Brian choose to use such a compelling word for his narrative? Most would simply refer to such things, those that creep in the night and in the memories of children, as monsters. Had she awoken this memory in him?

Such dark reflections, she scrawls.

"What made you choose to share this story today? Does the memory mean something to you?"

"I haven't thought much about the Scare Game or Little Paul in a very long time. It was what you told me earlier, the beast that lurches in the dark, that reminded me of the game." Brian's eyes wander around the room as she writes down her confirmed theory.

She was the one who woke the memory—with the help of Nina.

"What you said reminds me of something else; my son, Ben. Something horrible is happening to him. It's turned my whole life upside down and it's scaring the hell out of me." He swallows, gathering his thoughts. "As a boy, I thought that the Scare Game was the scariest thing that could ever happen to me. Now that I have my own son… I realize that what's happening to him is more frightening than anything I could ever have imagined."

Susan reaches back to grab a box of tissues from her desk and hands it over to Brian, whose eyes have started to well up. "How old is Ben?"

"Eleven," Brian takes a tissue from the box.

"Would you like to tell me what is happening with him?"

"It started the Sunday before last. He was attacked by ants in the middle of the night, which seemed to come from holes that began to form in his wall. At first, I didn't believe that he was being attacked. I thought that it was nothing but a nightmare. Well, my life has become the real nightmare.

"Over the week, more holes appeared in the wall of Ben's room. We used duct tape from the garage and started covering them up. Poor kid wasn't even sleeping. And maybe that's why he had an episode at school."

"An episode?" Susan interjects.

"Well, two things happened. He fainted in the middle of a biology lesson, talking about the holes in a fake lung, and then he was sent home after drawing an image that disturbed his teacher in a different class. It was of a Black boy covered in bloody holes."

"My goodness," Susan writes something down.

"Those were just the start," the father sighs. "The worst thing is what he did to Lady. That's my daughter Morgan's pet turtle."

"Okay, so what did your son do to your daughter's turtle?"

"He killed her," Brian says softly, hardly believing the words even now.

"He... *killed* the turtle? How?"

"Uhm," Brian shifts uncomfortably. "I don't know if you want to know the answer to that question. My daughter and girlfriend were kind of messed up afterward."

"I think it's important that I have the full picture," Susan says. "Trust me, there's little that can surprise me. These walls have heard many a sordid tale."

"He... We kept him at home because we thought a break would do him good—this was after the drawing— and he must have taken my electric drill from the garage around the time that Rosa discovered the beehive in the garden shed. I think she may have been avoiding him after he'd destroyed her painting the day before. He drilled holes into the turtle. And his bedroom wall."

"That's a lot of information to process at once," Susan murmurs. All the while, she continues to take notes. The mental image of the turtle, bleeding and full of holes, is an unwelcome one. "So, okay, he's become more than a little destructive. Is it fair to assume that Rosa may have been afraid to be alone with Ben after all that had happened?"

"Yeah... She's been warning me that something is seriously wrong, but like... I don't know, it's hard to explain."

"Try me."

Brian meets the psychologist's eyes and notes that she is unwavering. Throughout his story thus far, she's retained her composure. "She thinks that there's evil upon us."

"I see. And, do you feel that way?"

At first, Brian doesn't know how to answer the question. He certainly feels like something isn't adding up, but what that is, he can't say. "They say deaths come in threes. That's something I couldn't stop thinking about all weekend because, on Saturday, Rosa's uncle died. He's a handyman who also does pest control. We asked him to take a look at the holes because of the ants and the beehive, and he was attacked by a whole swarm of them right in my backyard. Had an anaphylactic reaction because he's allergic. Maybe that's why Rosa's always been so afraid of bees, even though it's not an allergy that they share." Brian shrugs. "I don't know. Who am I to say what's going on? When we were in Ben's room, I smelled this smoke, this sweet tobacco scent, but Rosa's uncle couldn't smell it. How do you explain something like that? How do you explain any of what's been happening lately?"

Susan brings the back of her pen to her lips pensively. She's at a loss for words too.

"You have a dead guy, a dead turtle, a dead career since I got fired because I can't keep my personal shit together, my ex-wife giving me hell about the week the kids have had, and a traumatized child making everyone scared of him. I mean, my whole friggin' life is upside down. I scheduled an appointment with a pediatrician and ADHD specialist on Thursday to seek some help for Ben."

"Well, whatever is happening to Ben aside, getting you the help you need is the first step. On a plane, when the oxygen masks drop down, what do they tell you to do?"

"What?"

"They say to put your own mask on first, and then attend to your children. It's a parent's instinct to protect their children, to put them first, but you can't help your children until you help yourself. What good are you to them if you can't breathe?"

"I guess that makes sense. Thank you," he nods. "I'm relieved to get a break from Ben and Morgan, to be honest. They're with my ex-wife at the moment."

"I can imagine that would be a relief, except for the weekend you ended up having."

"Seems to be a trend."

Another note. "Tell me more about yourself. Where would you say you're at in life and what would you consider the most important aspect that got you here?"

Susan knows she needs to take time to dig further into Brian's past using a technique she refers to quite simply as peeling back the layers of an onion. The Scare Game is the skin—she knew that instantly—but it's the beast that will lead her to the deep center of Brian's trauma. And it's there that she'll find the answers she's looking for; the ones that will help him.

"I've been dating Rosa for three years now. Got divorced five years ago. She kinda made it feel like I was pressing a restart button on everything that happened before I met her."

"What about before Rosa? How about when you were a boy, for example?"

"As kids, Paul and I moved around for a bit with our mother. Our father was in the Marines. He's a tough, disciplined guy. I wouldn't say our relationship is a loving one or that we have a very close bond. It's more like one of respect."

"That must have been tough."

Brian shrugs. "Around the time that Dad left the Marines, we eventually settled in Dennis on Cape Cod, Massachusetts. Those were some of the best times. And the worst."

When he clears his throat, Susan offers a bottled water. He gratefully accepts.

"Worst?"

"My mother left us for another man. Didn't see her much after that." He takes a sip. "The same thing happened with my father later on. I went to Boston for college and after that, I came here to Arizona. Didn't see Dad much then."

Susan returns to writing as Brian speaks. She knows their time is running out and as riveting as Brian's stories are, as much as she wants to get to the bottom of his being here, she can't turn away other appointments.

"What happened to him after that?"

"He moved from the Cape to his childhood neighborhood in Dorchester, Massachusetts. It's a mostly Irish community. There's a pub on every corner, which turned out to be great for him because he met and married a new lady named Connie. Now they live together, smoke, drink, and gamble. I check in every six months or so and we talk for a bit."

Brian runs his hands through his hair and Susan tries not to press. *Is this difficult for him because of his own trauma or because he hasn't faced it in years?*

"Last I heard, his health was bad. He suffers from COPD, Chronic Obstructive Pulmonary Disease." Brian gives a weak laugh. "No one gets to know this much about me the day they meet me."

"Therapy can be a very different experience, especially if you're not used to opening up about your past. Most people aren't. 'Leave the past in the past,' people like to say."

"Yeah," he murmurs, taking another sip. If he strains his ears enough, he can hear the whirring electronic machine out in the waiting room.

"What about your brother? Did he go to college too?"

"No…" Brian looks down and quite suddenly, he looks older. Worn. "Paul became a rebel as the years went on. He got into a lot of trouble when he was a teen, around the time he started high school. When he was sixteen, he ran away from home and got hooked on drugs."

"I didn't expect that."

"You're not the only one. When he was twenty, he overdosed on heroin. I hated the way he did that…" He clenches his fists, recalling the day he got the news. "I hated that he left me behind, that I lost my brother. I hated him for getting hooked, for OD-ing."

"How old were you?"

"Eighteen."

"Just a young man yourself," Susan remarks.

Brian ponders this. He didn't feel like a man. "I watched my father sink lower and lower after Little Paul died. He drank and drank, feeling guilty. My father was raised Catholic and he wasn't quiet about his beliefs. He believed Little Paul knew what he was doing..."

"That his overdose was a suicide?"

Brian nods.

At that moment, a timer on Susan's desk goes off. It's a subtle ring, but it's unmissable. Time is up.

"I can take a hint," Brian grins. It doesn't touch his eyes.

"I'd like to schedule a follow-up appointment if you are ready to continue your treatment, Brian," she says as he stands from his seat. "I think we made good progress today."

"How about after Ben's doctor appointment?"

"I think that will be good. You mentioned earlier that your children are with your ex-wife for the week. When are they coming back to you?"

"Friday. And Ben's appointment is on Thursday."

"Okay, perfect. Let's make it right after Ben's appointment. That way, we can prepare you for the upcoming week."

13

TRYPOPHOBIA

The woman who sits on the side of Ben's bed has perfectly coiffed blonde hair, framing her face in a long bob. It's early. The sun has only started to peek over the horizon, but she wears a perfectly painted lip and her lashes are a deep black, coated with mascara.

"Are you ready to see Dr. Sabin?"

Ben looks up at his mother apprehensively. "Yes," he pauses. "But do I have to tell him about what happened at Dad's house?"

"You should," Kim says. "It's the only way to make things better."

"I don't want to!"

It's hard for Kim to contain her surprise by her son's tone, but she presses forward. "Well, you can tell me then, and I'll tell Dr. Sabin."

The boy sitting up in his bed, pajamas wrinkled and sleep crusted in the corners of his eyes, cocks his head to the side and considers this offer. Eventually, he leans in and asks, "Can I tell you a secret?"

"Yes."

"Are you sure I can tell you?"

"Yes, pinky swear," she smiles and holds her pinky out.

Ben lifts his pinky and they curl their fingers around one another's. Then, pulling his back, he lowers his voice to a whisper, as if anyone can hear them. "I know where the ants are coming from in my room at Dad's."

"Okay, where?"

"They're coming from the holes in my wall."

"Oh, okay. Did the ants make the holes in your wall?"

"No," Ben shakes his head. "But I know who did."

"Did you?"

Ben suddenly sticks his hand out, points his index finger, and folds his finger forward. "No… Come closer, come closer."

Confused as she is, Kim leans in closer.

Raising his voice, Ben cries out, "So you can see the holes inside of me!"

Startled by the sudden outburst, Kim shifts back, standing up off his bed in time to see her son pull his shirt up to reveal that his chest is covered in six black circles, made with a black marker. Heart racing, Kim looks on as if the child before her is someone else's. There's no resemblance to the Ben she knows.

"I have holes too, just like the Black boy in my wall!"

Kim gulps, mortified and helpless.

•••

Determined to break his unwelcome late streak, Brian shows up to Pusch Valley Pediatrics 15 minutes earlier than the time of Ben's appointment. Even so, walking into the waiting room, his eyes instantly spot his ex-wife. Kim looks perfect as ever, but the pursed lips and long bob make her appear stern. She's wearing a crimson sun dress that calls for attention. When he approaches, Brian can see the cracks in the façade. They're in the barely concealed purple bags beneath her eyes and the makeup sinking into frown lines around the corners of her eyes and mouth.

"Hello," Brian mutters. He gives Ben a pat on the shoulder. "Hi, Buddy."

Kim shakes her head. "I don't know what the fuck is going on at your house," she says in a low voice filled with disdain. "But you are screwing up our son."

"Shhh," Brian hisses, flicking his eyes around the room pointedly. Another parent looks on, the magazine that previously held her attention is abandoned.

"Don't shhh me," Kim hisses back. "He told me everything. The poor kid was covered in ants. Does his room have holes in the wall? Really? He is scared to death. He doesn't want to go back." Kim looks up defiantly. "And I won't force him to."

"Okay, listen," Brian sighs. He's grateful when the other parent returns to her magazine. "First of all, keep it down. Now, I know how this sounds, but there is something else going on." At his feet, Ben has a handheld between his fingers but it's off and he's staring at the floor. "He has never acted like this in the past. Never."

"You're telling me!" Kim wags her finger at him, growing irate. "Your son drilled holes through Morgan's fucking turtle."

The woman who'd previously glanced their way looks up sharply, giving them a warning glare before checking on her children, who are coloring at a small plastic table. She slaps the magazine down on a table in the center of the room loudly, wordlessly informing them of her offense at Kim's shocking revelation. Brian catches himself checking on his own son. He's close enough, and unoccupied, that he has to be able to hear what's going on, but the kid doesn't react at all. Meanwhile, Brian is humiliated, wishing he could melt away while his ex-wife continues to berate him.

"And that's not all," she half-whispers, barely concerned about her volume anymore. "When I asked him why he did it, do you know what he told me?" The heat in Kim has slowly started to fade as her tone falls flat and, for a brief moment, Brian thinks she might start crying. Her emotions surface and the crack in her voice is sounding more familiar than Brian wants it to be. "He told me that a Black boy is living in his wall... And that he makes the holes with his finger."

To emphasize her point, Kim reaches for Ben, pulling him closer by the arm. She lifts his shirt and Brian's eyes widen at the sight of faint black circles on his skin. It's obvious that they've been scrubbed off and the surrounding skin is slightly red.

"He drew holes on his chest using a marker. I tried to wash them off, but, as you can see, it looks like it was a permanent marker. He wanted to look like the boy in his wall." She releases Ben and he, gratefully, makes his way over to the plastic table. Brian watches as the other parent takes him in, staring at Ben as if he's crazy, and feels his own heart sink. "He told me that he can see the other boy's eyes looking at him through the holes in his wall. And he's so afraid that he won't leave his bed."

Brian heaves a sigh. He knows this, of course.

"Did he wet the bed at your house?"

What's the point of lying? It won't improve things. He nods, resigned.

"Unbelievable," Kim concludes, pinching the bridge of her nose in irritation.

Brian's unsure what he can say at this point and, mercifully, he doesn't need to say anything at all because a door opens and a man with a handheld tablet calls Ben's name. Ben, probably as relieved as Brian, is the first one up and through the door, his parents follow after him. Brian makes the mistake of looking back in time to see the look of disgust on the mother in the waiting room's face. They walk through the back rooms and into an exam room, a path they've all taken many times before.

Morgan has been here far less than Ben, Brian thinks with some uneasiness.

This office is unlike Susan's and Brian, though he isn't the patient, feels uncomfortable. Everything is white and clean, pressing in on him. Posters are covering almost every wall, educational and informative, telling him about every illness his children could ever have. He notices, ironically, there are no posters on the mental health of children and its importance.

Ben immediately hops up onto the exam bed in the middle of the room and makes himself comfortable, oblivious to the squeaking of metal beneath him that makes his father jump.

"Okay, how are we doing today, Ben?" The man with the handheld tablet asks.

"Fine," the boy answers.

Kim and Brian watch as the man ticks off a few items on the tablet. "How has everyone been sleeping?"

It's a probing question. At this point, the man looks over at Kim and Brian questioningly, ignoring the second time that Ben unconvincingly mumbles that he's fine.

"Fine," Kim snips.

Brian looks between the three other people in the room. The man is a nurse and he has a name tag that reads "John." They learned early into Morgan's development the importance of the parent's sleeping habits, that children sleep well if their parents are sleeping well. Truthfully, he doesn't think anyone has slept well since the night Ben was attacked by ants. Hell, his son is only 11 years old and Brian can see faint purple coloring beneath Ben's eyes. Kim requires a deeper and longer inspection, but even all the makeup she has on her face can't hide that she's had some rough nights with Ben and Morgan at her house.

I'd have heard if holes were in her walls, so I'd say it can't be that bad.

"I see," John gives a halfhearted smile and nods at Brian. "Well, I'll let the doctor know you guys are ready!"

Brian almost feels bad for John. It's pretty obvious that things are less than kosher. He's relieved when John leaves, and he's almost certain the man himself is relieved, setting the tablet down on a tray used to cart around. The three are silent until the door once again opens, revealing their pediatrician, Dr. Sabin.

"Morning," the doctor says with a warm smile. His voice is like honey, perfect for bedside manner. Brian's always thought so. "How are we all doing today?"

"Could be better," Kim murmurs, though she smiles at the doctor, softening in his presence. "Things have been a bit crazy."

"So you said on the phone." Dr. Sabin doesn't look up at either Kim or Brian, but his brows do furrow as he stands before Ben. "How about you, Ben? How are you doing?"

"Good," Ben says with the first hint of a smile since Brian arrived in the waiting room. He looks up from the hole on the paper sheet that he's been picking at. This is his favorite doctor.

"What's new with you, young man?"

Ben looks over at his mom before shrugging. "Not much."

"Hmmm," the doctor hums and fills in the forms within the tablet. One by one, the empty fields are filled with checkboxes and notes. "Not much, eh? How's that game of yours? Last we spoke, you were stuck on the shark level."

"I got past that one ages ago," Ben says proudly. "I'm almost on the final battle level now."

He's already shone a light into Ben's eyes and ears. Now, he's prodding the boy's skin around his neck, checking his vitals. There don't seem to be any abnormalities as the doctor moves on.

"Really? That's so cool. You have to let me know when you win the final level."

"Of course," Ben beams as if this is the most obvious thing in the world.

"I'm looking forward to that! Open wide for a moment," a tongue depressor goes into Ben's mouth and the light gets shone on the back of his pink throat. "All right. Your vitals are looking good. Very clean ears. Looks like you have a few bug bites, that are healing fine. Do you want to step on the scale for me?"

With the confidence of someone who has been in this room a hundred times before, Ben hops off the bed and walks over to a scale on the far side of the room. It has a ruler attached to the side, which Dr. Sabin prepares and uses to measure Ben's height while he gets weighed. As soon as they're done, the doctor jots the details down in the tablet.

Finally, he has Ben get back up onto the bed and lift his shirt up, using the stethoscope around his neck to feel for Ben's heartbeat. First, he runs the piece of cold metal along Ben's back before moving around his sides and then his front.

"What are these?" The doctor asks, referring to the faded black spots that cover Ben's chest.

"Holes," Ben mumbles.

The doctor looks over at Kim, who simply shakes her head. There's a warning look on her face and the doctor seems to catch on. He goes back to checking Ben's heartbeat, listening intently with pursed lips.

"Breathe in deeply."

Ben does, his chest heaving.

"And out."

Ben exhales, huffing outward with an adorable, "Hoo!"

This happens a few more times before the doctor pulls away, lowering Ben's shirt and removing the ear tubes, the chest piece dropping onto his coat.

"Okay! Everything looks good! Healthy as always," Dr. Sabin grins at Ben and Brian is more than a little pleased to see some color in his boy's cheeks. "Is there anything you want to talk about today?"

Ben looks at his parents and Kim gives a small, encouraging smile. Brian is about to speak up, to tell Ben that it's okay to talk about what's been happening to him and that it will help, but Kim's voice is sharp.

"Actually, I was wondering if we might have a word in private, Doctor?" She tucks her hair behind her ear as Dr. Sabin looks between her and Brian.

"Sure," he says lightly. He doesn't take his eyes off of his patient. "Ben's more than welcome to go back to the waiting room and play."

"How's that sound, Ben?" Kim asks their son. "You know how to make your way back."

"That's okay, my medical assistant, John, is right outside. You can ask him to lead you back."

"Okay," Ben says unconvincingly. There's one last awkward glance from Ben to the doctor, to his mom, to Brian, and back to the doctor before he hops off the bed and walks toward the door. "Bye, Dr. Sabin," he says before he shuts it behind him.

"Have fun, Ben." He turns to Brian and Kim. He gestures toward a side door that's difficult to notice because it's painted white and covered in posters, much like the rest of the walls. "Would you like to convene in my office?"

They hear John's muted tones and Ben says something back, muffled by the door, before they're left in silence.

They don't need to answer because the doctor is already opening the side door and the three of them go through it, into an office that has beautiful wooden décor, inclusive of a desk similar to Susan Lew's, and bookshelves that line the walls. A faint odor of mothballs lingers in the air. The space reminds Brian of his late grandmother's house. She had the same uncomfortable, straight-back chairs at her dining table.

Seated across from the doctor, Brian isn't sure where to begin and he's grateful when the doctor clasps his hands together and exhales as if he has something to say. "All right, so I understand Ben has been going through some things lately. On our phone call, Mrs. Brennan, you sounded quite frantic, and I was surprised to find how Ben behaved today. He does seem a bit quieter than usual, but overall, I didn't observe anything overly abnormal. One question I do have regarding the marker holes on his skin." Dr. Sabin meets Kim's eyes. "I gathered by your expression when I asked Ben what those marks were that there is more to this than meets the eye?"

"I don't even know where to begin," Kim echoes Brian's thoughts. "I asked if he would speak to you, but he didn't want to, so he asked me to. That's why I didn't want you to push while we were in the exam room." She sighs. "Our son drew black spots all over his chest with a marker. It's taken hours to get it off. He's... Well, something traumatic happened to him at Brian's house last week. I think Brian should explain since most of it has occurred there."

"Something traumatic?" This time, Doctor Sabin looks at Brian.

"I don't know how to explain it, really, but he was attacked by ants in the middle of the night. We heard him screaming for help from across the house and when I got there, he was covered in them. Several left bite marks and there were even a few that crawled out of his nose and ears while I helped clean him up in the bathtub."

"That explains some of your concern. No offense, but that's a bit unusual for Ben, so I imagine that's something that has stuck with him. I also observed the bite marks on his skin here and there. They're healing well."

"Thank you. We've been applying calamine."

"So, what's this about the marker and holes? How does this relate to the ant attack?"

"That happened at my house," Kim answers. "He told me he wanted to look like a boy he is seeing in the holes in his walls."

"Holes in his walls?"

"Well, that's the weird thing," Brian says. "The ants came from a hole in Ben's wall. And Ben started to grow obsessed with holes after this." Brian pauses and glances over at Kim. He's uncertain how much he should be revealing. He doesn't want to mention Lady. "The day after this occurrence, a boy in Ben's school fell onto a cactus and Ben witnessed it. He described over dinner later that night, which is the day after the ant incident happened, that the boy's face was covered in holes. Then he had a little bit of a fit in our kitchen, pointing out that holes are everywhere, including in our sponge and strainer. It freaked my girlfriend and daughter out, but this was only one incident. Following it, Ben had an episode in school during a biology lesson where he had to hold a fake lung, which was, of course, covered in holes. We also caught him drilling holes into his bedroom walls."

"You're leaving out one very important thing, Brian. The poor child is so terrified that he's started wetting his bed because he doesn't want to get out of it at night." She groans. "Ben also told me that the reason he drew those holes on himself with a marker is that he wanted to be like that boy, the one that he's seeing inside his walls."

Concern is written all over the doctor's face and as Brian and Kim speak, it grows.

"He's been acting out ever since the attack and, to be frank, it's gotten quite scary," Kim interjects. "He even destroyed a painting with a broken brush, stabbing holes into it."

"That would be my girlfriend's painting, which Ben knew she'd been working on for an art exhibit. The destruction broke her heart. Afterward, Ben told me he didn't mean it and apologized, but it wasn't exactly something that could have occurred by accident, you know?"

"I'm worried that the reason he's behaving this way may be due to the medication he's on," Kim states bluntly.

Brian bites his tongue.

"The medication I've prescribed Ben is for ADHD. He's currently on a dose of thirty milligrams of Methylphenidate, which is not known to cause any such side effects." The doctor says gently, jotting something down on a pad in front of him. "That being said, based on your description of what's been going on, I think that I might know what could be causing this type of behavior in Ben. I think you'll both agree that out of all the events that have occurred recently, a prevalent symptom is an obsession with holes, down to the statement that they are everywhere. Am I correct?"

The parents nod their heads.

"From my own assessment of what you've told me, I believe what we are dealing with is a type of phobia. It's possible, Ben being within the hyperactivity disorder spectrum, that he had an extremely bad reaction to the ant infestation. It's not unheard of to have a very traumatic event trigger an instinctive cognitive response. Ben sees and feels the ants crawling all over his body. He then associates that with the hole whence they came. For many phobias, the average onset is as young as seven years old." Again, he jots something down. "There is a particular phobia known as 'trypophobia' which is the fear of tiny holes or clusters of holes. Environmental triggers can include things such as sponges, strawberries, and objects that have holes in them, such as hockey masks."

"Or a kitchen strainer," Brian murmurs.

"Yes, exactly."

"That makes a lot of sense for some of the things, Doctor, but what about his comments about the boy in his wall?" Kim asks. "Is it possible that there is something more serious going on in his brain?"

"He's not crazy, Kim!"

Kim glares at Brian. "I never said he was."

"If I may," the doctor interrupts their bickering before it can escalate. "It could be that Ben is simply trying to justify or make excuses for that which he does not understand. I do believe that we are dealing with a traumatic event that has triggered a severe phobia. For that reason, I am going to prescribe a medication called Risperidone."

"Risperidone?" The parents echo.

"It's a mild dose that should help keep your son's thoughts in check and prevent the mania he's been experiencing. We'll start with a small dose of one milligram twice a day with breakfast and dinner." He writes out the prescription and passes the sheet over to Kim. "See if you notice a difference and give me a call in a week."

Kim is hesitant, but she takes the piece of paper and murmurs a terse, "Thank you."

"Thank you, Doctor," Brian repeats.

The two head out and in the waiting room, Kim takes Ben's hand and almost literally drags him away from the small table where he sits.

"Brian," Kim nods goodbye.

"Bye, Dad," Ben calls.

"I'll see you tomorrow, kiddo!"

•••

With a slight glance toward Dr. Susan Lew, Brian leans back in the comfortable armchair, his mind full of thoughts.

"You seem more relaxed today," Susan remarks.

"Actually, I am. This morning, when Kim and I took Ben to see his pediatrician, Dr. Sabin, we told him about what's been happening over the past week and he thinks that Ben is suffering from a severe phobia."

"A phobia?"

"He called it trypophobia, a fear of tiny holes."

Susan nods, reminding Brian of Dr. Sabin as she writes on her notepad.

"Anyway," Brian continues, choosing his words carefully. "He prescribed this medication called Risperidone that he thinks will help."

"And what do you think?"

Brian meets Susan's eyes, surprised and impressed by her intuitive ability to sense his doubt. "Honestly, I hope it helps. I hope that this phobia is all it is. But the truth is that some really weird shit has been happening. Just this morning, at the appointment, I found out that Ben told his mother he thinks there is a boy in his wall; a Black boy who uses his finger to make holes in the wall. The same holes the ants come out of." His statements drop like bombs. "And the strange thing is… Every day last week, a new hole appeared in his walls. And these holes… They look like they could have been made from the inside out. There was even drywall dust on the baseboard."

"I want you to clear your mind," Susan sits forward in her seat. "Let's refocus for a moment. Many times, the secret to solving the problems of the present are hidden in our pasts. The behavior we exhibit, how we react, and even the way we interpret things come from a history of ingrained habits."

"Okay…"

"I think we need to make sure we have covered some of the indelible memories of your past and this may lead us to solve some of the challenges that you are facing today. Are you up for that?"

Taking her lead, Brian sits forward slightly, straightening his back and nodding in confirmation.

"Let's go back to the Scare Game. Did you ever tell your mother or father about the Scare Game?"

"No. It was just something Paul and I would do."

"Do you recall how old you were?"

Brian pauses, letting his mind wander through old memories. This is a technique Susan taught him last time he was here; simply closing his eyes and breathing as he shuffled through it all. They're like a Rolodex, an entire index of images being flipped back. "I must have been about eleven."

"Ben's age," Susan comments.

"Yes, about Ben's age," Brian continues. "I remember that we had just moved to Dennis. We had this nice little house in this wooded area. It was great. Little Paul and I could ride our bikes to this nearby bridge over the waterway. We used to fish off that bridge every chance we got."

"What else do you remember about the Scare Game?"

It's hard for Brian to think about the Scare Game, now that he thinks of it. So much time has passed by that he practically forgot about the terror of it all, the trepidation and anxiety that came with being under the covers, being unable to breathe. He tried to breathe through his nose because it made less noise than gasping for breath through his mouth.

"Brian?" Susan prods.

"I remember this smell. Like the smell of a cigarette. My father is a smoker, so I had smelled it before." Brian furrows his brows. He had smelled it before. "That reminds me... Ben's room had this smell. But it was more like a sweet burning tobacco smell."

"When was this?"

"When I entered his room over the past week or so, dealing with all the issues like the holes in the wall, I would sometimes get a whiff of this sweet burning tobacco smell. I even asked Uncle Reyes about it, but he said he couldn't smell anything when he was there to investigate the supposed ant infestation."

"Just to be clear, you recall a certain smell... from your childhood memories? And you also recall a particular odor in Ben's room?"

"Yes," he's getting excited now. This isn't something he's put together before. "Yes, it didn't have the same smell. I remember it smelled like cigarette smoke when I was a boy. Ben's room… That smelled more like a cigar or a pipe. Sweeter. Not as repelling."

"That's an interesting way to put it," Susan notes, writing on the pad again. The scrawl cuts into the noise of the outside traffic floating in from the window. "Did you hear what you said just then? The scent in Ben's room was more inviting and appealing, yet the smell from your childhood memories is more repelling and off-putting."

"That's deep, Doc," Brian says with a snicker.

Susan smiles, showing off a set of perfect teeth. "Well, I'm going to psychoanalyze a bit here, but the human mind is complicated. Smells, odors, and scents have memories associated with them much like the one you've described. There's a medical condition sometimes known as olfactory hallucinations called phantosmia."

Brian rolls his eyes.

"Brian, I don't want to lose you in my attempt to help you understand the different probabilities that could be occurring in your life. My goal is to help you find and recognize the places in your mind that hide your trauma. Then, I'll work on giving you the tools you can use to cope and heal, ultimately helping you deal with situations like the one your family now finds itself in."

"Sorry," he murmurs. "I don't mean to make light of it all."

"It seems that the Scare Game has left an indelible impression on you which we may be able to discover. I believe that what is happening to Ben is connected to that memory."

She makes a good point, he thinks. *Could it really be that my childhood has hidden traumas connected to what Ben is going through?*

Deep in thought, Brian tries to work himself back to the space he'd been in moments before, steadying his breath. It's not the easiest task when his heart is racing at the idea that he could be close to revealing something his mind has kept locked away. Part of him doesn't know if he wants to find out, but still, he pushes, forcing himself to go back to that bedroom where he and his brother slept in Dennis, back to his 11-year-old self.

"Thinking back... I remember finding these marks on my nightstand that made it all feel real."

"Marks?"

Brian nods. "Yes, they were like claw marks. At least, that's how I remember them. My nightstand had a dark wood finish and these marks were darker against it. I remember finding one or two of them." The nightstand is clear in his mind's eye, down to the concentric rings in the wood and the chipped edges. "They appeared along the edge of the nightstand. They were short, like a sharp fingernail had scratched into the surface of the nightstand, leaving behind a dark, discolored mark."

"Did anyone else see these marks?"

"No," he murmurs. "I hid them. I didn't want to get in trouble, so I covered them with a book or a magazine or something. My mother liked to keep things organized and clean in the house. I once got in trouble for putting a bumper sticker on my dresser and she made me peel it off."

"I see. Where do you think the marks came from?"

"At first, I didn't know, but later more marks appeared. At some point, there were five of them. It began to look like a hand with five fingers, five claws to be exact, had scratched my nightstand." He snorts. "I would tell myself it was the beast, that he was real. It made my Scare Game even scarier. More intense."

"It gave you a reason to believe the beast was real."

"Yes," Brian opens his eyes. "Perhaps we're dealing with mental illness? Maybe there's something wrong with me?"

His mind runs wild with the possibility that Ben's disability could be genetic, due to him.

"Now who's psychoanalyzing?" Susan gives a small smile and hands Brian a bottled water off the table. "Take a sip. And take comfort in the fact that generational symptoms of mental illness and psychological disorders don't tend to show themselves this way. I still firmly believe that we are dealing with two separate events between your history and current happenings, but you are the common thread between them." She pauses and meets his eyes over his water bottle. "I see some projection going on."

"Projection?" Brian sets the water down. "I'm confused."

Susan glances at the ticking clock on her wall. "Let's not go too deep here, but I do see you projecting some of your traumatic memories onto Ben's traumatic experiences. The smells, the nightmares, and the imaginary characters have all reappeared. I want you to know that taking the step to seek help was the first step to recovery." She hasn't written anything down in some time and her hazel eyes pierce into Brian. "You are already a great father because you've acknowledged that both of you need help. We as parents only ever want what is best for our children and you are doing the right thing, coming here, to help yourself. In turn, you're helping Ben."

"Thank you," he nods. "I appreciate your help as well. What we've discussed makes a lot of sense and I can see that I do have things I need to address."

"Great news! Okay, well, we are out of time for today. Let's get you back here next week." She stands from her seat and Brian follows suit. "Take into account what we have discussed and let's see how things go when the kids return."

Brian nods again.

14

JUST BREATHE

*F*riday
The sound of his kids flooding through the doors is the most comforting thing Brian can think of. It's not as noticeable in their absence, but when they return to him, he's reminded just how quiet life is without them. Although his psychologist might think reflection time is important, he's not so sure he likes it. There's far too much time alone with his thoughts and nothing else, especially with Rosa spending most of her days in her art studio, working on ensuring that every little thing is perfect for the pieces she's submitting, save for yesterday when she had to take her artwork to the gallery to prep for tonight while

Brian had two separate doctor's appointments to attend to. Between today and yesterday, he reckons Rosa has begun to go a little stir-crazy in the silence.

Bags are lifted over the threshold and Morgan argues with Ben that she wants to go in first as Brian locks the SUV, leaving it parked in the driveway. There's a tenseness between the siblings that wasn't there before—at least, not like this, not that Brian can recall. Brian knows he's lucky not to have seen the state Lady was found in firsthand, but he can't help picturing it and wonders if his kids are ever going to be as close as they used to be, or if they'll be scarred for the rest of their lives. Pets die all the time, sure, but this is a rather particular circumstance, and Brian doesn't know if they can overcome it. Truthfully, most of what they've been going through seems difficult to overcome. Kim swears that Ben and Morgan have been getting along fine—but she also swears that she and Doug don't argue and not only did Ben tell him about arguments during their time at Kim's house, but Morgan didn't look at or say a word to Ben throughout the drive home. It's usually a drive filled with catch-ups from both his kids.

Not today.

Rosa stands in front of the downstairs bathroom mirror, door open, while she puts her earrings in and finishes off her makeup. Either Ben and Morgan don't see her or they don't want to greet her as both carry their bags up toward their bedrooms. Brian hopes it's the former. These weren't concerns he had the last time he picked them up from Kim's house. His kids have come to look at Rosa as family over the past three years. Perhaps a lack of a job has made him cynical.

"I was thinking of ordering pizza for the kids tonight," he says, popping his head in through the bathroom door.

"Kids never tire of pizza but me, I am glad that we are eating out tonight," she grins.

"You're glowing today, you know," he says with a smile.

"I am excited!"

Rosa is beaming and Brian takes a moment to simply marvel at her. A black dress clings to her body, hugging her curves and standing out against the gold hue of her skin. Her dark curls tumble down her back and a pair of stockings highlights her legs down to a matching pair of black pumps. They're not high. Rosa would avoid the heels altogether if she could, this is her compromise. Brian would be lying if he said the effect of the heels doesn't make her legs and rear look fantastic. Plus, she's at the perfect kissing height.

"Are you going to take long?" Rosa asks, a faint pink taints her cheeks under his gaze.

"No, lemme go make that order and get ready!"

He dips out and what he sees in the living room stops him in his tracks, phone pressed to his ear. Ben and Morgan are sitting on the sofa together, in front of a music video channel. One look at the screen tells him that Morgan has the control, but even though they are on opposite ends of the seat, this is closer than Brian imagined seeing them.

Is this the medicine working? Ben is calm and quiet, eyes focused on the screen. Neither of his kids has their eyes down, for a change.

"Hey kids, how's it going in here?"

"Fine," Morgan says bluntly.

All right. Some improvement is better than none.

"Great! The holes in my walls are gone!"

"Yeah, we had that fixed for you while you were away."

Ben simply smiles and goes back to watching television.

"Rosa is getting ready for her art show this evening, and I'm gonna go change now too. Kylie is going to be here soon to watch you guys. How do we feel about pizza?"

Ben lights up at the mention of pizza and Brian is almost certain he sees the corner of Morgan's mouth twitch upward slightly.

"I'll place an order for the usual," Brian chuckles.

"Thanks, Dad," Morgan murmurs.

"Thank you!" Ben repeats.

Heart feeling the tiniest bit lighter, he leaves to place the order and get his suit on at the same time. He'd had the good sense to take a shower before picking the kids up, so his hair dried on the drive and he still smelled good. It's important to him that Rosa has a good evening, and he's going to do everything he can to ensure that, including keeping his promise to her that he wouldn't take long to get ready. A clean, black suit awaits him. They're going to look like a celebrity couple. Incidentally, the exhibit might happen to have a red-carpet entrance. He's kind of excited too. Mostly, he's proud of his girlfriend.

The doorbell rings while Brian is brushing his teeth and then again while he combs his hair and applies cologne. From upstairs, he can hear the excitement from his children both times, making it difficult to tell which doorbell belongs to the pizza delivery service and which belongs to Kylie.

Apparently, the babysitter is as cool as pizza.

"Ooohhh," Kylie calls as he walks down the stairs. Standing across from her is Rosa, ready for the evening. She's holding her wallet in one hand and is putting her card away; she paid for the pizza. "You look stunning, Miss Degardo!"

"Aw, thank you, Kylie. I appreciate that."

Kylie turns to face Brian and squeals. "You guys look so classy tonight! What's the occasion?"

"Rosa's paintings are on exhibit at the Southern Arizona Art Exposition in downtown Tucson," Brian says, coming to stand beside his girlfriend, and giving her an affectionate kiss on the cheek.

"We should be on the road if we want to miss the traffic," Rosa says. "Kylie, do you have everything you need?"

"Same old, same old, right? Since it's Friday, can they stay up a little later for a movie or two?"

"Yeah," Brian says. "But no horror movies, please. Ben's going through a bit of a rough time right now and we'd prefer to keep things light."

"All the numbers and everything are on the fridge and I made note of the Wi-Fi password for you," Rosa adds hurriedly. "And I'd like to request that my art room be left alone."

"No problemo," Kylie flashes finger guns their way. "And thank you guys for the pizza! I'm sure we're all gonna have a really fun night!"

"I'm sure you will," Rosa can't help but smile at the teenager. "Brian and I should be home by around eleven p.m."

"Speaking of which, let's head out!" Brian takes Rosa's hand and gives the babysitter a salute. "You know how to get a hold of us if you need us. Thanks for watching the kids, Kylie."

The pair says goodbye to Ben and Morgan, who are both already digging into the pizza in the living room, and they leave the house to the sounds of the kids wishing Rosa luck at her art exhibit.

•••

Kylie joins the kids in the living room and in no time, there isn't a single slice of pizza remaining. The babysitter relaxes in one of the armchairs and rubs her belly, giving an exaggerated groan.

"I don't know about you guys, but I love pizza."

"Yeah," Ben grins. He copies the babysitter, rubbing his belly. "Kylie, do you think I can go upstairs and play video games?"

"Since when do you ask, kid?"

"Mom made a rule that we need to spend time together and have less screen time while we are at her house."

"I see," Kylie strokes her chin. "Well, you're not at your mom's house anymore, but don't tell her I said that, and then sure, you can go play games."

"Promise, I won't say a word. Thank you!"

Ben wastes no time, hopping up from his seat and racing up the stairs. Morgan is happy to be left alone with Kylie, so she doesn't comment. Instead, she sits forward in her seat.

"How's it been going with you, girl?" Kylie asks her.

"Weird," Morgan answers honestly. "What about you? Did you ever end up going on a date with that Dean guy?"

"You remember that?"

Morgan simply nods, her cheeks pinkening slightly. Hearing Kylie tell her about college and the gossip of people she would probably never meet is always exciting. Secretly, she lives vicariously through her babysitter, looking forward to being 19 herself. Besides, she's never kissed a boy and the last time Kylie was here, they talked about a boy named Dean who kissed Kylie before he even asked her out on a date.

"Well," Kylie giggles. "If you must know, I did go on the date. Buuut, we didn't kiss again. Actually, we watched a movie and it was really nice."

"Do you think you'll go on another date with him?"

"Maaaybe."

Morgan tucks her hair behind her ear. "Will you tell me about it?"

"Of course. So, what's been happening around here? Why did you say things have been weird?"

"Uhm..." The words are hard to find. How does one begin to explain the strange ongoings? "Ben has gone crazy. Like really crazy."

"What do you mean?"

Before answering, Morgan looks around. She can't help it. Part of her is afraid that Ben will hear her and do something to hurt her or break something that she loves. She can't imagine anything being worse than what he did to Lady, but she doesn't want to find out what this new version of her younger brother is capable of.

"Hey," Kylie's voice breaks into Morgan's thoughts. "Is everything okay, Morgan?"

"I'm worried he might hear us," she whispers.

Confused as she might be, Kylie is curious to hear more about what's been going on with Ben. Only a few minutes into taking care of the kids and this is one of the most interesting babysitting experiences she's ever had. Apart from sharing gossip with Morgan, her visits to the Brennan household are generally standard; take care of the kids, maybe get takeout, watch movies, and use the unlimited Wi-Fi.

"I can take care of that," she tells the teenager in her care.

With a bloated tummy, Kylie makes her way up the stairs two at a time and heads left toward Ben's room at the top of the stairs. The door is wide open and Ben is on his bed, handheld game in his hands. The volume is on at full blast. Still, he looks up as Kylie enters the room.

"Hey kiddo, I think you should take a shower or bath so that you're all ready for bed later."

"Oh," Ben murmurs. "I thought I could play games a bit longer."

"Don't worry, you don't have to go to bed right away. It's just so you don't need to shower later. You can play games afterward."

"Oh okay. Sure, no problem."

With that, the babysitter heads back down the stairs. In her absence, Morgan has cleaned up the empty pizza boxes and poured two glasses of soda for them. Kylie grins at the sight of the glasses; they're wine glasses. There's nothing cuter than the way that Morgan tries to bond with her on the same level. Kylie remembers being that age and she likes hanging out with the younger teenager.

Taking a seat beside Morgan, she picks up a glass and holds it out. "Cheers."

Morgan touches her glass to Kylie's. "Cheers. Where did you go?"

"Just went to tell Ben to take a bath or shower and get ready for bed," Kylie winks, taking a sip of her drink. She's as hungry for gossip as Morgan. "He won't hear us now. How has he gone crazy?"

After giving a brief look toward the stairs, Morgan lowers her voice. "He's been messed up. He… He killed my turtle."

"He *what?*" Kylie sets her drink down on the coffee table. "Are you serious? Was it an accident?"

"No, it wasn't. He killed Lady with a drill. She was full of holes. I'm kind of scared of him and things are worse when we're at Dad's house. I lock my door at night so that he can't come into my room."

Upstairs, the sound of water starts running in the bathroom. Ben has left his room. Both girls wonder if he's heard their conversation since he would have had to pass by the top of the stairs. Kylie's breaths come out slow and shallow and her eyes flit toward the sound. She shouldn't be scared, but she doesn't like the uncomfortable sensation she feels on the back of her neck. It feels like she's being watched.

"My parents took him to a doctor and things were better at my mom's house, but I don't know how much the new medicine is going to help him," Morgan whispers.

"Do they know what's wrong with him?" The babysitter is whispering too.

"He has trypophobia."

"What's that?"

Morgan shrugs.

Tugging her phone out of her back pocket, Kylie signs onto the Brennan Wi-Fi network using the password Rosa left for her and looks the word up on the internet:

> https://web_search_results...
>
> Trypophobia
> /ˌtrɪpə(ʊ)ˈfəʊbɪə/
> *noun*
> An extreme or irrational aversion to or fear of clusters of small holes or bumps.
> Origin: early 21st century, from Greek trýpa 'hole' and English 'phobia.'

The babysitter chews on the inside of her cheek. She's grown attached to Morgan and Ben over the last few years of watching them, so much so that she continued to babysit even when she started college. What was meant to be a way to make pocket money in high school while occasionally getting to do art with Rosa turned out to be a large deciding factor behind studying language, so that she could eventually study abroad while Au Pairing. She loves kids and she realized that thanks to these two.

"Maybe he'll be okay," Kylie says. "Many people have some kind of phobia, you know. It's just a fear of some kind and sometimes some people have them worse than others."

"Rosa is afraid of bees," Morgan offers.

Kylie looks up what the phobia would be called and finds that there are two results. "Do you know if she's afraid of the bees or afraid of being stung by them?" She receives a shrug in answer and laughs. "Okay, well, if she's afraid of the stings, then it's called melissophobia. But if she's afraid of the bees themselves, then it's apiphobia."

"I'm afraid of spiders?"

"Oh, I don't need to look that one up. It's arachnophobia. I hear that one a lot."

"Are you afraid of anything?"

The babysitter takes note that Morgan has relaxed a bit. She isn't looking up the stairs anymore. The water stopped running some time ago and Morgan didn't seem to notice at all.

"I have a fear of drowning, I guess. I almost drowned in a swimming pool when I was seven and I've kind of been scared of water ever since." With the web search still open on her phone, she looks that up too. Morgan leans over so that she can see the screen.

"Aquaphobia," the two say in unison.

"Drowning is scary because with most phobias, you can just breathe and try to stay calm, but with drowning, you can't breathe which is scarier."

"You didn't seem to take a breath through that whole sentence!"

Morgan giggles and Kylie joins in.

"C'mon, let's look up some more."

The two sit close together on the sofa, arms touching, as Kylie enters one of the numerous links to a list of phobias available. Each one has a description beneath it. The one they've chosen is in alphabetical order.

"Fear of books?!" Morgan cries out when they reach Bibliophobia. "How can you be scared of books?"

"I mean, maybe they're scared someone will throw books at them."

"It's probably like the bee thing where, like, the fear of books is different from the fear of reading."

"That's really smart. It probably is," Kylie agrees.

They continue reading, calling out the strange ones, and laughing at others. Some of them are ridiculous, but Kylie tries to keep judgment out of the conversation. She doesn't want Morgan to think it's okay to be rude about the things others are going through. The introduction to the article mentioned that phobias are classified as illnesses. As far as she's concerned, college is the best place to discover how important mental health is. Besides, she's been going to therapy for her fear of water for years. It's easy to laugh about with a belly full of pizza and a 13-year-old's head on her shoulder, but it's something she's battled with for what seems like the longest time.

The list is a long one and Kylie is brought back to reality when they reach T and beneath it, trypophobia. It's easy to tell Morgan is feeling better because she skips over it without a second glance. Kylie, on the other hand, pauses. Checking the time, she realizes that it's been a while since she thought of Ben too and the silence upstairs has grown uncomfortable.

"I'll be right back," she says to Morgan, tucking her phone away.

She goes up the stairs two at a time, stopping at Ben's room just in case he had gotten out of the tub without anyone noticing. The room is empty, though the handheld has been left on and repetitive music comes from the pause menu. She goes to the bathroom next, hating how quiet it is upstairs, how still.

"Ben?" She calls from the hallway.

No answer.

Speaking into the door now, Kylie calls, "Ben... Are you still in the tub?" Her stomach tightens uncomfortably. "Ben?"

There's no sound of movement or water from inside the bathroom and Kylie begins to fear the worst as she firmly raps her knuckles against the wood.

How could this happen on my watch? My most feared phobia in the world... Drowning. Please don't let it be that.

"Ben, are you still in the tub?" She calls through the wood.

Again, no answer.

Kylie grabs the doorknob and turns. To her horror, the door doesn't open. It's locked.

"Ben!"

"Use the doorknob key!" Morgan shouts, appearing beside Kylie and pointing to the hiding spot above the door trim.

The babysitter's hands are shaking as she reaches for the

key and shoves it into the door, twisting it into the knob frantically. "Ben, answer me!"

When the door swings open, Ben sits in full view, frozen in the tub. He doesn't move when the girls enter the room, Kylie practically falling in. His skin is pale.

Kylie acts on instinct, grabbing the nearest towel and racing toward him, wrapping it around him without concern of it getting wet, and tugging his body out of the water. It's freezing cold by this point. The babysitter is covered in water and she's breathing heavily as she checks on Ben, pressing her index and middle finger to his throat and finding a pulse. His lips are tinged blue, but she thinks that's from the cold more than anything else.

"Ben?" She follows Ben's gaze, which hasn't changed. He's still and focused on one thing, as if his eyes have been screwed in place and he's unable to move them within their sockets.

Soap suds float on the surface of the water and his eyes are unmoving as they float like clouds atop the water, gentle, but popping by the second.

Hundreds of tiny holes.

"I told you, he has trypophobia!" Morgan shouts again, seeing where Ben is staring at the same time Kylie does.

"Shhh," Kylie whispers to the whole room; to herself as much as to Morgan and Ben. She remembers what Morgan said earlier—with most phobias, you can breathe, but not with drowning. *Ben didn't drown and he's okay.* "Ben, you're okay. Breathe. In and out, breathe."

While she speaks to Ben, she gently turns his head away from the tub and holds him close to her body, rubbing her hands up and down his back through the towel, using friction and her own heat to warm him up. With her other hand, she rips the plug out of the tub and watches as the water starts to disappear, taking the suds with it. She continues to comfort the child in her arms, relieved that nothing more devastating happened while her heart races and she tries to slow her breathing.

"Just breathe…"

•••

Later that evening, when only the streetlights remain on, Brian and Rosa return home, high on the rush of a successful night. Parking in the garage, they can already see that the house is quiet from the outside. There are only two lights on and one of them is the living room, which is where they find Kylie chilling on a sofa and watching something on the television.

"Oh hey, you guys are back," Kylie says nonchalantly. It doesn't take a genius to figure out that Brian and Rosa had a good evening and she doesn't want to do anything to spoil that for them. Turning off the TV, Kylie hops up from the sofa and grabs her bag. "I'll let myself out. The kids were great. They're both already asleep in their rooms."

Following her lead of keeping their voices down, Brian and Rosa slip her some cash and give her their thanks and lock the door after she leaves.

Rosa has a bright smile on her face and she's a little tipsy from the sparkling wine that floated around on the trays of suited waiters and waitresses at the gallery. Brian takes his girlfriend's hand and leads her up the stairs toward their bedroom, as quietly as they can.

Behind the closed door, Brian raises his arm, fingers still clasped through Rosa's, and she playfully does a spin beneath it. They mock dance and both are laughing quietly. The dances at the gallery had been far more structured and Rosa had been the belle of the ball. People came up to her all night to compliment her artwork.

"I think it's safe to say your exhibit was a huge hit," Brian says. "You were the lady of the evening."

Rosa smiles. "My cheeks hurt from smiling so much."

"You know," Brian murmurs, pulling her body close to his. "I've never had sex with a famous artist before."

"I never sleep with a groupie before," Rosa says, her Spanish accent is thicker under the influence of alcohol. "I hope this isn't a mistake."

The sexiest smirk plays on her full lips and Brian slides his hands down her back, tugging at the zipper of her black dress. In the dark, with moonlight streaming through their window, the sequins glitter and sparkle as light hits them. He spins her body around and slips his hands over her shoulders from behind, watching as the dress slides down her body, crumpling in a heap on the floor.

Brian brushes her curls over one shoulder and leans in to press his lips to the back of her neck, gently kissing her. Under his attention, Rosa moans in appreciation, before turning and wrapping her arms around his shoulders. Her fingers slide into his hair and tug, pulling him down toward her, kissing him deeply. Their tongues dance together while her hands get to work on unbuttoning the dress shirt he wears, wasting no time in gliding across his bare chest and going lower. When they break away from one another's mouths, both are breathing heavily.

Reaching his belt, Rosa begins unbuckling it and undoes the buttons of his pants, lowering his zipper. Feeling what awaits in his pants, she takes a hold of him and strokes gently.

"Slide it inside of me," she whispers.

Brian's not about to say no, and he spins his famous artist around until she's bent over the side of the bed, kissing the top of her spine before following her instructions, making love to her until they're spent.

•••

Bzzz bzzz. Bzzz.

The sudden vibrations jolt Brian from a deep sleep. His eyes open to the bright light illuminating from the cell phone ringing on the bedside table. He grabs it and rolls out of bed to avoid waking Rosa.

In a groggy voice, she mumbles after him, "Baby, is everything okay?"

The split second it takes to look back at her and find that she's fallen back to sleep instantaneously is how long it takes for Brian to miss the call. Gathering himself and blinking in an attempt to wake himself up, he grabs a pair of pants and a T-shirt, quietly exiting the bedroom and heading into the master bathroom, shutting the door behind him.

Two missed calls? I must have slept through the first one.

It's his dad's phone number. His immediate thought is that something must be wrong. It's 4 a.m.

Brian returns the call.

"Brian?" Connie answers, her voice broken and hoarse. "Brian… It's about your father."

"What happened?" Brian asks, hardly trusting his voice.

"He passed this morning, in his sleep…" There's a sniff from the other end of the line.

"How could this happen? He's not old enough." The statement makes no sense, he knows.

"We… Well, I think you should come to Dorchester, Brian. There are things to take care of and I don't think any of this is going to make as much sense over the phone."

"Of course," he nods even though his father's partner can't see him. "I'm so sorry, Connie."

Another sigh, static in his ears. "Will you come? Will you help with the arrangements?"

"When do you need me to come?"

The door opens suddenly, startling Brian. He spins to see Rosa entering. She mouths, *sorry*.

"Sure, I'll be there," Brian says to Connie, who had asked if he could catch a flight and come to Boston that day.

Hearing the final exchange, Rosa embraces Brian in a hug, wrapping her arms around him. He hangs up and embraces her right back. The warmth of her small frame against his in such a cold moment in his life cracks what's left of his hard exterior and, unable to hold them back, the tears fall from his eyes silently. "I feel like I'm drowning," he says in a shallow voice. "Everything that has been happening…"

He breaks off at the thought of it all, his body contracting with the force of emotion flooding through his body. No longer are the tears silent. His chest is tight as they turn violent, his shoulders convulsing and his chest tight. Each breath he takes is a choked rasp. The emotion he feels is intense and no matter how hard he tries to reel himself in, he can't seem to control it. Somewhere deep within, something is broken, and all he can do is hold onto Rosa.

"It's okay, love," she whispers, rubbing his back. "Just breathe…"

•••

Sometime later, Brian sits up against the headboard exhausted but unable to return to sleep as the sun begins to peek through the gap in their curtains. The tears have left Brian numb and for the last hour, he has simply sat with Rosa in his arms. She's moved around to get ready for the day and make coffee here and there, but mostly, she's been his source of comfort while he stared straight ahead at the wall.

> Brian 6:34 AM
>
> Hey Kim, could you take the kids for a few days? My father passed away.

> Kim 7:01 AM
>
> Brian, I'm so sorry. Of course. I'll be there to pick them up whenever you need. Let me know.

When Kim arrives, she doesn't come in. Rosa ensures that the kids have everything they need and both of them are understanding about the fact that their father isn't going to say goodbye to them today. It's the second death that they've experienced in the space of a few days. Brian hates to say it, but the family is beginning to become familiar with tragedy and trauma. An old saying comes to mind… That deaths come in threes.

Reyes. His father. Who will be next?

"I'm terrified to get on a plane," he admits when Rosa returns from handing the kids off to Kim for a while. "You know I hate flying…"

"You will be okay, baby," Rosa touches the cross around her neck. "I know it."

"Can't judge Ben for his trypophobia. Look at me, scared as shit."

"Take a moment to pray with me. Pray you will have safe travels."

15

LURCHES IN THE DARK

Brian lands at Logan International Airport, happy to be on the ground. The first thing he does is rent a car so that he can drive to his father's apartment.

His father and Connie live in an apartment in Dorchester, Massachusetts. Brian is intrigued by the amount of information he's covered with Susan, information that hasn't cropped up in his daily life for years, that all seems to be coming to the surface. Never did he expect to be back here so soon. The town retains all the evidence of a dated New England suburb. There are breaks in monotony in the bodies of water he passes by. Being back on the road here brings back all kinds of memories.

It's like being in one giant memory. All the feelings of nostalgia come back to him and for a moment, he almost feels like he's never left. The apartment he's looking for is an old three-story row house on a quiet street. They live in a two-bedroom unit on the third floor and the door opens before he has the chance to knock.

"Brian," Connie breathes, hugging him and standing to the side to allow him to pass by her into the apartment.

"How are you, Connie?"

"I've certainly been better," she coughs. "Make yourself comfortable. Can I get you something to drink? Some coffee?"

"Sure," Brian follows her into the kitchen. "Do you mind if I look around?"

"Go ahead. Today has been a crazy day. Sorry, I've got a lot going on."

"I can imagine. This came out of nowhere." He walks through the house to where he knows his father's room is while the coffee maker warms up.

Connie's voice drifts to him down the hallway as he opens the door. "It wasn't a surprise for us," she calls.

"What do you mean?"

The room is dark and dated. Heavy curtains cut off most of the outside light and it smells of smoke. Brian can almost see the smoke lingering in the air, swirling in the minimal sunshine coming in through the gap in the drapes. The left side of the mattress is sunken where his father had been confined for months in his limited mobility.

Connie appears behind him, "Paul's health had been deteriorating for months. The COPD was taking its toll.

He started using oxygen and still tried to smoke."

Chronic Obstructive Pulmonary Disease. How could Brian forget? "Sounds like Dad."

"Well, he lost sixty pounds after that. Went down to one-forty."

"Why didn't you call, Connie?" Brian sighs.

"He made me promise not to bother you. He just wanted to die in peace." Connie runs a hand over her face. "He said nothing fancy, just wanted to be cremated."

"Oh," is all Brian can muster. Then, he walks over to the curtains and rips them open, letting the daylight into the room. "This room is so dreary."

Connie shakes her head. "Oh Brian, I know you and your father were not as close as he would have liked, you being in Arizona and all. But over the past few months, he was not right in the head."

"What do you mean?" From down the hall, the coffee maker percolates to a stop. Brian hasn't faced the room in the daylight yet. He looks out over the town, seeing nothing but roof tops in the distance.

"He started talking nonsense. Seemed to be carrying enormous guilt and thought his past was catching up to him."

Brian turns to face Connie, but anything he'd thought to say dissolved on the tip of his tongue. In the wall, there are six holes, directly across from the bed. He blinks, for a moment wondering why his son's bedroom is so vividly coming to mind. When he opens his eyes again, he finds that the holes haven't disappeared. In an eerily similar pattern to those in Ben's room back home, there are six holes in the wall. He goes toward them, running his finger across the outer edges. He's stunned by the strangely familiar pattern. *This can't be a coincidence, can it?*

"Where did these holes come from?"

Connie hesitates. "They're bullet holes."

Surprised, Brian tears his gaze away from the wall and faces his late father's widow. She reaches into a dresser near where she stands and removes a small-caliber revolver half-wrapped in a white cotton towel. Holding it out, she brings it in toward him.

"Here, you should take this. I hate guns."

Brian takes the revolver and unwraps it, staring down the cylinder. "It's empty of bullets."

Wrapping it back up firmer than it had been, he goes to place it back in the dresser it came from. It's not something he wants. "I can't take it on a plane anyway."

"He kept it in his nightstand. About two weeks ago, I woke up to him screaming at nobody. He was acting crazy," she waves her hand in the air. "Next thing I know... Bam. Bam. Bam." She closes her eyes, clearly bothered by the memory. "I nearly had a heart attack. He could have killed someone."

"What was he screaming? Was he having a nightmare?"

"He was screaming about nonsense. Stuff like, 'They're coming for me... My sins are coming for me...' I turned on the light and there was nothing there. Just him lurching in the dark."

Brian's heart is pounding.

"Anyway, you should take a look around. Take whatever you want." She walks over to the closet and opens the door, gesturing to some boxes. "These are all his personal papers and pictures. He would want you to have them."

After that, she leaves the room and Brian is left alone with nothing but memories that don't belong to him. The room doesn't look much better in the light. It's musty and smells damp. Various areas are cluttered with things and Brian wonders where he should begin "taking a look around." He decides to investigate the nightstand beside his father's bed first since he spent so much time in it. The nightstand is covered in clutter too. When he opens the drawer, a small stack of unopened bills falls off of it onto the floor. As he leans down to pick them up, his eyes widen.

Beneath the clutter, he catches sight of the same dark claw marks he recently remembered being on his childhood nightstand. Five dark lines in the wood. A chill runs up his spine and he involuntarily glances back over his shoulder to the wall filled with bullet holes behind him.

The claw marks of the beast, he thinks. Only now, being older and wiser, he recognizes the marks for what they really are... Cigarette burns.

"Here are some of his Celtics and Red Sox clothes you can look through," Connie returns, dropping a pile of sports attire onto the bed. She finds Brian on his haunches, rubbing at the cigarette burns on the nightstand. "It's a wonder the place didn't catch on fire. Your father had a bad habit of leaving a lit cigarette on the edge of the nightstand and forgetting about it."

For the first time, Brian begins to realize that his and his father's pasts are intertwined. Dr. Lew told him that his past may be related to his present issues. What if his father's past holds some clues to everything that's been going on? One coincidence he can buy, but there have been so many at this point. Eager to investigate and learn more about his father for possibly the first time in his life, he heads toward the open closet where Connie said his father kept all his papers and photos and begins tugging boxes out of the bottom until he has a collection to carry through to the kitchen, desperate to finally have that cup of coffee.

"You're right on time," Connie says, setting an English muffin down on the table. It's easy to see they're store-bought, which doesn't surprise him.

"Thanks." He sets the boxes down beside his chair and begins emptying them.

"If you happen to find…" She pauses and checks a note next to a phone on the countertop. "Uh, the funeral home asked me if I can provide them with a DD 214 form. They said they need it so that they can provide him with a military funeral service."

Digging deeper into the boxes, Brian pulls out an old green envelope with a string-wrapped closure. He opens it up and removes a stack of documents from within and carefully shuffles through them in search of the form for Connie. The DD 214 form comes up quickly and he hands it over.

"Thanks, Brian," she murmurs, tucking it under the phone with the note.

Brian barely notices her, digging through the remaining papers. He finds one letter in particular that draws his attention and begins to read:

UNITED STATES MARINE CORP
CRIMINAL INVESTIGATION DIVISION
2ND BATTALION, 2ND MARINES
CAMP LEJEUNE, NC 28542

November 12, 1994

From: Marine Corps – Criminal
Investigation Division
To: File

Subj: CIVILIAN DEATH INVESTIGATION INTO
PFC. PAUL HOWARD BRENNAN AND PFC. SCOTT
RICHARD LYNCH – OPERATION UPHOLD
DEMOCRACY, PORT-AU-PRINCE, HAITI.
SEPTEMBER 29, 1994.

Encl: (77) Victim, Jonas Biassou, age 11
     (78) Witness, Sister: Tamara
            Biassou, age 13
     (79) Witness, Grandmother:
            Lourdes-Gina Fatiman, age 55
     (80) Crime Scene photos

1. PFC. Brennan and PFC. Lynch under
   orders LtCol. (b) departed Echo
   check point beta on route, Blvd du
   Cap-Haitian. At 22:30 PFC. Brennan
   and PFC. Lynch were directed to
   investigate residential district
   for gun fire.
2. 1-day prior Echo company engaged in
   firefight with coup-supporting
   elements of the Haitian police. ROE
   – Self- defense, deter armed attack
   on armed forces.

3. House to house search of armed coup elements ended at [location of incident] Rue Soleil 17. Search resulted in hostile exchange with individual (79) and service weapon discharge.
4. PFC. Brennan and PFC. Lynch acknowledged an accidental discharge of USMC issued M4, resulting in death of victim (77).
5. Victim (77) sustained multiply (6) gun shots to the torso, death was instant. Per (80)
6. Witness (78) confirmed events.

Investigative Conclusion:
1. PFC. Brennan and PFC. Lynch confirm accidental discharge of weapon.
2. Conduct within orders given and Rules of Engagement guidelines.
3. Witness testimony (78)

No recommended disciplinary action be taken against PFC. Brennan and PFC. Lynch.

TRENT C. MCCULLAN

CC:
USMC CID
Cmdr MARSOC

"A Black Haitian boy, age 11, is accidentally killed by gunfire, leaving him full of holes…"

Brian is blown away by the strange contents of the letter he's read. He knows that it's crazy, he's well aware that the angle of justification his mind is taking is both bizarre and unbelievable in so many ways. Still, he can't help but connect the dots. Is it possible that this terrible incident from his father's past is somehow related to what is happening in his own life now? All of this could shed some light on the events with Ben.

Common sense would lead anyone to question such consequences, wouldn't it? Perhaps his mind is projecting again, as Doctor Lew said. Maybe he's allowing the puzzle to fit the pieces rather than the pieces fitting the puzzle.

"Did Dad ever talk about his time in the Marines?"

"Once in a while. You know your father, he kept to himself until he was three sheets to the wind," Connie waves her hand again, sitting at the table across from Brian. She eyes the papers littered all over it. "He told me on more than one occasion that he was a man made of guilt. I think when he lost Paul Junior, it broke something inside of him."

"Yeah, that one hurt. For a long time, I was just mad at him—my brother, I mean. You know, because of how he left us, ran away to Boston, and got hooked on drugs. What a waste. But now…" Brian shakes his head. "Now, I just miss the fun times and wish he could see the family I made."

"You've done well for yourself," Connie nods. "And you're a good father. Remember, they are together now and they are watching over you." Catching sight of the letter in front of him, she pauses. "Is that about the death of that Haitian boy?"

"Yes," Brian says, eyes wide. "Has he ever talked about it?"

"Just once... I remember it was a long time ago. He had a few drinks in him, and had heard through a friend that one of his old Marine buddies—a guy named Lynch—died."

"Go on..."

"Well, he was all upset. Lynch had apparently committed suicide and your father was saying he had already died in Haiti... when that boy was killed. He said that our sins are coming for us all someday. I guess Lynch couldn't get over what had happened in Haiti and took his own life."

16

DEATH COMES IN THREES

It's the crack of dawn when Brian shoves Valium down his throat in the hopes of ridding himself of the panic thrumming through his system. The sun hasn't started to shine brightly yet, but there are pink and purple streaks through the clouds, before metal aircrafts fly through and split them apart. The airport hotel shudders each time a new plane takes off—at least, that's how it feels—and Brian finds himself gripping the nearest object so hard his knuckles turn white every time that happens. Looking down at his watch gives him heart palpitations and he's almost sure his vision has gone blurry a couple of times. Maybe it's the dizziness he feels. It's hard to say with the distracting screams of airplanes taking off every few minutes. Why he thought it was a good idea to sleep this close is beyond him. Sure, he didn't want to sleep at his father's apartment, despite Connie's offer, but he could have picked any other hotel and not have had to deal with the exhaustion after a night of spending more time throwing up than he did sleeping. This is quite possibly the most anxious he's ever felt about flying. The flight to Boston was a safe one and he's not so sure the flight out will be.

The little sleep he had was filled with strange images of Haiti and a little Black boy and girl. They had Ben and Morgan's voices when they cried out for help, but he couldn't reach them before a machine gun somewhere out of sight went off, leaving both children bloody with holes bigger than the ones in Ben's bedroom wall. A demon with a red face and fangs for teeth laughed and cried at the same time. Its claws were cigarettes, long and dark, and it took a drag from its index finger before blowing the smoke in Brian's face, instantly waking him from the nightmare, coughing and spluttering, and surrounded by the sounds of an airport.

Brian could swear he smelled smoke in the room.

Death comes in threes, he keeps thinking. *Death comes in threes.*

Uncle Reyes, his father, him next. It's irrational and he knows it. That doesn't stop the thoughts from swimming around in his brain.

The flight coming here hadn't been nearly as terrifying. Then again, now that he thinks of it, he was probably in shock from the news. Besides, Tucson has a few things Dorchester doesn't; for one thing, Rosa isn't here. He considers praying and then decides better of it. Instead, he texts Rosa.

Brian 5:43 AM

I'll be home soon, boarding starts at 7:00 a.m.

Rosa 5:54 AM

Miss you, things have been quiet around here since you left.

Brian 5:55 AM

Miss you too. Took Valium. It's not helping yet.

Rosa 6:00 AM

You'll be okay, baby. I know you'll have a safe trip. I love you.

Brian 6:01 AM

I love you more.

Boarding the plane back home to Arizona, Brian is numb. He'd meticulously followed the bottle's instructions to ensure he was calm by the time they needed to board and although he can breathe easily and his heart isn't trying to break through his ribcage anymore, his stomach appears to be doing somersaults with each step he takes down the aisle between the seats. He barely recalls what the flight attendant said to him when he showed her his ticket, but he's memorized his seat number and having been the first to board—a perk, if one could call it that, of being intensely paranoid—he doesn't need to worry about stopping and waiting for other passengers to place their luggage in their compartments before getting into their seats. The aisle before him is clear, unlike his mind. All he cares about is reaching the seat that matches the number he's mentally repeating to himself.

Brian is one of the first passengers to be seated, with his carry-on, which is all he brought, safely tucked away and his seatbelt firmly fastened. It seems that all at once, while he was preoccupied with getting to the window seat on the furthest right, other passengers had shuffled in and the plane is now filled with commotion while he presses noise-canceling earphones into his ears. He doesn't notice they're in the air until the world below is minuscule and when he does, he's relieved to know that he missed one of the worst parts, take-off. The passenger beside him, a woman with short ginger hair and neon orange nails, makes conversation with the woman to her right, in the center aisle. It's another small blessing that no one, flight attendants included, bothers him.

With little else to do, Brian finds himself focusing on the tiny details of the plane, such as how many windows there are, what color the threads on the carpet are, which directions the lights point in, and where the earphone hole ports that he won't use are located. Looking down isn't a desirable option, not when everything looks so small and reminds him just how high in the air they are. In the bottom of his window, he notices a tiny hole and, without wanting to, finds himself unable to look away. *Is Ben right, that holes are everywhere? They certainly seem to be once you begin paying attention.* This trip alone presented him with more holes—holes in his past, in his father's wall, in the boy that was killed all those years ago.

Stop fucking with my head, he thinks. And even as he thinks it, he drifts off to the thoughts of all the events that have been doing just that.

•••

The light telling everyone to fasten their seatbelts comes to life with a low ding. Moments later, the plane jolts forward, jostling everyone in their seats. Brian wakes to the turbulence as the pilot's calm voice sounds out. They're mid-flight and it's clear skies outside.

"Good afternoon, ladies and gentlemen. We're experiencing some minor turbulence at the moment. Please remain seated and relax. We'll be through momentarily and then our lovely flight attendants will come around with some snacks for everyone. Thank you for flying with us today."

Brian's heart races from the rude awakening and receives a sideways glance from the woman beside him. He shakes his head, wiping his eyes.

"Ahhh!" He suddenly gasps, shoving himself back from the window when he notices a cluster of tiny holes around the one that he'd seen in the window before he fell asleep. Six perhaps. Panicked, he hits the call button on his seat controls.

A flight attendant hurries over in a pair of heels. The woman beside him tries to speak to him, but he only tugs the earphones out when the attendant arrives.

"Look! I just noticed there are holes in the window," Brian says, pointing. He's disoriented from sleep and his heart is getting faster by the moment.

"Yes, sir. Those are bleed holes. They are designed that way to balance air pressure."

"No," Brian snaps, irate. "You don't understand. There was only one bleed hole. I get that. But look, now there are a bunch of them."

He looks at the window again, seeing more holes than before and, even as he watches, a new one perforates the glass. There are dozens of them. Every inch of his body is covered in goosebumps and the hairs on the back of his neck stand up on end. Another appears, piercing through the glass, and another one. Again and again, more appear. He can scarcely breathe and it's getting worse by the second.

"Look… More holes are popping through the window! There's something wrong!" Brian raises his voice.

The flight attendant holds her hands up, "Sir, you have to calm down. You're scaring the other passengers."

"I don't give a shit," Brian's eyes flit back to the

window, and to his horror, he sees that tiny holes are emerging in the fuselage around the window. He breathes in shaky, quick gasps. "You need to tell the pilot... You need to tell him, there's something wrong. Tiny holes are popping through the side of the plane." As he speaks, more holes drill through the surface of the metal.

"You need to calm down, sir. I'm warning you!" The flight attendant says in a loud, firm voice.

Around him, Brian sees the faces of other passengers looking over at him like he's insane, including the ginger woman and her center aisle friend. The edges of his vision are blurry. Panic has set in and fear billows in his throat. When he looks back at the fuselage, it's almost entirely covered in holes. There are so many of them that they're all he can see, a contrast of light in a thousand dark circles. Every part of his body starts to itch at the sight of them and he can't move. More and more of them appear, splitting through the plane. All he can do to reach down with fumbling hands and tighten his seatbelt as much as he can.

Suddenly, a section of the fuselage rips away from the plane and with it, the flight attendant standing in the aisle is sucked from the plane. Wind and pressure ravage through the cabin and Brian's hands fly down to the sides of his seat. He grips onto it as hard as he can. Debris, papers, and personal items fly like projectiles out of the huge opening in the fuselage. Oxygen masks fall from overhead and all around him, people are screaming, drowned out by the roar of the sky and the jet engines.

The whole plane begins turning downward in what

Brian can only assume is the pilot's fight for control. Up front, a light indicates that someone is speaking to them from the cockpit, but whatever they're saying, Brian can't hear them. His seat is beginning to tear away at the anchor bolts, which tremor uncontrollably. He looks out into the vast sky beyond the opening and suddenly his seat rips away. In one chilling moment, Brian feels himself succumbing to pressure as his body, still belted into the seat, gets sucked out into the sky.

Brian is instantly thrown forward in his seat, wide awake, back in the plane.

Another mind fuck, he thinks.

●●●

It's a quiet morning at Kim's house, which is exactly how she likes it. Morgan is, as she casually puts it, "hanging out" in the living room. She's not allowed her phone, so she's reading a book on phobias and she's on the last few pages. Kim has something cooking and a tangy aroma wafts through the air.

"Mom, can I go play in the yard?"

The sound of Ben's voice surprises Kim almost as much as the question does. It's been so long since her son asked if he could play outside. She's been complaining about the kids no longer wanting to get dirty for ages. Prim and proper though she may be, she fully believes that children shouldn't have this screen time nonsense so encouraged by the day's age and she misses seeing Ben without a handheld going *pew* every five seconds.

"Of course," she says. "But be careful around the pool."

Ben nods and heads out through the glass sliding door

while his mother chops vegetables. Outside, there are piles of dirt everywhere, with one main pile taller than Ben. The yard has a huge hole in the middle, from where all the dirt has been dug up. It's been excavated in the shape of an oval pool, deeper on one side. Inside it, the pool company has already run the rebar. Number fives each way, along the bottom and up the side walls. Ben walks on the edges of the pool, kicking at the dirt piles.

Inside, Doug walks through the house on what appears to be an aggravating phone call. A vein in his forehead pulses. Morgan and Kim give him a look, though Kim's is more scathing.

"You're disturbing the peace and the baby is sleeping," she hisses. "Take it outside."

Doug rolls his eyes but opens the sliding door and lets himself out. "Hold on," he growls into the phone, loud enough for Ben to hear through the opening. They meet eyes across the space and Doug shakes his head. "What do you want?" He snaps at Ben before he turns away and starts yelling into the phone again.

What do 'you' want? Ben thinks, annoyed. *Doug doesn't know how to speak in normal volumes.*

As Ben watches, Doug paces along the edge of the new pool. He stops suddenly and Ben glances down at the ground to find that in the spot next to Doug's foot is a red ant hill. His heart skips a beat at the sight and he watches on in a trance-like state, unable to look away even though he's freaked out by the ants. A few reddish-brown dots start crawling up Doug's shoes, then up his bare legs. Ben is suddenly glad that he isn't wearing shorts himself.

In the kitchen, Kim catches sight of Ben through the glass. She finds it odd that he's just staring at Doug, who is swatting something off his legs.

Weird. She furrows her brows and is somewhat perplexed, returning to her task of rinsing the rice.

A moment later, the rice is done and Kim looks up to see that Doug is gone. She dries her hands off on her apron as she walks over to the sliding door and steps out. Only Ben is there. He hasn't moved and is staring straight ahead.

"Ben, where did Doug go?"

Her son raises his arm and points to the pool hole.

Hesitantly, Kim walks over to the edge and, her throat already tight, looks down into the hole. Doug is face down in the hole, his body impaled on the rebar in several different areas, spikes stick out of his back, head, and legs. Blood plumes out from the wounds, soaking into his pants and dripping down the metal into the dirt beneath. Ants crawl up and down his calves.

Kim screams out in horror.

•••

Rosa takes the stairs two at a time, rushing toward her bedroom.

"Brian!" She shakes her boyfriend's shoulders frantically. He arrived earlier that day from Boston, drove home from the airport, and took a nap. "Brian, wake up! There's been an accident!"

"What happened?" Brian mumbles groggily, sitting up in bed.

"Check your phone! Morgan tried to reach you. Doug is dead!"

She may as well have thrown a bucket of cold water over his head. Brian grabs his phone off the nightstand in distress. "Damn it," he mutters. "It's still in airplane mode."

Brian turns airplane mode off and reconnects to the Wi-Fi. Text messages stream through, filling his notification bar up. He only catches a few words.

Morgan: Dad, call me… It's an emergency!

Immediately, he dials Morgan's number. It rings and rings. No answer.

"Call Kim!" Rosa waves her arms.

Brian does so hurriedly.

"Oh my God, Brian, where the hell have you been? I have been trying to reach you! Doug is dead! Jesus Christ… He's fucking dead!"

"Kim, calm down," Brian says softly. "Are the kids okay?"

"Yes. I mean no… CPS took them. They took our kids!"

"Took them? Where?!"

"Are you back? Are you in town or are you still in Boston?"

"I'm back, but I need you to tell me what the hell happened!"

"I'm afraid to talk on the phone," Kim says. He can tell. Her voice is shaking. "I'm freaking out… This is bad!"

Brian does his best to remain calm, knowing that if he freaks out, it will only make things worse for Kim. "Okay, take a deep breath. Don't be paranoid. No one's listening. Just tell me what happened?"

"Doug was outside, Ben was there too. Next thing I know… Doug is gone. I went outside and—" Kim's voice breaks and she cries into Brian's ear. "He was dead… He was in the hole they dug for the pool and…" She takes in a deep, shuddering breath. "The metal rods… They went right through him… Oh, my God, it's horrible. I can't believe he's gone…"

"I don't understand. Did he fall?"

"You don't understand. The police are here—they are investigating it. CPS took our kids. And there is something else… When it happened, I was looking out the window, cooking in the kitchen… I looked up, they were both out there. Doug was on his phone with Ben just standing nearby, staring at him. I looked away for one second, then I looked again and Doug was gone." She lowers her voice. "I'm not sure, Brian, but what if Ben pushed him?"

"No, Brian breathes. "He wouldn't have done that."

"How do you know? With all the stuff going on, the fucking meds he's on… I looked up Risperidone. Did you know that it's an antipsychotic? They give that shit to psychos, did you know that? What if our son is a psycho and he did push Doug?"

"You can't think like that!"

"He was just standing there looking at him! He did nothing… Like that fucking kid in *The Omen*."

"Listen," Brian reels the conversation back. Rosa is chewing her nails, sitting on the edge of the bed. At some point, he stands up and paces lines into the rug. "You're in a bad place. We both are. Ben is suffering from something and I'm starting to think that it may not be medical."

"Oh, my God, do you think he is possessed? Do you think our son is evil?" There's static on the end of the line. Brian isn't sure what Kim is doing to cause all the white noise but he needs to move the phone away from his ear due to the sudden ruckus. "I need to go... I'm losing my mind."

Kim ends the call.

●●●

Brian and Rosa find the Child Protection Services number for their area and dial it the moment they get off the phone with Kim, who was loud enough for Rosa to catch the gist of their conversation.

"I'll direct you to the mental health center where your children are. They'll be able to tell you more," a cold male voice on the other end of the line tells them.

The phone rings and rings. If not for the horrible nightmare he had on the plane, Brian might consider more Valium to calm his nerves.

"Hello, this is Karen," a woman's voice cuts through the dial tone.

"Hello, this is Brian Brennan. I was told that my children, Morgan and Ben Brennan, are currently being held at your medical health center. CPS directed me to you."

"Ah, yes. Your children are undergoing some grief counseling and a psychiatric evaluation. We understand that they were in their mother's care at the time of the incident. Can I assume that you are aware of the circumstances under which they were taken from her custody?"

"Yeah, I am," Brian says. "Are they all right?"

"We'll be able to say more after their evaluation."

"Am I able to come to the center?"

Karen pauses. "Yes, but only the evaluation results will determine whether you can see them."

That's enough for Brian. "Thank you."

He and Rosa hit the road and they are at the center within minutes. Inside, a woman greets them at the front desk and Brian recognizes her voice.

"Hi, I'm Brian Brennan. I called earlier. This is my girlfriend, Rosa."

"Mr. Brennan," she steps around from the desk. "Rosa. I'm Karen. I'm one of the caseworkers here."

"Do you have an update on my kids? How are they?"

Karen purses her lips. "Well, Morgan is shaken up, but she's doing fine. You can see her and visit with her."

"What about Ben?"

"Based on what we know about Ben's recent history and the events that occurred at the house with—Doug?"

Brian and Rosa nod.

"Right. A psychologist asked us to run a series of tests and an MRI."

"An MRI? Has this already happened?"

"I'm afraid so. Come with me, I'll take you to the doctor."

They walk down a hallway and Karen grabs a file folder along the way. Moving through with ease, Brian hates the clean white walls. They feel more claustrophobic than ever. The smell of medicine and disinfectant hangs in the air. The trip required them to sanitize their hands at one of the doors and before long, they stopped outside a half-open door.

Karen pokes her head in. "Doctor, the father of the Brennan children, is here."

"Of course, send him in."

Rosa slips her hand into Brian's and they walk into the doctor's office.

"Hello," he says. "I'm Dr. Sanchez."

"Brian. And this is my girlfriend, Rosa."

Karen closes the door behind them as they take a seat across from the doctor.

"Can you tell me what's going on with my son?" Brian asks, his fingers still gripping Rosa's. "The caseworker told us that you ran tests and did an MRI?"

"Yes, we were checking for brain lesions, among other things," the doctor nods, pulling up one of the folders on his desk. "Sometimes organic brain lesions can cause psychiatric symptoms such as depression, anxiety disorders, schizophrenia, and other cognitive dysfunction."

As he speaks, the doctor flips through a file that Brian sees Ben's name written on.

"Something could be wrong with his brain? Is that what you're telling me—us?" He corrects himself.

"Actually," the doctor pulls out a sheet with a negative image of a brain. "The MRI report determined that no brain lesions or any other possible cause is evident. The psychologist who evaluated Ben states that, according to your son, the victim was swatting at ants that crawled up his leg. Doug slid off the edge of a dirt bank around the pool and fell to his death."

"Oh my god," Brian breathes.

"The psychologist who saw Ben has also determined that Ben is suffering from an acute anxiety disorder categorized as trypophobia. Ben's persistent and excessive fear of tiny holes, as corroborated by his sister in her evaluation, triggered by the ant trauma that occurred a few weeks earlier has gotten a bit out of control. We are recommending an increased dosage of Risperidone."

"Really? More antipsychotics?"

The doctor narrows his eyes. "Please don't read into the categorization of the medication, Brian. Many people benefit from antipsychotics and they are by no means indicative of a person's psychosis. Mental illness comes in all shapes and forms, as does medication."

"What if it doesn't work?" Brian asks hopelessly.

"If it doesn't work, or if Ben's condition gets worse, there are other options to consider such as cognitive behavioral therapy or hypnosis. And, either way, I highly recommend that your son receive weekly counseling so that he can get the necessary tools to cope with what's going on, especially given that he is on the disability spectrum."

Brian nods.

"Thank you, Doctor," Rosa offers quietly.

"The CPS caseworker will be helping you to transition the children back into the households."

"They said that we could see Morgan. Are we able to see Ben before we leave?"

"Yes," the doctor says. "That will be fine."

17

THE BEAST

A return to Dr. Susan Lew's office starts with Brian sitting quietly across from his psychologist, fidgeting with his fingers. Susan is equally quiet.

"Did you get my message? I'm sorry I missed our last appointment."

"Yes, not a problem. It's understandable. I'm sorry for your loss, how are you coping?"

"Not good. It's been a rollercoaster if I'm being honest. First, I get the call about my father dying. I had to fly back east to deal with that." He takes a sip of water. "I wanted to talk to you about what happened. While I was there, I made a disturbing discovery about something that happened in the past, in my father's days as a Marine—I also discovered that my dad hasn't been right in the head for a while."

"Oh?"

"Remember what you told me on the first day that I was here? About things that lurch in the dark? Well, my stepmother told me he woke up one night near the end and thought something was coming for him. He put six bullet holes in the wall."

"Was anyone hurt?"

"No, thank God, but that's not it. You're not going to believe what happened next." Brian shakes his head back and forth, an expression of disbelief on his face. "Doug, Kim's boyfriend, fell into a hole in his backyard that had been dug up for a new pool and died, perforated by rebar."

"Oh, my God," Susan covers her mouth. She's not normally easily shocked. "That's terrible, Brian."

"The worst part is that Ben actually witnessed the whole thing. Kim is convinced that he watched it happen or even somehow instigated it. I mean, everything that has happened these past few weeks... it all makes no sense. I talked to Kim and she agreed. To be honest, I'm starting to think that Ben is possessed or maybe we are dealing with some kind of evil spirit or something. Think about it... What else could it be?"

"Okay, let me stop you there," Susan holds up a hand to stop Brian from going any further. She's been furiously taking notes, but the more he speaks, the more distressed Brian becomes. "Take a deep breath."

Brian does, taking a quick pause.

"Okay, good. How are the kids? Are they still with Kim?"

"CPS took the kids while they investigate the incident with Doug."

"So the kids are okay?"

"Yes, they're both safe. CPS ordered an evaluation. They ran Ben through a bunch of tests, an MRI, and all that shit."

"That's good though. Brian, that's a good thing! Did they find anything?"

Meeting his psychologist's eyes, Brian begins to calm down. Speaking without letting his thoughts run wild has helped. "Nothing bad. No lesions or signs of brain trauma. They just think he has an extreme case of trypophobia."

"Okay, Brian," Susan sits forward on the edge of her armchair, the notepad on her lap. The pen sits precariously between the open pages. "I want you to take a moment. Don't speak. I want you to think about everything you just told me, everything you've said... All of your ideas, theories, and fears."

Brian nods slowly and does as he's asked.

"Then, I want you to think about what you found out from the doctors. They have told you this more than once, that Ben has trypophobia, which is a fear of holes. I want you to digest that information for a minute." To indicate that she literally means a minute, she points to the clock on the wall and then taps her wristwatch pointedly.

Taking another deep breath, Brian gives a nod and runs through the exercise. At first, when he thinks about all the crazy events—from the moment he related the six holes in his father's wall to the ones in Ben's room, to the moment he woke from that nightmare on the plane, to Kim questioning whether their son is evil, and everything in between—his heart starts to pound again. Panic races through his system. *What if he really is evil?* Brian turned away from religion so long ago and part of him is starting to think that this is his karma. When he puts his hand to his chest and feels his out-of-control pulse beneath his palm, Susan sits forward even more, about to say something, but he holds up an index finger to ask her to wait. If she interrupts his thought process, he isn't sure he'll be able to pull himself out of the spiral on his own. Though, in a way, she's reminded him that he needs to, that there is a purpose behind allowing his mind to run through all the recent events.

"Trypophobia," a word that currently holds so much power over his life. His son has a fear of tiny holes, or clusters of holes. The thought alone brings images swimming to the surface of his mind, of the walls, his daughter's poor turtle, beehives, kitchen strainers, and, unbidden, the terror he'd experienced when the fuselage of the plane ripped away because of the holes perforating the structure.

God, if Ben is as afraid of holes all the time, if he sees them everywhere, and experiences the same fear I do when I'm on a plane, I feel for the kid…

A fear of holes. Not evil. There have been no recommendations for an exorcist—only medication.

The doctor at the medical center told him and Rosa that no one is at all insinuating his son is a psycho.

No, the only people who've done that are his own family.

Brian sighs while his mind fires reality his way. Somewhere along the way, his heart rate has started to slow. And he knows that he's failed the one thing he promised his son, that he would be there for him no matter what.

The clock tells him that it's been two minutes since Susan asked him to mull things over and she is simply waiting, watching him.

"The funny thing about holes," he starts, after another deep, calming breath. "They're all around us, yet kinda invisible in our everyday movements through life. We just do our thing, never paying too much attention to them. Until we do. Then, like a bull's eye, we see them everywhere. Your eyes lock onto the simplicity of their form; round, black voids, almost like a portal into darkness." He presses his palms together in front of him, fingers out, creating a line of sorts. "This is what haunts me. I look at life as a line, a solid, unmovable line. If I do this, I get that. For example, if I'm good, I will get good in return. You know?"

"Somewhat," Susan says. "I imagine there's more to this?"

"Yes," Brian looks from the psychologist back down to his hands. "So, this line brings me closure. It has two ends and they meet in the middle. They have a beginning and the end. But a hole... That's more like an open wound. Being a circle, it will always be open in its center. And it's that blackness in the middle that can lead anywhere. It can go through a wall, a door, through my heart, or even my mind. For all I know, that hole could lead to the gates of hell. Not knowing what's on the other side is frightening to me, never knowing how deep it may go, or anything. I could end up in a dark void with the world around me on the outside."

"What you've described here is profound," Susan grins simply. "When I hear your words, Brian, I hear a man, a good man, a good father. You are perhaps realizing that you have a wound to heal."

Brian reaches for his bottled water. He's spoken a lot in today's session.

"It's not the holes that haunt you," the psychologist continues. "It's not supernatural. It's your mind digging here. Ben is a part of you and your inability to control everything in your life has resulted in a break. In that line, you described a loss of control. Now, the line you live by, a straight path with a beginning and an end is clean and easy for your mind to comprehend, but the symbolism of a hole, a circle with no endpoint where you go around and around, that is what haunts you. That is what your mind cannot comprehend."

"That kind of makes sense, in a way…"

"As humans, we fear what we don't understand."

"Okay, so what do you think this all means? Do you fully understand?"

Susan gives a small smile. "I wish that I could say I fully understand, but sometimes, that's not even a possibility. Plus, I would expect that it may take some time for us to get there. These are early days in your therapy."

"Fair enough," Brian nods.

"I believe what haunts you, the darkness in the hole, what you've described as a void... I believe that began in your childhood bedroom. I believe the answers that you seek reside in that stage of your life when you would play the Scare Game with your brother." Susan sets her notebook aside on the end table beside his seat. "I want to ask you to go back to that moment. I want to see if we can go any deeper than we already have. If you are willing to allow yourself to remember, I believe you, too, will see that all that is happening to you and Ben is not related to anything supernatural or any kind of hocus pocus at all."

Brian can't help but chuckle at the use of the term "hocus pocus."

Softening, Susan continues. "It's about a boy who is afraid to face his childhood trauma, Brian."

"I remember I was very scared," he lowers his head in thought. "I would measure my breathing, telling myself that the beast could probably sense my fear or hear me if I breathed too loudly."

"Would you like to press further into the past?"

"Yeah..."

"Okay, tell me a bit more about how you felt when you were under the covers and measuring your breathing."

"I could hear creaking in the house. Like, I don't know... It seemed real and not real at the same time, because I had made the beast up, didn't I? Still, after the creaking came the subtle squeak of my bedroom door, as if it was being pushed slowly open, like someone was sneaking into the room. Then, I could feel movement as the beast searched around the room." Brian pauses as he thinks back to those times, putting himself beneath the blanket mentally. "There was this shift in the volume of the air around me, a change in the way my blanket felt over my curled up body. I could hear the beast breathing, a heavy pant and at times, a deep grunt. I often prayed my brother was safe, that he was hiding as well, that he wouldn't surrender to the heat or the sweat or the fear or the lack of air. I hoped he would remain covered until the beast had left."

"You once said that you usually won the game, outlasting your brother."

"Yes, I had a greater imagination than my brother. I think my imagination of the beast was so real, so powerful, that I would never have come out from under the covers."

"You must have been curious," Susan gestures. "In all the times that you played the Scare Game, do you ever remember taking a peek, just to see if the beast was real?"

"I don't remember," he answers immediately.

Narrowing her eyes, the psychologist probes. "How did you picture the beast? What did you see in your head when it came to mind?"

No response as Brian thinks on it. "Probably like a devil or something..."

"With long sharp nails, allowing it to make the claw marks on your nightstand?"

"Oh!" He gasps, eyes wide open. Brian adjusts his chair and leans forward. "I forgot to tell you! The five claw marks. I found out what they were when I was in Dorchester. They're not claw marks. I mean, from the point of view of an eleven-year-old boy imagining a beast in his room, I always thought they were claw marks. But when I flew back east after my father died and I discovered the holes in his bedroom wall, I also noticed the same marks on the nightstand beside his bed. They were cigarette burns."

"Cigarette burns?"

"Yeah, Connie, my stepmother, told me... Apparently my father had a bad habit of leaving a lit cigarette on the edge of the nightstand. When the cigarette burned down, it left these pointed brown burn marks etched into the wood."

"I've seen them before," Susan nods. "They could have been anything you wanted them to be."

"All these years and I never realized that's all they were," he murmurs while his psychologist watches him.

The two are silent for some time. Susan reaches out to the bottle on the table and hands it to Brian, who gratefully sips some water. She goes ahead and drinks some of her own before she speaks again, keenly aware that this appointment will be longer than usual.

"I have a difficult question to ask you. Think about it before you respond, all right?"

"Okay."

"Why would there be cigarette burns on your nightstand? Remember, you told me in the past that you could smell cigarette smoke in your bedroom when you and your brother played the Scare Game. Who would be smoking a cigarette and leaving one on your nightstand in your room at night?"

"No one?" Brian answers, troubled.

"We can assume the beast is a fabrication of your eleven-year-old mind, right, but the cigarette burns were real. Those were not manifestations of a fearful child. What did your imagination of the beast look like? Can you give it a face?"

"I don't remember... It was just a scary beast I imagined in my head. Nothing tangible."

Brian has a smile on his face, but Susan isn't as amused. After passing the bottled water to Brian and sipping from her own, she had picked up her notepad and it was once again on her lap. "Try to remember. Close your eyes."

He does.

"You are under the covers, hot and sweaty. The blankets shift after that subtle squeak of your bedroom door. You feel the presence of the beast as it walks into your room."

Breathing in, he concentrates, once again going back to his childhood bedroom. The funniest thing is that every time he thinks back to being covered, he can feel the heat again. It's as if he's there. Listening to Susan describe the scene throws him back to the memory. He's 11 years old and curled up in the darkness.

"You smell the cigarette smoke..."

He does. It's thick and pungent, making it harder to breathe than it already is. He has no openings, not a single hole.

"You hear the beast breathe, hear it pant, and maybe a deep grunt. It's out there. All you need to do is take a little peek outside of the covers."

Heart starting to beat faster again, Brian recalls the seam

around him where the blanket is shut, where it meets the mattress. He's hot, too hot, and sweating. His own breath comes back into his face, hot and wet. He's scared; he's never looked before and for that, until now, he has survived the Scare Game, being stronger than his brother.

Tonight is different. His curiosity is getting the best of him. He wants to look. *Just a peek,* he thinks.

Slowly, Brian stretches his arm out, careful not to move the blanket around him. He only wants to see, he doesn't want to get caught. One at a time, he wraps his fingers around the edges of the blanket and lifts it. At first, there's nothing but darkness. There are no lights on in the bedroom. As his eyes begin to adjust and he blinks the darkness away, the edge of his nightstand comes into sight.

A little more, he thinks. Shadows are shifting and he squints to make them out. On the other side of the room, there's some kind of movement.

"What do you see? What is the face of your beast?"

Susan's voice sounds far off now. Brian's eyes focus on the nearest object. Part of a cigarette, the orange part, hangs off the lip of his nightstand. It's lit, slowly burning into the wood, making it smell stronger. Smoke swirls upward and dances in the air, floating over his head, blocking his view of anything beyond. Agitated, he rolls the blanket a bit further, wanting to see more. Something is moving over by his brother's bed.

Could this be the beast? A shadowy form thrashes in the darkness, muscles bulging and protruding. Now that the blanket's seal has been broken, he can hear it clearly; heavy breathing and low grunts as it moves around Little Paul's bed. Brian's nerves are a wreck and, eyes wide with fear, he works to make sense of the grizzly form of the beast within his bedroom, the beast attacking his brother, while he lies in his bed and wins the Scare Game.

Struck by the memory he's pulled from a place deep within his subconscious, a memory he'd lost on purpose, pushed away so that he would never need to find it again, Brian opens his eyes. He's back in the office, back in the comfortable armchair that suddenly feels uncomfortable, back in front of his psychologist, but mentally, he can't rip his thoughts away from what he saw. He's not looking at the memory through the eyes of an 11-year-old boy anymore and he's retrieved it, for better or worse, never to be returned to that place of obliviousness again. Brian can now see it for what it was, through the eyes of a man in his late thirties, a father.

His throat constricts and he can scarcely breathe.

"Brian, look at it. It's okay," Susan says gently. "What is the face of your beast?"

"I remember now," Brian splutters, his eyes watering up. "I did peek... and I didn't understand what I was seeing..."

"You were a child."

"It was my father, not a shadowy form thrashing in the darkness. It was my father's hairy back facing me, his bulging muscles, his heavy breathing. His grunts were so frightening. A beast after all..." Brian bursts into tears, his body convulsing into a violent array of uncontrollable motions. "... sodomizing my brother, Little Paul."

How many times within this short space of time has he

cried, after years of not shedding a proper tear? It's a long overdue cry, one only found in grown adults, one that comes from years of living with trauma. It does not bring a cleansing feeling upon him, not one that peace will follow. Each tear that leaves his system has exhausted him, sucking a great deal of energy out of him, simply finding a way to exit his mind and soul.

"Brian, it's okay," Susan hands him a box of tissues. It's familiar, like the first time he was here. "Let it all out... Let it all out..."

And, once again, Brian does as she says. He cries and cries, trying to force the image out of his mind, and in between, he wipes the tears away and blows his nose. There are three crumpled tissues by the time he starts to regain control over his own emotions.

"I am very proud of you, Brian," Susan says when he starts to come back to her. He wonders if she's been taking notes—if she has, he hasn't seen it. "You've been through so much more than you deserve. What your father did was horrible, absolutely inexcusable! And you did all you could to bury the trauma that it caused you. No eleven-year-old boy wants to see their father, or anyone for that matter, like that. So, your young mind gave him the face of a beast, a mask of sorts, so as not to destroy what the person behind it meant to you. There's a deep betrayal that comes from an act of abuse suffered at the hands of people who are meant to be our loved ones, people who, despite the horrors we may endure at their hand, we still love."

Brian can only sniff, blinking tears away. He's almost numb after expending his emotions.

"Now, you can see what Little Paul must have suffered too. It's very possible that these events are what drove him away from your family, into running away and his life of addiction. Please, don't feel guilty about this because what happened is in no way your fault." She pauses, but Brian says nothing. He takes another tissue from the box. "I want you to know that all that is happening right now, all that has happened, is explainable. Once we understand it, we can work on fixing it. And remember, you are not your father."

The clock on Susan's watch beeps.

"I'll see you next week, back here again."

18

THE LOTUS POD

Things are different in the Brennan household. Certainly, things have been different since that night with the ants, but things have grown steadily worse and the only remaining occupants in the house, in the absence of Ben and Morgan, are Rosa and Brian, both of whom can feel that a funk of some kind has set in over the house. Perhaps it's set in over them. They have been through so much and the effects show in the most basic of behaviors, in the lack of playfulness and romance that comes with waking. When the kids aren't with them, things are a lot livelier.

As it is, Brian is filled with melancholy and Rosa's

bubbly personality is muted. They wake with less enthusiasm than usual, though Rosa leans over to kiss Brian the moment her eyes are open. She's not one to ever leave him wondering if he's loved or wanted. They're all they have. Incidentally, she's also not one to remain in bed, regardless of how much of a *funk* they find themselves in.

When she climbs out of bed, Rosa walks over to the large window and pulls the curtains open. Outside, it's a beautiful day; the sky is clear and the sun shines down brightly, not unusual for Tucson. Acreage of natural desert land borders their backyard, giving them an endless view of the land as the eye can see, broken only by the occasional green cactus. In the distance, the Catalina Mountains create a bold silhouette, a sentry standing watch over them, keeping the secrets of thousands of years to itself. Those slopes are home to wildlife, the line of the peaks on the horizon looks like a heartbeat, and between the bright blue sky and the greenery at the base of the trees and ferns too far away to make out further than their lush coloring, Rosa can only look on in admiration.

"It looks like a beautiful day, my love," Rosa says.

Brian sits up in the bed and glances over to the window. "It does," he nods in agreement. "Let today be a new day."

Rosa smiles and Brian returns the smile. "A new day. In that case, let's do away with the funk. Will you pull the sheets off the kid's beds? I'm going to do laundry today."

Without waiting for Brian to leave, she begins pulling the sheets off their bed. Brian rolls out of it with the smallest smile on his face. He heads to the bathroom to relieve himself before he makes his way toward his daughter's bedroom. The billowing of bedding can be heard behind him as Rosa strips their bed. It's just as well. Brian wouldn't have been able to get out of bed without her.

Entering Morgan's room, Brian notes how empty it feels when she's gone. The posters and colors are only lively when she's here. He strips the bed and drags the laundry to the stairs, creating a pile near the top and closing the door to Morgan's bedroom behind him. He's happy to be out of there, but something tells him, as he opens the door, that Ben's room will leave him feeling much the same.

When the door swings open, he stops dead, all thoughts and expectations of what he thought he might find disappear from his mind. What he sees is spine-chilling, so debilitating that he stands frozen, to the point that he resembles a statue of ice in the doorway to his son's bedroom. The signals race from his optic nerves behind his retina, carrying the image his eyes are seeing to his brain so that it can be interpreted, but no sensible mind could understand what Brian sees at this moment. His body's reaction to the wall before him is visceral and his skin crawls with the sight, causing his pores to drip with sweat and his skin to crawl in discomfort. It's illogical... Unreal... Terrifying...

"What the fuck," he mutters aloud, barely able to hear his voice as the pressure of anxiety presses down on him from every side.

"Baby?" Rosa calls from behind him, noticing the way he stands motionless in the doorway of Ben's bedroom.

"Baby, the sheets…?"

Brian hears nothing.

Walking up to him, she instantly sees what's tethering him to his spot, holding all his attention.

"Oh, dear God," she gasps.

Together, side-by-side, they look upon the bedroom wall that Uncle Reyes repaired and patched. Dark voids of depth leave the wall filled with bumps that stand out and, because of the number of them, seem to move. Covering the entire surface, end to end, are thousands upon thousands of tiny holes, creating one giant cluster.

•••

Outside, the only sounds that can be heard are those of crickets. Night has once again fallen, bringing with it a sky devoid of stars, thanks to the clouds that hover above the house. It's windy out there. A storm could be brewing. The rustling of tree branches is hardly noticeable, not from inside and not on a night such as this one. Instead, the branches loom threateningly outside the windows, their shadowy forms are transformed into monsters under the influence of imaginations driven by fear.

Inside has been no different. Barely two words have been spoken between Brian and Rosa since they discovered the holes in Ben's bedroom wall. The two are curled up on a bare mattress, covered only by a comforter left behind on the stripped down bed. They've been here for the majority of the day, both lost in their own thoughts. Every time they blink, they see the wall, and their eyes burn with the effort of trying not to. A once beautiful sunny day had disappeared in seconds, leaving behind a pile of dirty sheets at the top of the staircase.

"Evil is real," Brian whispers. Rosa turns her head to meet his eyes as he continues. "Evil has found us somehow."

Whispering back, as if evil is right there with them, listening in on their conversation, Rosa asks, "Why us? What did we do?"

"I've been putting a lot of pieces together over the past couple of weeks, and I think it has to do with my father. Something that he did a long time ago in Haiti."

Interest sparks in Rosa's doe eyes. "What did he do?"

Brian's been thinking about this conversation for the past several hours, playing it all out mentally, but having prepared responses doesn't make talking about it any easier. The light of day brings scrutiny with it, whilst darkness comes with hiding spots. Right now, he likes neither option. He's barely started to process his own past. Sharing it with Rosa is a difficult task, but one he knows he has to do, not least because she's the person whose opinions he values most. She wouldn't judge him, right?

You didn't do those things, a rational voice in the back of his mind whispers to him.

"My father, it turns out, did some terrible things. I discovered in one of my recent appointments with Dr. Lew that I've had some trauma buried somewhere inside… like some kind of repressed memory. And it was about my dad." He pauses. This is another image he'd rather keep off his mind. "He raped my older brother."

"Paul?" Rosa gasps.

With a nod of his head, Brian continues. "That's when we

were kids, only... When I went to Boston, I went through a bunch of old personal papers of his. Connie let me. I found this letter from his Marine days, and basically, there was a shooting that he was involved in where a young Haitian boy was killed. It was supposedly an accident."

"Supposedly?"

"I don't know..." He shrugs and takes a deep breath. "That's not the weirdest part though. The boy... He was shot. Multiple times, potentially. And he was Black."

Rosa furrows her brows. "I don't know what you mean, baby..."

"Remember what Ben drew? A little Black boy full of holes."

Eyes wide, Rosa gasps.

"Yeah," Brian murmurs.

And just like that, the two return to laying in silence. Rosa has no idea what to say and, until she's ready, Brian has said all that he can.

•••

At some point, Brian climbs out of the bed and goes down to his office. The light is the first and only one he's turned on since dusk fell, and only because with darkness came a foreboding sensation that he and Rosa weren't alone in the house, that the entity that may be lurking in the shadows is something else. Then again, he'd felt that way for the majority of the day, since entering Ben's room. All the light had been sucked out of *him* at that moment. The computer boots up with a low hum and Brian tries not to lose his mind with boredom while it comes to life.

The second his system is up and running, he opens the

browser and enters "trypophobia" into the search engine:

> https://web_search_results...
>
> Trypophobia
> /ˌtrɪpə(ʊ)ˈfəʊbɪə/
> *noun*
> An extreme or irrational aversion to or
> fear of clusters of small holes or bumps.
> Origin: early 21st century, from Greek
> trýpa 'hole' and English 'phobia.'

Right underneath the definition of the phobia, a row of related images appears. To his surprise, he sees pictures of lotus pods. He doesn't have to suffer from trypophobia to be disturbed by what he's seeing. Two weeks ago, he mightn't have blinked twice, but the images make his skin crawl. Nevertheless, he clicks on the image link to review more of them. Both living and dead lotus pods show up in the feed and his body is instantaneously covered in goosebumps as he's faced with an entire screen of them, and they're equally creepy in every way. The living pods, from the moment the flowers are ripe, have tiny buds inside tiny holes. In a way, they remind Brian of worms, of maggots whose heads are ready to burst through. When he closes them because they gross him out, the ones that are dead, where the buds are missing and the holes are brown, empty, and dried out simply remind him of Ben's wall. Never did he think flowers, dead or alive, would ever be disturbing, but the dark voids where buds once nested have him scratching his scalp in discomfort.

Scrolling through the web search, Brian comes across several articles related to lotus pods and trypophobia. He finds out that the pod is one of the most commonly known triggers to those suffering from the fear of tiny holes. Other things that are triggering, he's less surprised to come across; beehives, honeycomb, and sponges. Strawberries appear and Brian feels bad for people who can't eat strawberries due to phobias and allergies for a second. Some of the images that show up are graphically modified pictures of people's faces, hands, and bodies, clusters of tiny holes burrowing into their skin, bumpy and swollen, black in the center, ringed with either pink or blood. Some were created by special-effects makeup artists. They all look too real for his liking. A few results lead to an internet hoax that trypophobia is like some kind of disease or virus one can catch by contagion.

Eventually, it's time to come back out of the rabbit hole and Brian opens a new tab, typing "lotus pod" and "Haiti" into the search bar this time. He's not one to go to the next page; the first one usually has everything he needs. Skimming through for different keywords that make sense, as if something will pop up that has a direct correlation. One catches his attention quite suddenly: "Inside Vodou Spells."

Brian clicks on the link and begins reading the article. The clock tells him that it's already past four in the morning and his eyes are burning from having to stare at a screen for so long. He came down here over two hours ago. Blinking and rubbing his eyes, he reads on:

"Vodou, dolls, rituals, Haiti, and lotus pods..."

There are a lot of strange—albeit obscure—pieces that fit the puzzle that Brian's been mentally entertaining summarized in the article.

"Vodou curses and spells have been used for love… and revenge. Some choice ingredients are herbs, flowers, and other organic items of the earth such as lotus pods."

Upstairs, he hears the sounds of Rosa heading to the bathroom in the middle of the night.

This is crazy, he thinks. *But somehow, as crazy as it seems, it makes the most sense. Things haven't added up or been as simple as the doctors and psychologists suggest it is. Too many coincidences.*

But this article. It makes sense.

Brian shuts down his computer and steps away from his desk, groaning as he gives a huge stretch and his knee joints pop. His limbs and muscles are all stiff. It's almost dawn and he has no intention of going to bed yet. He's far from tired. After using the bathroom, he finds himself in the kitchen. He makes himself some toast and, while the kettle boils for a cup of coffee, he wanders into the garage where he's stored the box of items he brought back from Boston. The only thing that gives him pause is the sight of his drill on the workbench, disconnected with all the different rivets locked tightly away in a toolbox. It wasn't his intention when he came downstairs to continue investigating. All he wanted was a cup of coffee, but his brain hasn't stopped processing through everything that came up in his search results and he's more convinced than ever that Haiti is the center of everything and his father's past holds the key to figuring it all out and, hopefully, returning his life to some semblance of normalcy.

With a sip of coffee and a mouthful of buttered toast, he begins fishing through the contents, thinking back to the letter he discovered in Connie's apartment. Funny how he's started to refer to her as Connie on her own, and not Connie and his father. There are several papers and he's not surprised to find that none of them are organized. Ruffling through them, he finds a newspaper clipping with the heading: "Catholic Priest Dies Before Trial."

"A Catholic priest has been charged with multiple counts of sexual abuse," Brian read the article aloud. Apparently, the priest in question had been abusing altar boys for years. "My father was an altar boy," he murmurs to himself.

If my father was a victim as well, sexually abused as a child himself, then he grew up only to later abuse my brother. Abusers become abusers, they say.

Brian creates a new pile, starting with the newspaper clipping. He stands up from the table and grabs the letter from the Marine Corps and adds it to the pile. Everything of no interest had already been tossed out. This is the first item that means anything until he comes across a small, old manilla envelope. In the top corner, it bears the notation "(80)."

Opening up the envelope, Brian slides the contents out onto the table. Four colored photographs land on the table. He takes a sip of coffee and, after catching sight of the first image, he's happy that he's already finished his toast because any appetite he might have had has disappeared. In fact, he's feeling a little ill all of a sudden.

The first photo is of a body at the base of a wall. It's a

young Black boy, completely expressionless with his head tilted back and his eyes wide open. There would never be another expression on his face again. The boy is dead, his bare chest is full of six bloody bullet holes, and the once-white wall behind him is smeared with his blood. In the midst of red, there are holes in the wall, holes that go all the way from the top of the wall down to where the boy's body slid down to settle at the base. The entire scene plays out in Brian's head, of the boy being shot again and again, his body slamming back against the wall and eventually collapsing, leaving a red trail behind.

The second photo depicts a small, dark room. It takes Brian a moment to see that it's the same one that the boy died in. His body is on the floor to the left, rather than at the center. A bed is now in the center, with the door to the room on the right, across from the boy's body. The room is cluttered, messy, and drab, with the bed and bedding in disarray. If not for the small numbered marking on the floor next to it, Brian would have missed the military name patch lying on the ground beside the bed. The picture is too grainy to be able to read what the name patch says.

The third photo isn't in a dark room; it's of an elderly woman with dark skin, standing outside a house. Her hands are held out in front of her, palms up and open. They're covered in crimson blood. Brian sees that there's blood on her clothing as well. Wrapped around her hip, comfortably resting in a blanket, is a young Black girl. The child looks as if she's been crying, fear and sadness in her eyes. It makes her look younger, but if she were happier, Brian would say she is perhaps 13 or 14 years old.

The fourth and final photo is of PFC. Brennan, Brian's father, and PFC. Lynch. They are standing beside a vehicle. PFC. Lynch has a name patch on his uniform, whilst PFC. Brennan is missing his own and he is covered in dots of blood on his face and shirt.

These are the pictures that were taken by the Marine Corps—Criminal Investigation Division. They're the ones that were referenced in the letter. Now, more than ever, Brian knows what he must do. He no longer cares how crazy or unreal this connection seems, nor does he care about the fact that all the so-called professionals are telling him there's nothing more to it. The playground he passes on his route comes to mind and he remembers that he promised his son that he would help him and to do so, to help his family, he will try anything.

I have to go to Haiti. I have to. He rereads the letter from the Marine Corps: '*Rue Soleil 17.*' *That was where the incident took place.*

Brian doesn't return to bed. In the time he's spent shuffling through a box on the kitchen table, the sun has risen. It's past seven and Rosa doesn't sleep late. She walks into the kitchen wearing a T-shirt and panties and kisses him.

"Have you been up all night?"

"Since two," he says. "And I found something. I… Well, I think I have to go to Haiti."

"You do?"

Brian notices Rosa holding onto the cross at her throat and he knows she won't judge him for this. She's a devoted Catholic of Mexican descent, and she's told him herself that there may be something more going on. "I think there's something more going on here. The evil started in Haiti, by my father's hand, and to fight it, I have to go back to the root of it. I want to help our family."

"Okay," she says simply. "I support you."

"You believe me? You don't think that any of this is crazy?"

"Baby, all of this is loco. We saw holes reappear in Ben's room after those walls were patched up by Uncle Reyes and now he is dead. Everything that has happened. If that doesn't prove evil is with us, I don't know what else does."

PART III

"Hell is empty and all the devils are here."
William Shakespeare

19

RUE SOLEIL 17

Slightly soberer than the last time he took a flight, Brian lands at Toussaint Louverture International Airport in Port-au-Prince, Haiti. The new dose of Valium—after the last time, he knew he had to reduce it—leaves him numb to the palpitations that he's used to experiencing whenever it comes time to step off the plane, despite the relief that comes with his feet being planted firmly on the ground, but unlike last time, he's in complete control of his mental state. For the first time in a long time, he feels like everything is going to be okay. He finally knows what to do, how to help, and he's following the clues in his backpack in the hopes that they might lead him to the next one.

It will. It has to.

This time, he had the forethought to arrange a taxi to pick him up and take him from the airport to the Royal Garden Breeze Hotel. Getting lost isn't part of the plan. The driver greets him and they're off on a short, quiet journey. It seems the driver doesn't speak a lot of English and when he does, it's almost unintelligible due to his accent. Brian wishes he at least spoke French.

When they arrive, the driver hops out of the car and opens the back door. He stands in front of Brian and holds out his hand so fast that it takes Brian a moment to understand that it's time to pay. A quick fumble for his wallet and he hands the cash over, apologizing.

"Merci!" Another person has already taken Brian's place in the backseat of the taxi and they're off before he's taken in his surroundings.

Under any other circumstance, it'd think he was on the coast of Mexico. The sky is a clear blue and it's warm, with a gentle breeze. An outdoor pool, bar, and summer terrace are among the features the hotel boasts, and everywhere he looks, he's greeted with beachy decor, shells, and blues. It's exactly the kind of atmosphere he expected for an impoverished Caribbean country. Before he checks in, he tugs his cellphone out of his back pocket and dials Rosa's number.

"Hey baby, I'm safe in Haiti. I'm at the hotel, about to check-in."

"Be careful out there, Brian. Will you keep me posted?"

"Wi-Fi is included," he chuckles. "You know I will."

"I love you."

"I love you," he ends the call.

At the check-in desk he provides his details and obtains his keycard. At this point, he's antsy, both anxious and excited to do what he came to do. The concierge comes over to him.

"Bonjour, monsieur. Puis-je vous aider?"

"Parles-tu Anglais?" It's the only thing he knows how to say in French.

"Oh, of course. Welcome to the Royal Garden Breeze Hotel, sir. Is there anything I can do for you?"

"Thank you! It's nice. My name's Brian Brennan, I'm staying in Room 32. I was wondering if you could direct me to Rue Soleil 17?"

The concierge raises his eyebrows, taken aback. "Rue Soleil is not far, but Monsieur, I would not suggest walking. It's located in the Cite Soleil district, and it's not in the best neighborhood. It is a few miles away."

"How dangerous are we talking?"

"I think you will be fine, but you must take precautions and be careful. Unfortunately, crime is a problem in some parts of the city for tourists. Especially after dark. You must not wear this," the man taps on his wrist pointedly, which bears no watch. "Carry your money, your phone, and your ID in your front pockets instead of your back. Tourists get pick-pocketed in such places."

"I understand. Thank you. How do I get there? I used the airport taxi service to get here."

"I can call you a Tap-tap. This is recommended."

Brian anxious, "I'll drop my stuff off and be down in

fifteen."

"I will make the arrangements for you," the concierge confirms.

Brian rushes toward Room 32 and he's ready to ditch the backpack and leave, but a change of clothes is in order. Determined not to stand out, he opts for a pale brown cotton shirt. Casual, not touristy. He wears sandals and ditches his watch, putting his phone and wallet in his front pockets. The criminal investigation letter and the photos are inside a large envelope he can easily tuck in his waistband and hide under his shirt.

The Tap-tap cab, it turns out, is a gaily painted truck. It's intricately and lavishly decorated, painted in stark bright colors of reds and golds and greens. The windows of the big colorful vehicle are covered with hand-carved lettering. Many people are boarding the cab and Brian follows everyone else's lead, hurrying to join them in-route to Rue Soleil 17. He's happy to find that he blends in well with his low-key clothes. Port-au-Prince is built on a hillside, set up in such a way that the neighborhoods are indistinguishable, at least to Brian's eyes, from one another. Building's blend into one another for both travelers moving up and down its slope. The one thing that does stand out to him is the difference between the hotel and the lanes that they drive down. Climbing into the Tap-tap was like stepping through a portal into another dimension; the mostly maintained clean blues and whites, that he experienced at the hotel the second he arrived, are replaced by an impoverished society. Buildings changed from consistent, solid structures with foundations that have been present for years to resemblances of shanty towns while Brian watches the locals on the truck. He enjoys seeing the culture even if he can't understand the language. They don't go too deep into the city and no one pays him too much attention along the way.

Thanks to the concierge, the driver knows where to drop Brian off and the vehicle comes to a slow halt outside a one-story house plastered in a melon color. Wrought iron bars cover the windows and the wooden door, behind a metal screen. Brian recognizes the building immediately. It's well-kept, bordered by walkways on each side. One is three feet and the other is about eight, seemingly for off-street parking. There's a Suzuki SUV parked in the bigger spot. The paint has changed since the photo was taken and the wrought iron bars are a new addition, but there's no mistaking that this is the house in the third photo, the one with the elderly woman. How could he forget?

Before stepping off, Brian turns to the driver and quietly asks, "Do you mind staying here while I check if someone is home?"

The driver nods and Brian walks up to the small house, knocking on the metal screen with a loud rattling as metal smacks against metal, alerting everyone to his presence. A glance over his shoulder confirms that he's being watched. Several neighbors glance through their blinds and the gaps in the curtains. On the other side of the yard, he hears a commotion and waits patiently until the door opens. Behind it is a dark-skinned Haitian woman with narrowed eyes, framed by long lashes, and attractive features. If he had to guess, he'd say they're in the same age group and she's somewhere in her late thirties.

"Bonswa," she says.

"Hello... Bonswa," he corrects, even though he doesn't understand Haitian Creole. "Uh, parlez-vous Anglais?"

The woman's lips twitch in amusement and she leans closer, opening the door a little more. "Ou vle di, eske ou pale angle?"

"No understand," Brian says, shaking his head in confusion. "Anglais?"

The woman smirks. "English. Yes, I speak English."

"Oh good, that's a relief."

"How can I help you?"

"Is this Rue Soleil 17, the home of the Biassou family?"

"Yes..." The woman says, drawing a serious expression. "Who are you?"

Brian's eyes drop to the floor and then up again. He knew it was coming, but he wants to approach this as sensitively as he can. "My name is Brian Brennan. I just arrived from the United States... In 1994, something terrible happened here. And, as a result, I believe my son is now in danger."

The woman's eyes widen as she takes in the words. "This is Haiti. Many terrible things happen here," the woman glances over his shoulder, taking in the cab and most certainly the audience of neighbors. "I am sorry. I cannot help you!"

With that, she shuts the door in his face.

"Wait, please! I just need a few minutes..." He knocks on the door again, murmuring, "Please."

Behind him, more people are watching. Some of them

stand in the street openly, others continue to look at the scene from their windows and doors. Their presence concerns him—the whole situation does.

"Please, are you Tamara Biassou? I have come a long way. I just need some answers, for the sake of my son." A shadow moves near the window next to the door. He gives it one last shot in the hopes that she hears him from her spot near the door. "Look, I'm staying at the Royal Garden Breeze Hotel. If I could have a few minutes of your time, please, I won't return. I'm begging you."

Desperate to get out of there, away from the scrutiny, Brian walks off the porch and gets back into the Tap-tap cab.

•••

"Any messages for Brian Brennan?" He asks at the front desk the following morning.

The concierge shakes his head.

There's no hesitation as Brian boards the Tap-tap cab and returns to Tamara's house, growing a bit more comfortable with the idea of traveling around Port-au-Prince. He's written a note for her and when he arrives, there's no vehicle in the parking spot and he assumes that she's not home. He slips the note under the metal screen.

He hops back into the cab, expecting to head back to the hotel, and at the sight of a bustling hub in walking distance from it, he asks the driver to stop. While he's here, he may as well take advantage of the local market. The city streets are lined with stores, restaurants, and street vendors. It's a live, never-ending market, and locals flock to it. A local marché stallholder sells fresh produce of all kinds—

barrels and baskets are piled high with different shapes of brightly colored fresh fruit, vegetables Brian doesn't recognize, mushrooms, grains, and mountains of raw spices with aromas wafting up to his nose at every turn.

"Bonswa!" Store-holders shout at him as he makes his way down the lane.

"Bonswa," he says back, never stopping long enough to be pulled into a conversation he won't understand.

The market shifts from fresh produce into cooked foods, food vendors chat over bubbling cauldrons of legume stew while Brian's mouth waters. Some others flip fried plantains and fold pastries for lines of locals that stretch around the block beneath the baking sun. If the scent is anything to go by, Brian doesn't blame them.

Outside of the queues, local women carry sacks on their heads. Only a few people in the crowd stand out, visitors in the mix of people. Here, Brian feels more of an outsider than anywhere. The clothes he wears can't help him fit in no matter how much he wants them to. He's a sore thumb.

So is the small shop he catches sight of in between the buildings, interrupting the row of street vendors. An unusual array of items glint at him beneath the sun and curious, Brian walks over. A quick look at the labels over the items and Brian recognizes some of the names of ingredients found on the website about Haitian Vodou.

"Holistic medicine," one of them reads. There are bottles of what appear to be oils and herbs.

"American?" A younger Haitian man greets him.

"Yes."

"Welcome, I have many medicines to cure many

sicknesses."

Brian glances around the shop.

"Some are natural and some… supernatural," the man offers.

"What do you know about trypophobia… the fear of tiny holes?" Brian looks at the man.

"Ahhh, you seek a cure for fear."

Brian nods.

"The sickness of fear can only be treated with supernatural medicines," the man turns and reaches for a bottle off the shelf behind him. The majority of the bottles on this shelf contain dark substances and have no labels. Some of them are coated with dust, including the one the man hands over. "This is a Cerasee plant. Prepare it as a tea and it will cure you of your fear."

Anything is worth a try at this point, Brian thinks, taking in the bottle skeptically. "How much?"

"Five hundred gourde." Then, when he sees Brian's face contort with concentration, "That's five U.S. Dollars."

"Okay." He hands over the cash and tucks the Cerasee plant medicine into his pocket, leaving the shop.

•••

Knock, knock, knock.

Brian sits upright. He's been resting on his bed for a bit, having explored the market for the afternoon. Ultimately, the only thing he bought was the medicine at the Vodou shop. He walks over to the door, hoping there's news of a message.

His eyes widen as the door swings open. It's the dark-skinned woman from Rue Soleil 17.

"Tamara Biassou?"

"Yes," her eyes take him in. His shirt is wrinkled, making him look disheveled. "Freshen up and meet me in the lobby. You are taking me to dinner." She turns away and walks off down the hall, a sultry sway in her hips.

Pleasantly surprised, Brian hurries to get changed, opting for a dress shirt. He brushes his teeth and applies cologne, running a comb through his hair. Grabbing the photographs and letter, he heads down to the lobby.

He spots her easily. "Thank you for meeting me!"

"Well, don't thank me yet," her mouth twitches with amusement, the same way it did the day they met. "I am taking you to an expensive restaurant."

With a smile, she walks toward the exit and Brian follows her this time. He doesn't mind. All he wants is to get some answers. The Suzuki is parked across the road from the hotel. He doesn't need to be told to hop into the passenger side and something about the fact that this woman drives an SUV makes her more attractive.

"You speak English really well," he tells her once they're on the road.

"I work at a reservation call center, so I get a lot of practice."

Driving through the busy streets of Port-au-Prince, it becomes clear that the city's nightlife is a world apart. The sun has already set and the dark hides much of the dirt and grit Brian noticed during the day. Poverty is all but outshone by the colorful lights painting the exterior of some of the hotels, businesses, and restaurants. The city comes alive in a different way. It's wild and surreal. They dart through throngs of people, in between cars and motorcycles, with ease. Brian couldn't imagine navigating through these roads himself and in the passenger seat, his heart is beating the slightest bit faster than he's used to. Seat belt or not, the experience is panic-inducing.

"Deplase ou moun fou!" Tamara yells out of her window when a motorcycle slows down ahead of her.

The outbursts happen once or twice and Brian stays quiet, glad he doesn't experience road rage so readily. He understands enough to know that she'd yelled something with the word "fool" in it.

The SUV slows down outside a restaurant with an outside seating area, a patio in full view of the ocean, right on its edge. Lights sparkle colorfully and the scent of salt drifts over to them. Brian takes a deep breath.

There's nothing like the smell of the ocean.

They walk over and Tamara requests outside seating. A hostess in a colorful red sundress leads them over to one of the tables overlooking the stunning view. She passes them menus as they relax in their seats. The only thing Brian's paid attention to is the view. Now that they're sitting, he wants to finally get what he came all this way for.

"Thank you again for giving me your time. I have traveled a long way."

"You are welcome… I got your note and read your words about your son being in danger. What is it you think I can do? I am nobody to him."

"My son has been diagnosed with a mental disorder; a phobia called trypophobia. It is the fear of tiny holes. It's taken over him, it's like he's possessed…" Brian pauses.

"He was fine a few weeks ago and then it happened out of nowhere. One night, he had this episode and I found him covered in ants… and in the wall, a hole appeared. A hole we never saw before. It's been haunting him since— haunting all of us."

"Ants?"

"Yes."

"How old is your son?"

"Eleven," Brian answers as a waiter appears.

"Bonswa, non mwen se Peterson. Mwen ka pran lòd ou yo?"

"Do you know what you would like?" Tamara asks Brian.

"Not really. I'm not familiar with the dishes."

"If you like chicken, we can have my favorite dish. It is called poulet aux noix."

"I do," he nods. "That would be great."

The waiter takes their order.

"Tell me more. What else has happened?"

And so, Brian begins the long tale he's beginning to feel as if he's told a hundred times over. At this point, he knows that he sounds crazy, going on about holes that keep appearing and reappearing out of nowhere, and a son who sees a Black boy in his wall. How did Uncle Reyes get killed by bees in the same week that his father and his ex-wife's boyfriend, Doug, did? While he speaks, Tamara is silent. Under the soft glow of the night sky, her eyes are intense. She doesn't interrupt and no expression of disbelief crosses her face. It throws Brian off marginally.

She must be one hell of a poker player, he thinks to himself.

To elaborate on his story, he pulls his phone out of his pocket and shows her the holes that he'd photographed in Ben's bedroom before Uncle Reyes could patch them up.

"Brian…" She starts. "Perhaps you have come to the right place for answers. But I am not sure you will want them… and I am not sure you will be able to stop what has already been done."

"I know something evil is going on!" He insists in a hushed tone. "I know what happened in ninety-four. My father, Paul… He was a Marine. I discovered that he was deployed to Haiti and I found this." Reaching under his shirt, he tugs the letter out of his waistband and places it in front of Tamara. "He was involved in a civilian shooting." He points his finger at the page. "Look, your younger brother, Jonas Biassou, was accidentally killed. I found out that my father and another Marine were involved and that your brother was killed by accident in a scuffle. The other Marine, Lynch, I found out that he couldn't live with it and took his own life not long ago."

He continues, taking the photographs out. "Look," he points to the photograph of Tamara as a 13-year-old girl on her grandmother's hip. "That is you… you and your grandmother, Lourdes-Gina Fatiman, right?"

Finally, he takes out the photograph of his father and his partner. "And this is my father and the other Marine, Lynch."

Tamara stares at him, her mouth agape with shock. She's quite clearly taken aback. "Yes, it is me!" As she reaches for another one of the photographs Brian has in his hand, he pulls them away from her.

"No, wait… I don't want you to see the rest of these! They will be painful to see!"

Tamara takes no pause, accepting his assessment. She glances down at the photographs, and a moment later, she tosses them back at him furiously. "Lies!" She spits. "This is nothing but American lies!" Brian blinks in shock, the sudden change of behavior is not at all what he was expecting. "Your military, your government… They hide the truth!"

As gently as he can, Brian tries to take her hand. "Please, if this is a lie… Then tell me the truth. I came here for the truth."

"What you said, what they said in this letter is shit! I know the truth… because it was my brother who was killed that day. I was the little girl in that room." She purses her lips angrily. "Let me tell you what really happened, and then you will know why your son is cursed."

"Tell me everything," he breathes. "I can't fix this unless I know the truth."

Tamara leans in close, whispering. "You can't fix this no matter what you learn tonight." A chill runs up his spine and before he has a chance to fully register the idea, Tamara continues in a lower voice, sharing what she remembers.

"It was a hot night. Hotter than usual. My brother Jonas and I were asleep in the back room of the house on Rue Soleil 17. That night, my grandma Lourdes-Gina was caring for us. My mother worked nights and my father was gone. He died in prison during the rule of Raoul Cédras." She closes her eyes, as if preparing to go on. "That night, sometime after dark, Jonas and I awoke to screams coming from my grandma. We could hear the voices of American Marines… We were very scared. Soon after, a man entered the backroom… A Marine. He had his big gun pointed at us. He was not nice and kind like in your TV shows, he was not himself at all. I could smell the cigarettes and alcohol on his breath.

"Jonas was very frightened. He stood in the corner, dressed in nothing but his shorts. I can see the tears that formed in his eyes, I can remember this clearly, even today. I too was only in shorts and a T-shirt. This is how hot it was. The Marine gave me a sinister smile and grabbed me by my arm. I could see in his eyes that he was a bad man. He whispered to me and Jonas… to keep quiet or he will have to kill us both. He then pushed me onto the bed face down…" Tamara's voice shakes to a small degree. Brian can't help glancing around uncomfortably. It's not the kind of conversation one would want to have at all, let alone in the middle of a restaurant. "I can still feel his coarse hands on my skin… He ripped off my shorts and all I could do was cry, focused on being as silent as I possibly could, afraid he would kill me if I cried too loudly. I heard him spit into his hand and felt him force his fingers inside of me. Then I could hear him undo his belt… It was at that moment that another Marine entered the room."

He wants to know more as much as he doesn't. "Who entered the room? My father or Lynch?"

"It was Lynch!" She snaps.

For years and years, Brian was convinced that there hadn't been a dark side to his father. He had never seen it, not once. He's torn at the seams, wanting to fight against this revelation and defend his father, but he knows now, after his last session with Susan Lew, that his father has been the face of the beast all along. So traumatized was he by what his father had done that he'd repressed the memories of it, lived in complete denial all this time.

"Lynch tried to do good. When he entered the room... He stopped your father. But then they fought. Your father demanded that Lynch leave the room. 'Detain the old lady,' he'd told Lynch." A look of disgust pulls at her mouth. "I could see in his eyes, he still wanted to rape me. He told Lynch to leave and to forget about what he saw, but Lynch would not... Your father pointed his gun at Lynch, told him to back off. It was like the Devil was in him and he was angry. Lynch pushed back, they struggled, and then it happened. Your father pulled the trigger and shot Jonas in the chest.

"When my grandma entered the room, Jonas lay dead. It was terrible. His chest laid bare and bloody, full of bullet holes. My grandma reached down to check on my brother, but he was dead. Her hands were covered in his blood, like that picture you just showed me. She screamed and attacked your father, launching herself at him and using her bloody fingertips, she poked them all over his face and uniform. Your father looked on in horror while she covered him with red polka dots of blood."

Brian picks the final photograph up, the one of his father and Lynch in front of the military vehicle. He hadn't noticed it before. His father is covered in dots of blood, his face and his top.

"Yes, that is how it looked," Tamara nods, taking in the same thing. "See, Brian… There was no accident. It was not their place to be in our home. It was Grandma Lourdes-Gina who cursed your father, your son. I remember her screams, her words." Tamara's voice changes and she speaks slowly, quoting her grandmother. "*Twou say o se peche ou yo*… These holes are your sin, your curse."

"Are you telling me she put a curse on my father? And why my son?" Brian runs a hand over his face. "He didn't even exist in '94! For God's sake, I was only a boy!"

"Not just a curse," she says seriously. "A spell. Grandma Lourdes-Gina… last name, Fatiman. She is an ancestor of Cecile Fatiman, a Mambo who helped start the Haitian revolution back in 1791."

"What is a Mambo?"

Tamara looks right into his eyes. "A Vodou High Priestess."

Brian sits back in his chair, finding himself falling deeper into the unbelievable. Where is the line at this point?

The waiter arrives with their food and drinks before he has a chance to think about it. After placing the plates and glasses on the table, soda for Brian, which he gratefully sips, he murmurs to Tamara. A glance over at Brian and he has a feeling this is in regard to their loudness. Tamara answers briefly in Haitian Creole and the waiter gives a nod, walking away from the table.

"You do understand, I'm American. None of this makes sense to me, it's not as casual as the way you mention it. I still don't understand how the so-called spell, if it was cast, would be on Ben after all these years. Shouldn't it be on me? Or what about my brother?" He looks at her as she takes a bite of her meal, a tender piece of meat gliding into her mouth with a forkful of vegetables. "He was a victim of my father as well... stuff I don't even want to share. The poor kid OD'd at twenty years old. We were both sons of my father. Shouldn't we be cursed?"

"Yes, and just because I am Black and Haitian does not mean I know all the details of the Vodou ways," Tamara says with a smirk.

"Sorry," Brian chuckles nervously. "I get it. It's just... You know a hell of a lot more than me."

She takes a sip of her wine, eyeing his food pointedly. He hasn't touched it, or paid it any attention at all, but now that he sees it, the dish before him looks delicious. It smells great and Brian hasn't noticed how hungry he was until now. His belly grumbles at the sight of succulent vegetables and chicken, golden and saucy. Nodding, he takes a bite and the taste melts onto his tongue.

"That's so good," he says.

"I know," Tamara says simply.

They continue to nibble and sip.

"Let's say there is a spell," Brian says. "Is there a way to remove it? Do you think Grandma Lourdes-Gina would be willing to end the spell?"

"She died several years ago."

Brian sighs, frustrated that every turn leads to a dead-end. "Today, I was at the market and stopped at a Vodou shop. The man sold me Cerasee medicine. He told me to use it in tea and it can help."

With a mouthful of food, Tamara covers her mouth as she laughs. "Cerasee plant?" Her tone is incredulous. "Yes, that is helpful if you want to cure heartburn."

His shoulders slump somewhat, but the humorous twinkle in Tamara's eyes makes him grin sheepishly. "Okay," he rolls his eyes. "It was worth a shot. I know it sounds stupid."

"Brian, seriously… I may be able to help. Your son was not at fault for what happened all those years ago and I have no ill will toward a child. I have an aunt who was very close to Grandma Lourdes-Gina. She will remember that night." She wipes the edge of her mouth with a napkin. "She may know what to do to help your son."

"When can you take me to her?"

The Haitian woman looks at him thoughtfully. "Tomorrow. I will pick you up from the hotel and drive you to meet with her. Together, we will try and help your son."

20

AUNT FATIMAN

When they arrive at Aunt Fatiman's house, an older woman with dark, pock-marked skin answers the door. She wears a traditional Haitian dress, dark blue with white frills, and a shrewd expression. Tamara's greeting is friendly whilst Brian is left feeling as if the only reason he received one at all is that he came with Tamara. It's fairly obvious that Aunt Fatiman does not have as much forgiveness as her niece. To her, it doesn't matter that Brian is not his father. The fact that they are related seems to be enough to harbor loathing for the White man who crosses the threshold into her house.

"Tamara has already informed me of what ails you and

brings you to our country," she tells him as they walk through her house.

Most of it appears normal, but the shelves have items that look similar to those Brian saw in the shop. He tries to keep his eyes forward. The house is dark and somewhere within, a wind-chime moves gently, making Brian feel like they aren't alone at the same time as making him feel entirely alone.

"Yes," he says. "My son, Ben, he's—"

"Cursed," she says simply. Her voice has a rasp to it and Brian wonders if she is a smoker. "Yes, I know. I was there when it was done."

"You were at the house? The investigation letter doesn't mention you."

They've reached a room with a wooden circular table in the center, six seats with purple velvet cushions on them are placed neatly around it. In the center, a small wooden chest sits. It's old, with a rusted lock and dust between the gold etched patterns on the outside of it. Brian doesn't recognize the symbol.

"Not there," she hisses, her voice lower in this room. It's poorly lit, with only a few black candles dotted around the room. "That's only where it began."

"What do you mean?" Tamara asks.

Aunt Fatiman takes a seat and the other two follow suit.

"Grandma Lourdes-Gina created a Vodou doll after what happened to Jonas," Aunt Fatiman tells them. "She used the military name patch that had been ripped from the uniform. She stuffed it into the doll so that it would have the essence of your father within it."

"*What?* So there *is* Vodou involved!" Brian looks between the two women, aghast.

"Yes," Aunt Fatiman gives a slow nod. "The Vodou imprinted its host. A dry lotus pod was attached to the doll and with it, a spell was cast, one that would create the fear of holes."

"Where is the doll?"

Aunt Fatiman lazily gestures to the chest in the center of the table. She reaches for it and whispers something in another language before she undoes the clasp. Inside is a small object wrapped in cloth, which Tamara pulls out. Together, she and Brian unwrap the covering.

"There it is," Tamara whispers.

Stitched by hand in a tan fabric is a doll shaped like a person. Unseen, somewhere within the stuffing, is the old military name tag that PFC. Brennan once wore. On the doll's arm are 11 red stitch lines, circled and threaded through the material.

"They indicate the age of the doll's host," Aunt Fatiman tells Brian and Tamara. "They are the age that the host must be for the spell to begin. Eleven. It's the age Jonas was. Such a loss, such a young soul."

Brian tries to ignore the venom that he's certain he hears in Aunt Fatiman's voice and continues to take in the features of the doll. Stitched onto the chest of the doll from the inside is one of the most disturbing things Brian has seen. It's worse than the image results he came across when he searched for "trypophobia" on the web. The chest is covered in holes, those dark lotus holes without the pods inside.

"Grandma Lourdes-Gina's spell would incite the fear of holes and the pod was meant to be symbolic of a resemblance to Jonas' chest, which was full of holes. I recall the night that the spell was uttered, the words that she recited. They would strike at the first-born grandson of PFC. Brennan at that age. It was revenge for the hole-filled death, you see."

"What were the words?" Brian has a feeling he already knows an answer to the question."

"*Twou say o se peche ou yo*… These holes are your sin, your curse."

Tamara and Brian are silent as they absorb what Aunt Fatiman has told them.

"Since Grandma Lourdes-Gina has passed on to the spirit world," she continues. "Only Papa Legba, a Loa in Haitian Vodou, can deal with the spells that were left behind by the dead."

"Who is Papa Legba?"

Tamara gasps, her eyes wide. "He is a Loa or a God who serves as the intermediary between this world and the next. He presides over the spiritual crossroads."

It's obvious that this is someone well-known to her, someone most likely well-known to all the locals. "Can we go see him?"

"Yes, if you are prepared to cross over into the world between worlds," Tamara smirks. "The crossroads, like your purgatory or the astral plane… is the space in between."

"Is Papa Legba good or evil?" Brian asks, fearing the worst.

Aunt Fatiman shakes her head. "No… No… He brings good upon our people!"

"It's hard to say, unfortunately," Tamara interjects. "You are not one of our people. But he is generally good." She turns to Aunt Fatiman. "Do you have paper and a pen?"

The woman nods and stands, heading over to a dresser in the corner of the room and returns with the items.

Tamara takes the pen and paper and begins to design a symbol. "This is the veve of Papa Legba."

Glancing at it, Brian can't help but see some similarities. It's a pattern that he recognizes. He takes out his cell phone, scrolling through the gallery until he finds the photo of Ben's wall with the holes, the one he took before they were patched up.

"Look," he shows Tamara. "The dark round holes that you drew, they are the same pattern as the holes in Ben's wall back home. They also match the holes that I found at my father's apartment, which were almost an exact replica."

Aunt Fatiman leans forward, looking at the picture. Suddenly she cries out, "Wi papa legba louvri yon pasaj!"

"What did she say?"

"Yes," Tamara says. "She said yes, it is Papa Legba and he has opened a passage into this world."

Tamara takes the pen and labels the drawing of the symbol. "The six holes are the six turns of the key that open the passageway to our world." Then she labels other parts of the veve of Papa Legba, adding further symbolization and telling him what she's sketching as she goes. "The ant heads, the body of the bees, the cane, and the four keys."

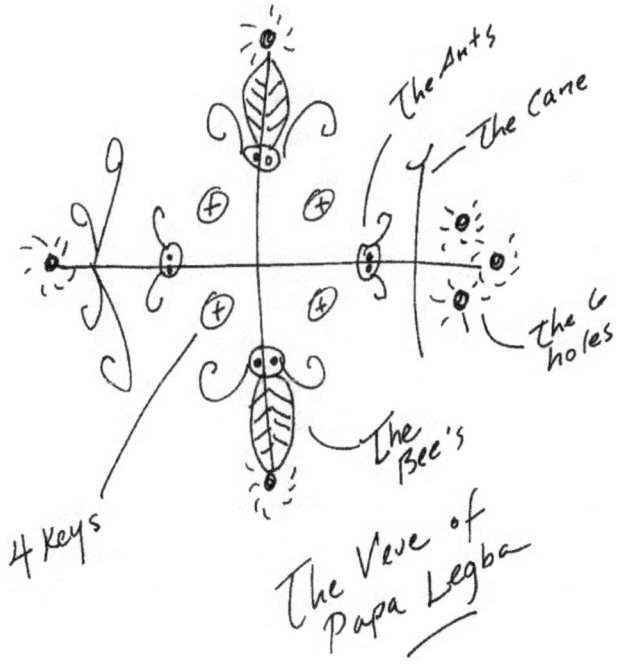

"We had a bee attack," Brian jumps in, starting to recognize the patterns between the veve and the things happening in his family's life. "They killed a relative. There was an ant infestation in Ben's room. It all makes sense now."

"The four keys are for gates, doors, passages, and locks. He can access all of these things. The head of the ant symbolizes his control over the earth and all below. The dead," she clarifies when Brian raises his eyebrows. "The bee symbolizes his control over all above, the sky and the heavens."

"Okay," Brian nods. "What does the cane mean?"

"The cane symbolizes his being, the body of a frail old man. But don't be fooled. He is a Loa of great strength and power."

"This explains so much," Brian whispers, glancing between the drawing and all its labels to the doll and back again. "I kept smelling the odor of sweet tobacco in Ben's room. Could this be related to Papa Legba?"

Tamara shakes her head in disbelief. "He is known to smoke cigars of sweet tobacco. There is no question. It is Papa Legba himself. He used his keys to come through from the crossroads into our world, into Ben's bedroom, and your father's. You must go to him if you wish to end all of this."

For one moment, Brian imagines what his father must have seen. Did he see a Black boy full of bloody holes the same way his son did, or was he faced with Papa Legba himself?

"How?" Brian asks.

"Titanyen!" Aunt Fatiman cries out.

"Yes," Tamara purses her lips. "We must go to Titanyen. It is not far, but we must wait until it's dark."

21

FIELDS OF THE DEAD

"**B**rian, Rosa answers the phone. Her voice is soft and it makes him miss home for the first time. He's been too preoccupied to think about Rosa.

"Hey, love. How's it going?"

"Good, quiet," she says the same thing as last time. Is time flying for her like it is for him? Does she feel as if she's running out of it? "How about there?"

"I'm making progress. The clues that I've found have led me somewhere, but I don't want to talk too much about it on the phone. I must go to a place called Titanyen to meet with Papa Legba."

"Papa Legba? Brian, do you know who this is?"

"I had a feeling that you would," he says with a nervous chuckle. "It's the only way to undo the curse that's been placed on our family, on Ben."

Rosa is silent for a moment and Brian wishes he could hug her.

"Be careful," she finally says. "I love you."

"I love you more."

They end the call and Brian spends the rest of the afternoon mentally preparing himself for what's to come. Rather than stress himself out with what could be irrelevant to his situation, he avoids the internet. He doesn't want to focus on the fear that he feels beneath the surface. Purgatory, Tamara had said—*like* purgatory, anyway. No good is associated with it. That much, he knows.

After dark, Brian receives a message from Tamara and leaves his room to meet her. The nights thus far in Haiti have been cool ones and he wears a jacket for the trip. The road is going to be a long one. They're traveling outside the city limits and north into the countryside, moving through the older structures into shanty towns and then, for the longest time, nothing but hills and greenery on either side. The ocean becomes distant and the city lights fade away. All at once, a thousand stars sparkle in the night sky. In his inner jacket pocket, he's carrying Ben's Vodou doll, close to his heart.

"What is Titanyen?" He asks along the drive. He's in the passenger seat, watching the road ahead.

Tamara has changed too; she's wearing a different dress than earlier that day. She doesn't look up from the road.

"A village. In Titanyen, there is a place called Lakou Mackandal. It was founded by the Vodou community based in Plaine du Nord, the historical site where the battles between colonizers and slaves took place. It dates back to Mackandal himself. This village, however, was established in 2010 after the Haiti earthquake."

"I remember that."

"I would be surprised if you did not," she says, her Creole accent as strong as ever. "The village is surrounded by the field of the dead. It is the site of mass graves that were dug for the victims of the earthquake."

A lump forms in Brian's throat. "That's terrible…"

"It has become the place that Vodouists believe is the doorway to the other side, a doorway to the crossroads."

There's a finality to the statement. Brian and Tamara are quiet, both thinking about their destination. After about an hour's drive down what has been a straight road, they turn and travel into a narrow, dark lane. It's completely desolate, with trees that grow densely together. Comically, it reminds Brian of the stereotypical road up to the haunted mansion in horror films. As ridiculous as the thought is, it doesn't remove the panic thrumming through his nerves. He knows they're traveling into the village now and he feels like he's found himself in a real-life horror story.

They finally come to a cluster of small buildings, a community of sorts. The trees had only been a wall, a protective barrier. Here, there are fields of emptiness as far as the eye can see. Tamara parks on a gravel road and they hop out of the small SUV. The doors echo when they close and they begin to walk toward the dwellings. There are a few local Haitian residents, sparsely dressed despite it being evening. They look on, but they steer clear of the new arrivals who walk between the dwellings. Some of them whisper amongst themselves and Brian is struck with the idea that these people have been expecting him. The village knew that there would be people joining them this evening. Without fully understanding why, Brian's heart beats a little faster. He can swear it's pulsing against the Vodou doll in his pocket and he wishes that he hadn't worn a jacket, that he had as much bare skin as Tamara and the residents of Titanyen. The air is thick with tension and the jacket sticks to his clammy skin. A crackling sounds up ahead and Brian tries to identify the sound, to hear something beyond the indecipherable whispers he knows his paranoid mind is imagining.

At the end of the walkway, flickering orange shadows glow and Brian realizes what the crackling is. The space opens up onto a large courtyard and in the center is a large bonfire. In the light of the fire, Brian takes in women in white who surround it, looking on in silence. There are many of them, some on whom the flames shine and others who are only silhouettes in the shadows of the courtyard. They wear white garments, covered from head to toe in a white dress marginally different from the one Aunt Fatiman wore. On their heads, a white head wrap. The eyes of the women follow Brian and Tamara, peering at the visitors intensely. It isn't until they move that Brian sees the woman in the center, dressed differently. She's wearing a colorful pattern of tribal-style garments, yellows glow and appear to dance in the patterns of her dress beneath the fire, and a crimson red head wrap. The women in white move in synchronicity, doing a kind of dance while chanting and singing around the one in the center. Their eyes continue to follow Tamara and Brian and although their words sound joyous, their voices and harmony bright, their faces remain stern.

Behind the bonfire is a huge mapou tree. It looks menacing with the flickering shadows of flames dancing along it. The thing must be hundreds of years old and it looks as if it could once have walked the earth, mastering the ability to move with branches bent in such a way that they look like arms. Meanwhile, the roots poked through the cracked ground as if they had once tried to free themselves but were frozen mid-step. The tree's branches are stretched out, sharp like claws, reminding Brian of the tree in his yard and, not for the first time, he thinks of the face outside the window. He gulps, taking in everything before him. Beneath the tree is a chicken, its foot tied to a fine wire and fastened to the tree's roots. To his surprise, the chicken is alive, occasionally flapping its wings, but generally calm.

Suddenly, the singing is joined by a series of drumming, a rhythmic sound that starts soft and slow and then ascends in volume with each passing second. Following the sound he hears, Brian scans the courtyard until he spots the source. The drums are strung with a cord, turned by adjusting small pegs in the interlaced chords all along the body of the drum. There are two drummers, a Bonga, and several of the women, including the woman with the red headwrap, who play with rumbas, all entrenched in a religious and complex rhythm. They are led by what appears to be an elderly man, a master percussionist. This is like no other musical performance Brian has ever seen.

The words of the song are unfamiliar to him:

> *Papa Legba nan ounfò mwen!*
> *Atibon Legba nan ounfò mwen!*
> *Alegba Papa nan ounfò mwen!*
> *Ou menm ki pote drapo nan Ginen!*
> *Ou menm ki pote chapo nan Ginen!*
> *Se ou menm k a pare solèy pou lwa yo.*

"What are they saying?" Brian asks Tamara in a whisper.

"They are calling Papa Legba to join them in this temple."

Brian finds himself looking at the courtyard differently after this explanation. As they watch, the woman in the colorful garment pulls a knife from the handle of her rumba. Her dance has stopped but around her, the men and women continue and she raises the knife, bringing it back down and driving it into the chicken tied to the roots of the old tree.

At once, the music and chanting come to a dead stop. Silence draws down over the courtyard like the curtain call of a stage performance, closed. The only sound is that of the chicken's final high-pitched squeals of life and the crackling of wood in the fire until the bird lies silent and its blood flows over the roots and absorbs into the dirt of the ground below. The woman flicks her head back like a whip and glances over her shoulder with wide eyes.

All at once, all eyes are on Tamara and Brian.

The walls of the courtyard feel like a cage around him

as all are still, staring onward until the moment that the Vodou priestess turns away and walks into one of the nearby dwellings. Just like that, all the others begin dispersing, leaving Brian blinking in shock.

He turns to Tamara, whispering, "What the hell just happened?"

"The chicken was a gift to Papa Legba. The spirits of the tree will carry the blood down the roots of the mapou and find him at the crossroads. Then, he will grant good fortune in return for the gift he has been given."

"Who was the woman in colors? She looked right at us when she killed it…"

"She is who we seek," Tamara whispers. "She is the Vodou priestess, Rose-Merline St. Juste. She may or may not help you."

"That sounds promising," Brian mutters in a low voice.

Tamara simply shrugs and a man walks up to them, wearing only cloth around his waist. He says something to Tamara in Haitian Creole and then walks away. Tamara follows him and Brian assumes he should be doing the same if he doesn't want to be left behind.

They are led to a guest room in the village where they will be sleeping. Tamara whispers to him along the way, which is the only reason he has any idea what is going on. The decor is scant, two low single beds with thin mattresses. There are no blankets but Brian can tell he won't need them. There's a straw basket in the corner, as well as a small basin.

"I'm going to speak with someone who can meet with the priestess. We will find out if she is willing to grant our request. Stay here."

"I will."

Tamara says something in the other language to the man who led them to their guest room and he nods his head vigorously, pointing out of the door. They leave together and Brian settles onto one of the beds, waiting.

It's not long before Tamara returns.

"The priestess has agreed to help you meet with Papa Legba at the crossroads. To do so, she will need you to give hair and a fingernail."

He raises his eyebrows.

"She must fabricate a Vodou doll of you. It will be used to guide you to the crossroads. They say they will conduct this ritual tomorrow evening."

•••

The next day, Brian can tell that he's an outsider in this village. It was harder to see in the comfort of darkness the night before, but they stayed away from *him*. They continue to do so in the daylight. Perhaps in a last-ditch effort to calm himself down, he'd convinced himself that it was both he and Tamara, the strangers in their village, that they didn't want to approach. There's not much to do in the village. People have their own routines and mostly, it's a quiet place. There aren't many children and the language is alien. At one point during the day, he is sitting on the grass under a small sandalwood tree when he spots Tamara walking with the Vodou priestess, deep in conversation. They must feel his eyes on them because they look right at him and quite suddenly, they fall silent, walking faster toward a house ahead of them, all whilst giving him a side-eye.

The moment leaves Brian's heart racing and as he scans the area, he sees several of the locals watching him from afar. There's no friendliness in their expressions. It dawns on him that he's come here alone, that he has trusted a stranger with his life. The shock of the night before, of witnessing the priestess kill the chicken, has worn off, replaced by sharp fear spiking through his system. There's no signal out here, no one to contact, and besides, who would he call? He's alone—in the middle of nowhere.

It occurs to him that these lands are burial grounds, bodies and bodies rest beneath the earth.

And he's never felt so vulnerable before.

•••

That night, the ritual begins, bringing with it a sense of déjà vu. Unlike the night before, when they're in the courtyard—temple—Brian knows what's coming. The bonfire crackles beneath the tree and the chicken sways, unaware of the ultimate fate that will soon befall it. The Vodou priestess, the women in white, and the music all repeat much the same way they did before. This time, however, Rose-Merline St. Juste draws the veve of Papa Legba into the earth, using her fingers. It's a dance of its own, watching her trace the shapes into the earth.

Then, she cries out the words of the song from before:

> *Papa Legba nan ounfò mwen!*
> *Atibon Legba nan ounfò mwen!*
> *Alegba Papa nan ounfò mwen!*
> *Ou menm ki pote drapo nan Ginen!*
> *Ou menm ki pote chapo nan Ginen!*

Se ou menm k a pare solèy pou lwa yo.

Brian is grateful to be seated this time, next to Tamara on a log. If he wasn't, he doesn't think he would be able to trust his own feet. He watches the priestess cut into the throat of the chicken, blood splashes onto the ground and specks of it land on her dress. She doesn't notice. The blood pours over the lines in the dirt of the veve of Papa Legba, spreading out but never spilling from the lines in the earth. Brian is shaking with fear, staring on in horror as the bird gives its final choking squeal, feathers fluttering through the air and floating down onto the dirt, white soaked in scarlet.

Rose-Merline holds a Vodou doll into the air, the one she made of Brian using his nail and hair, and then places it into a glass jar on the ground while everyone watches in silence. The jar sits under the mapou tree and it once again crosses his mind that he's trusted people that he doesn't know. How stupid is he to have given a priestess permission to create a doll of him? His anxiety heightens with the idea of it being in her hands.

"It's okay, Brian," Tamara whispers, breaking into his thoughts. She takes his cold hand in hers and squeezes. "You must be strong if you want to save your son."

Brian nods slowly. He can't find words right now.

"Be careful, Brian. Remember why you are here. The crossroads is a world between worlds. It's not just a place in Haitian Vodou—it's known in Catholicism as well. It's a place to deal with the Devil. Beware of others who may wish to trade in souls."

The father stares back at Tamara, wondering what he

has done by coming here. His soul may be at stake. He'd been Catholic long enough to understand the danger he's in and he's shaking with it.

Under the tree, the priestess places a lid on the jar holding Brian's Vodou doll. She begins twisting it on, closing it tight. Brian's heart is in his throat, pulsing so fast that he can't breathe. His windpipe is too tight for his heart, but it keeps pulsing, attempting to move up his throat and out of his mouth. Brian swallows, but it's no use. He's going to die because he can't breathe. Each breath is slower, harder to pull into his lungs due to the blockage. His eyes focus on the glass jar while the corners of his vision start to blur and he realizes why he can't breathe—the doll is sealed tightly inside.

He's suffocating. Panic fills him and Brian opens his mouth, gasping for air. Nothing happens. The space around him is devoid of oxygen and even with his mouth wide, his face stretched out and his eyes protruding as he clutches at his throat, he can't taste the relief of air. Falling forward onto the ground, Brian crawls toward the tree. The jar is all he sees, blurry, and his fingers clutch at the dirt as he works to reach it. He doesn't move. There's no strength in him to do so. The world around him spins.

Stop, his mind screams. *Stop…*

Without oxygen, nothing comes out of his mouth. No one can hear him.

Brian looks around and quickly comes to find that no one would help him even if they could. They are watching. Their faces haunt him and the situation dawns on him, from the bizarre ritual that he's made himself a part of to the strange culture he's entrusted his life to.

What have I done?

Tamara leans over him and he sees the corner of her mouth twitch upward. She smiles as if she's content with his death. It's the last thing he sees before his eyes close.

22

THE CROSSROADS

Brian's cheek is pressed into the ground, small stones stick to his skin. His eyes open and he gasps for air, sucking a breath full of dust into his mouth alongside sweet oxygen. Slowly, he uses his hands to lift his body from the ground.

Where am I? He's disoriented and the last thing he recalls is falling forward, not being able to breathe. Reflexively, he sucks another breath in now. It comes easily and he presses his hand to his throat.

The movement brings it all back. The jar. The ritual. He was at the ritual.

Did it work?

Brian's standing in darkness but he feels... free. It's not like he's in a dark sealed room, rather it's like the darkness of a night without stars, no faint light of any sort in the distance. There's more of a dark mist that seems to move slightly. A subtle, cool breeze blows against his face, indicating that he's outdoors.

Blind though, he thinks. *But I can't stay here forever...*

Straining his ears for some indication of what to do beyond the whisper of the breeze, Brian allows himself to tune in on senses apart from sight. He stretches his arms and feels nothing. One step forward, his feet crunch on gravel and dirt. He stops, listening. There are no trees, no voices. And then... a distinct sound of a shovel carving into the dirt can be heard.

With a gulp, Brian walks toward the direction of the sound. His steps are slow. The darkness leaves him feeling no less vulnerable than he had in Titanyen. The ground crunches beneath his feet, still the same gravelly sound, though his path is flat and firm. It's a smooth walk. Soon, he glimpses something up ahead. Though cautiously, he speeds up, desperate to see more, to no longer feel blind.

The dark mist clears slowly, a low-flying cloud drifts apart to reveal a dirt road. It leads down a slope to a valley below. On the horizon, fields ripe with tall grass gently swing and undulate in the breeze. The sky above is both beautiful and terrifying, it violently shifts and circles with the intensity and cadence of storm clouds in a hurricane. Grays and blacks swirl, touches of reds and oranges spark within their depths. Beyond the immediate sights he's greeted with, Brian sees four dirt roads. They converge at the base of the valley.

This must be the crossroads.

To his left, the tall grass recedes the moment he looks at it, revealing once-hidden lotus flowers. Their blossoming petals float over a marshy pond. Entranced by their movements, Brian almost forgets why he's here until the sound of a shovel cutting into dirt rings out again.

On the edge of the slope, filling in a hole amidst the tall grass stands a man. Brian walks over to him. At his approach, the man stops digging and stands beside the hole with his shovel, driving the tip into the dirt so that it stands freely. The man rests his elbow on the handle and tilts his head to one side, watching Brian silently.

Above the hole, Brian spots a granite gravestone. Carved into the face is the name of the person to be buried: "Benjamin Brennan."

"Nooooo!" Brian yells out. "No!"

He dives into the dirt hole, landing on a pine casket. Brian bashes the outside of the casket and begins prying the edge of it open. He forces his nails under the wooden frame of the lid and pulls back as hard as he can. His fingernails bend back to the point where they nearly tear off as he manages to pull up one edge and then another and another, finally pulling the lid off.

"Argh!" He falls back in disgust.

Inside the casket is a young Black boy, perhaps 11, his bare chest is full of bullet holes. He wears only a pair of shorts. Crawling all over his small body in a hungry frenzy are thousands of tiny red ants.

Looking up and out of the hole, Brian sees the

gravedigger standing over the edge, looking down at him. His face is covered in white paint, dry and cracked. So are his lips. On his head, he wears a top hat lined with tiny yellowing bones. The man's black pupils are surrounded by bloodshot veins. His attire is black, with an overcoat, and he's in no short supply of jewelry. Rings, necklaces, and trinkets hang from his body while silver rings with emblems and gems atop them sit on his thin fingers. A gaudy belt is wrapped around his waist and dreadlocks hang over his shoulders.

Removing his elbow from where the shovel rests in the dirt, the gravedigger pulls a cane out from his coat. With a slight limp in his walk, he takes a step forward and positions the cane to lean on it while balancing his stance. Brian realizes, watching the man, that he's found what—who—he came for.

"Papa Legba," he whispers.

Papa Legba cracks a smile, his yellow teeth are spotted black with decay. From inside his coat, he removes a hand-rolled cigar and with a twist of his fingers, a match ignites. With a series of puffs, the cigar burns hot. Plumes of smoke circle above his head.

Brian looks down at the dead boy in the casket and asks, "Jonas Biassou?"

Papa Legba exhales a puff. "The sin of your father." Papa Legba gives out a creepy chuckle. He speaks in English, yet with a deep Creole accent. "And I know why you are here, you come to the crossroads in search of redemption for your son. A spell has been cast. A curse upon your family has been made."

"Yes… I have since learned many things about my father and his sins that now haunt my son, my whole family."

"That is good. It is better to accept than to deny the truth."

"I do accept the truth," Brian says from the grave. "I know the evil deeds he has done to my brother Paul, Tamara, and Jonas. That is why I am here. I stand here at the crossroads to beg you to lift the spell on my son Ben. He is an innocent boy."

Papa Legba laughs again, exhaling cigar smoke. Brian recognizes the smell. It's the same sweet scent he'd come across in Ben's room. "Innocence has no value here. At the crossroads, you only have one choice. It is between the spirit world," Papa Legba points one way and then the other. "And the mortal world."

"Please," Brian implores. "I was told you can bring good upon people as well, that you are the only one who can deal with the spells left behind by the dead."

Papa Legba's pupils seem to expand. "Ah, if it is a deal you seek, what gifts have you brought for me?"

The hole is shallow and Brian climbs out over the edge, kneeling on the ground. He clasps his hands as if in prayer, pleading with Papa Legba. "All I have is myself. I would trade myself for the sake of my son."

"Yourself? Are you sure? Would you rather take the place of Jonas in the hole, in the pine coffin? With bullet holes through your body… ants devouring your cold flesh down to the bone… You'd be trapped in the dark, confined, and unable to move. Only when I open a passage from this world to the other can you open your eyes, wiggle your finger through the pine lid, and see into the bedroom of your son." Brian can scarcely breathe as he imagines the picture being painted for him. "Your eyes peer through the hole, ants crawl from your corpse, and invade your perfect world. Your voice calls out to your little Ben, *'Come closer... come closer... so you can see the holes inside of me.'*"

"No, that is not what I want, but I will give whatever I have to save my son!"

Papa Legba puffs away on the cigar. Smoke fills the air around him, blowing some in the direction of Brian. Brian smells the smoke, the same smell he knows, and he wonders how many times he's been this close to Papa Legba without ever knowing it.

"If it's not your rotting body you are offering, perhaps it's your soul you're willing to trade?"

Brian swallows hard. The price of his soul is frightening and a higher price than he had hoped for. He hardly recalls what Tamara told him before he suffocated. With hesitation, he says, "If there is no other way."

Seeing the hesitation and fear at such a request, Papa Legba chuckles louder. "Ahw, the crossroads are busy today... Perhaps it's the Devil you seek?"

The two look down toward the crossroads and in the distance, the figure of an elderly man can be seen walking down one of the roads toward the intersection. He stops. From so far away, Brian can't make out the man's features no matter how hard he squints. Within moments, a larger figure approaches the elderly man on the crossroads, partially covered by a hooded black cloak. It's bigger, clearer than the elderly man, a giant it seems from this distance.

The Devil looks down upon the elderly man, who kneels exactly as Brian has and clasps his hands together in a pleading request. His head is down, like he's avoiding looking into the eyes of the Devil standing over him.

In a grizzly voice that leaves Brian's arm hairs standing on end, causing the same sense of discomfort that comes from nails scratching along a chalkboard, the Devil speaks. "For this request, my price is the same." The Devil's voice grows into a thunderous scream. "I take your soul into my kingdom of fire and pain!"

The elderly man stands. Before walking away, he turns and looks up toward Brian from the bottom of the slope.

"Father?" Brian breathes, his heart skipping a beat.

"Yes," Papa Legba grins. "He has only recently passed, but all those who come to the spirit world shall travel through the crossroads."

"What has he done? What deal has he made with the Devil?"

"Forgiveness perhaps. A soul for a soul."

The elderly man nods and returns into the darkness of the road from which he came.

"Where's he going?" Brian asks.

Papa Legba laughs. "Into the pits of hell's fire, burning with brimstone and sulfur."

"No…"

"Save him, Brian," the Loa laughs once more. "All you have to do is go down there and make your own deal with the Devil… Your soul for his."

Stay focused on Ben, Brian remembers what Tamara told him about deals with souls. He watches in fear, but he needs to focus.

The Devil looks up at Brian, his eyes deep red, like blood. His pupils are snakelike, focused on the father kneeling on the edge of a hole.

Looking back at Brian himself, Papa Legba continues. "Perhaps He Who Comes With Many Faces—Satan, Lucifer, Mephistopheles—would be a better suitor for your request?"

The Devil's hood drops, revealing a creature covered in boils and scars, animal-like hair protrudes from the pores of its skin in patches, and monstrous deformities. It shifts before his very eyes, its skin bursting into flames, head replaced by the horrifically unnatural horned beast that he saw outside the bathroom window that fateful night. Once more, it becomes a man with veins pulsing with flowing lava and the head of a vicious snake, a tongue whipping out with a hiss so loud Brian's ears hurt. Finally, it becomes a winged creature with singed black feathers and large horns ripping through its skull.

Each transformation sends Brian scurrying further backward, the beast growing larger than life, before suddenly shrinking back down to the hooded figure he first saw.

"Ahw," Papa Legba murmurs condescendingly, as if Brian's a cute puppy. "The face of Lucifer for the man who worships the God of the holy cross."

"No, please, Papa Legba... It is you I am here for."

Down at the crossroads, Lucifer grins, a low chuckle

echoes through the land. It's as if it comes from the thunderous sky. He walks back the way he came, fading into the darkness.

"I beg you... Please, I swear to Almighty God, I will give my life for my son."

Papa Legba's eyes widen. "You swear upon the God of the holy cross?"

"Yes."

"The symbol the Whites have used to cause my people so much sorrow?"

Raindrops begin to fall from the sky. Papa Legba looks up into the storm, which has turned dark and angry, as rain pelts his face. Brian feels the warm droplets pelt his own body and looking down, sees that they're drops of red, standing out against his white skin.

"My people still weep tears of blood. Dutty Boukman led our people to revolt against our slave masters in revolution. It was not uncommon for slave masters to hang a slave by the ears, to pull teeth out, to mutilate a leg or genitals," Papa Legba pulls open his coat, revealing his naked torso marked with tattoos, scars, and scorched pigmentation. Turning to the side, he reveals a large scar that runs along his side. He adds, "Sometimes they would gash open one's side and pour melted lard into the incision."

Papa Legba takes a fresh puff of his cigar. "For the women, it was worse... Rape, their sexual parts burned by a smoldering log, or boiling cane syrup poured over their heads. These heinous acts were committed to force slaves to perform their duties..." Papa Legba's voice rises. "All this while the symbol of their God, the cross, hung from their necks."

Brian drops to the ground, pressing his face to the dirt. He is distraught, tired in ways he's never been tired before, and still does not have any answers. All he's found for himself is horror, a place of great fear and horror. A tear forms, then another and another, and in his sobs, arms to his sides, he looks up at Papa Legba.

"Please, tell me what I need to do." He asks again. "I was told you can bring good, that you are the one who can deal in the spells left behind by the dead. Please help my son... He is without sin. He should not have to pay for the sins of my father."

With more seriousness, Papa asks him, "Will you do anything for your son?"

"Yes."

At his words, all the petals of the lotus flowers that had been floating across the marshy pond fall away, leaving behind giant pods similar to the dry lotus pod attached to the Vodou doll of his son. Eerily, the field of pods across the pond twist and all at once face toward Brian. A chill runs up his spine at the sight, but he can't turn away, mesmerized. Within their small bud holes, what looks like hundreds of tiny eyes protrude, all staring at Brian. They wiggle and squirm, blackened tips rolling around like eyeballs in a socket the longer he stares back at them.

He's reminded that it's the lotus pod full of its tiny holes that gives power to the spell that haunts his son and the terrible vision before him, making his heart pulse wildly.

"What do you see, Brian?"

"Tiny holes... Thousands of tiny holes."

Suddenly all the lotus flower pods slip beneath the watery surface.

"Where you see holes, I see death and reemergence. The lotus flower is like no other flower. Its roots are latched in the mud below and it submerges every night. In the morning it is reborn, rising from the mud clean and in full bloom. You only fear what you do not understand."

"Help me understand," Brian pleads.

"Are you willing to trade a son for a sin?"

"Yes, my father's sin for my son."

Papa Legba arches an eyebrow, holding a finger out in the air. "A son for a sin cannot be undone."

Without another word, he turns and begins walking away. Brian calls after him, "Is it a deal? Do you accept our trade?"

"Only time will tell if you made a good deal!" Papa Legba calls back over his shoulder.

"Please," he whispers, knowing that he won't receive an answer. He puts his head to the ground, devastated and filled with a sense of failure. "I need to know..."

Papa Legba walks into the distance and disappears into the high grassy hillside.

"Brian?" A soft voice comes from behind him.

Brian turns around and is perplexed by what he sees, "Tamara?"

It is Tamara. There's no doubt about that. She's naked, her dark skin is smooth and her body is beautiful. Long legs lead up to a place he knows he shouldn't be drawn to and everywhere he looks, he's met with a sweet curve that begs to be touched, to be kissed and tasted. Moving toward him, she joins him on the ground and Brian, still confused by her being here, is unable to resist. He takes her into his arms and his desire only grows when his fingers find that she's real, that her skin feels even better than it looks, and that she folds into his body so readily.

They kiss, lips ripe with a devious passion. Brian groans at the taste of her and Tamara unsnaps his pants, tugging them down a bit. That's all she needs, settling on top of him.

Who am I to resist? Brian thinks. His hands run free across her body, his mind in a dreamlike state. Everything about this seems surreal and above their heads, the clouds continue to swirl, bursting with grays and blues and shades of fire. The same fire lights up Brian's body and when Tamara palms him and guides him toward her entrance, slipping into her warm place, it feels so real as she rides him.

Willfully, his mind plays tricks on him. First, he sees Tamara, hips rocking against him as she moans into the stormy sky above. Then, in the next instant, a glimpse of Rosa's face is imposed over Tamara's. The dark skin and difference in Tamara's body are present but Brian continues to slide in and out of her, breathing heavily.

The breeze brushes by their writhing bodies, the sound of the crisp high grass rustles in the wind while they give into the overpowering lust and temptation, passion carrying itself out in this strange place. Across the marshy pond, the lotus flowers rise from their muddy roots and blossom upward, petals slowly spreading out from their ovaries, moisture rolling from their sepal. Each part glistens with moisture, widening outward into full blossom.

Tamara moans loudly as a feeling of warmth erupts inside of her. Brian's mind is completely lost to the moment and as they slow and their bodies relax, Brian opens his eyes to the sight of blood smeared between their legs. Tamara's hands cup her abdomen and she pulls them away to reveal her palms, covered in blood.

Below her navel, Brian sees a tattoo that hadn't previously been there—the veve of Papa Legba.

Brian screams out, "Ahhhhh!"

23

NO PLACE FOR A WHITE MAN

Brian wakes up to Tamara setting down a tray of tea and fruit. He's in the guest room in the village.

"You've been out for over fifteen hours," she says when he blinks his eyes open. "What happened?"

"I saw Papa Legba at the crossroads. I think that we made a trade... I told him I would give my life for Ben's and he told me..." Brian recalls what Papa Legba told him. "A son for a sin. I agreed, but I'm not sure if the spell is lifted. It was very strange."

"What do you mean?"

"Dreamlike... I'm not sure which part was real or a dream."

"Papa Legba can sometimes be a trickster. What did he say exactly?" Tamara presses.

"He asked if I would trade a son for a sin and I agreed. Then he said a son for a sin cannot be undone."

"Okay, perhaps the spell has been lifted. You will need to see if your son is better. And if so, you must destroy the Vodou doll." She hands the doll of himself over. "You must destroy both of them."

The two of them get dressed and pack up their few items, including the dolls. They leave the compound to return to Port-au-Prince, the locals remaining far away from them. The priestess has all but disappeared. Brian hasn't seen her or any of the women from the temple. Only a couple of loiterers remain on the edge of the dwellings while he and Tamara make their way to the SUV. That suits Brian just fine. He doesn't want to speak to or see any of them ever again.

Driving back to the hotel is a quiet trip. Brian is still trying to figure out what happened in his dream-like journey and what it all meant. Deciding not to share the parts that she appeared in. Did it mean anything? Tamara doesn't mind, focused on the driving aspect. He doesn't want to read too much into her silence.

When they arrive at the hotel, he gets out of the SUV with a breath of relief. "Thank you," he says to Tamara.

"Good luck," she says before driving off.

Inside, the first thing Brian does is take a long shower, staying under the water until it goes from hot to tepid and eventually ice cold. He steps out and sits on his bed with a towel wrapped around his waist, calling Rosa.

"Baby! I was so worried!"

Brian checks the time. It's been over forty-eight hours since he told her he was traveling to Titanyen. "I'm sorry. There was no signal in the village…"

"What happened? Did you do it?"

"I think so," Brian whispers, allowing himself to feel hope for the first time. "I think everything is going to be okay. It may have worked."

"So you're coming home then?"

"Tomorrow," he confirms.

"Okay. I can't wait to see you. While you were gone, Kim called four times. She wants you to call her back the second you can."

"Sure. Did she say why?"

"You know she'd never tell me anything," Rosa says. "Call her. I love you. Have a safe trip tomorrow."

"Thanks, baby."

The call ends and Brian dials Kim's number next. It's answered in seconds. "Brian! Where have you been?"

"Long story. Is everything okay?"

Kim sounds happy when she responds, happier than Brian has heard in a while. "CPS released the kids back into our custody. And Ben is in great spirits." She whispers. "He seems like a new kid. I think the medication must be working."

His spirits soaring, Brian says, "I'm so happy to hear that. I will plan to see them on Friday when I pick the kids up."

When they end the call and Brian gets dressed, he's feeling more confident that the ritual and the deal with

Papa Legba worked. He packs his backpack with newfound excitement, ready to leave first thing in the morning. He doesn't want to waste any time checking out of the Royal Garden Breeze Hotel and going home.

•••

The next morning, Brian gives the concierge one last request in calling a Tap-tap cab. Before the airport, he has one last stop: Tamara's house. He wants to say goodbye and thank her before he leaves.

I owe her so much.

When he arrives, he knocks on the door with less care for the neighbors than he had a few days earlier. She answers it in her pajamas, her hair a bit mussed from bed.

"Brian," she exclaims. "What are you doing here?"

"I wanted to say goodbye. I'm on my way to the airport after this." He gestures to his over-stuffed backpack.

"Come in. I'll make some coffee."

The Tap-tap cab drives away when Brian steps over the threshold. They head to her small kitchen and Brian sits at the table while she prepares the coffee.

"I think the curse has been lifted," he tells her excitedly. "I talked to Kim and Ben is acting normal. She says he seems better. I'm flying home as planned since it worked."

"That is good news," Tamara smiles. "As I told you... Papa Legba can do good deeds as well."

Looking at Tamara, Brian has a flashback of her naked form riding him. "What happened at the crossroads was strange..." He starts. "I'm not sure I fully understand any of it."

"The spirit world is unnatural. It's hard to

comprehend."

"I saw the Devil… in its many forms. One of them… I could swear I've seen it before, right outside my window. How close they've been without me knowing."

"You must let it go. It will haunt your mind." She places a cup of coffee on the table for Brian and walks out of the room. "Let me go and change into something."

She walks into the next room, the bedroom and bathroom area. The house is small. She continues to speak to him from there. He can hear her moving around as she does.

"Brian, you must have faith and believe that Papa Legba granted your request and that your son Ben no longer bears the curse of the spell my grandma cast all those years ago."

Brian glances toward the open door and catches sight of Tamara changing. Her bare back and curvaceous ass come into view and he's about to turn away, not having wanted to catch a glimpse of her nude form, when he notices something. She's standing in front of a full-height mirror and as she pulls her shirt up over her head, her belly is reflected at him. Under her navel, he sees the tattoo of the veve of Papa Legba inked into her skin, the same tattoo in the same location he saw at the crossroads.

Feeling as if he's been jolted out of his own body, his eyes widen and he finds himself rising out of the chair and walking toward Tamara's bedroom door. Noticing him in the mirror, Tamara's eyes widen and she turns to confront him at the entrance of her room. He's pale with shock.

"Brian, stop!" In a firm voice, she continues forcefully, "You have saved your son and now you need to return home to your family."

"No... You need to tell me what the fuck happened. Was it you at the crossroads?" He's confused but he knows what he saw.

Tamara looks down for a moment, then back up. "What is done cannot be undone."

The chill of her deception washes over him. It's true. Tamara *did* appear at the crossroads and she did, in fact, fuck him. It's all exactly as he recalled. What seemed like a strange memory trapped between two worlds is actually reality.

"Why?" Brian raises his voice, angered by Tamara's deception. "You've been playing me... You've been playing me since I got here, all of you. Why?!"

"Brian, go home," Tamara says calmly, her voice unwavering. "You do not understand our ways. You must accept this and go."

Grabbing ahold of Tamara's arm, he continues in a furious tone. "I'm not going anywhere. You need to tell me what the hell is going on! What happened at the crossroads?"

"How dare you?" Tamara rips her arm free and pulls away, pushing back at Brian and raising her own voice. She's frightening in her resolve, seeming taller for it. "Papa Legba sees all. Papa Legba knows all. Papa Legba, with a snap of his fingers, could drain the life out of you... out of your Ben!" She tilts her head, standing with her chin strong, and points her finger at him, pacing around him like a lioness.

Brian retreats, paling at her words. She's naked, but

Tamara's a sight to behold even in her fury.

"You made your trade and I made mine," she hisses. "I carry a child now. Unable to conceive a child in this world, I made my own deal with Priestess Rose-Merline St. Juste. I made my own deal with Papa Legba to conceive a child in the world between worlds. What is done cannot be undone."

A son for a sin…

Brian backs out of the room, shocked and helpless as Tamara stands up to him.

She turns on him. "You made your deal. Go home to your family while you still can… This is no place for the White man."

Hurriedly taking his backpack, Brian heads for the door and leaves the house. Tamara walks with him toward it. He gets a Tap-tap cab by walking up the road, its colors visible from a mile away, and makes his way to the airport.

24

BLACK HOLE SON

Rosa picks Brian up from the airport. Valium runs through him but he doesn't think any dose would have been able to clear the anxiety. Everything that happened since he arrived in Haiti has replayed in his head, sometimes in the order they happened, sometimes backward, sometimes in bits and pieces. During the flight, he couldn't calm down and he didn't get a wink of sleep as he tried to pinpoint the exact moments where he thought he was safe even though he wasn't. How many people exchanged glances of true intention that he'd completely missed throughout the journey? In the end, Papa Legba honored his people first, before anyone else, exactly as

Brian should have expected. The car ride home is spent in much the same state of mind.

They get to the house and Brian's out-of-sorts behavior does not go unnoticed. Rosa has no idea what he has been through, what he experienced out there.

"Are you okay?" She asks him while she makes him something to eat. He looks exhausted.

"It was horrible..." He looks at her as he sits down at the table but he doesn't seem to see her. "The experience in Haiti was just so strange and bizarre..."

She waits for him to say more, setting a can of soda and leftover lasagna in front of him. He doesn't elaborate.

"I'm sorry you had to go through this, Brian. You're so brave."

"I hope everything will be okay now. Kim told me Ben has been acting like a new kid, that he's better."

"I hope so too," Rosa murmurs, squeezing his hand gently. "By the way, I had one of Uncle Reyes friends come over and patch up Ben's wall. I didn't want him to have to come home to that scary sight."

"Thank you love, you're amazing."

After that, Brian returns to his thoughts and in a single glance, Rosa knows that he's gone back to the space he was in on the way home. She presses a kiss to his forehead.

"I'm going to do some chores around the house and get your laundry in. Don't worry about anything for a bit. Maybe you should take a nap?"

Brian doesn't answer and Rosa knew that he wouldn't. She takes his backpack upstairs and for the rest of the afternoon, he keeps to himself. It haunts his thoughts that he willingly conceived a child with another woman, that he witnessed all that he did at the crossroads and he knows for certain that evil is real, the Devil is real, that the Devil has many faces.

Eventually, he goes up the stairs to sleep and he sleeps for the longest time as the jetlag settles over him.

•••

Friday.

The next day, Brian wakes past noon and takes a shower, feeling a bit fresher. He's nervous to see his children. It feels as if it's been ages since he saw them last, like he's gotten older, grayer. At the same time, hope blooms in his chest. The whole mix leaves his stomach turning and despite its grumbling, he doesn't trust himself to keep food down and leaves the house on an empty stomach.

Arriving in the school lot, Brian steps out of the car and waits for his kids. He's early enough to hear the end-of-day bell go off and witness kids spill out of the doors. He eagerly scans the crowd for his kids and warmth floods through him when he sees that they're walking out together, chatting. There doesn't seem to be any tension from where he stands and the second they spot him waiting, they run toward him excitedly.

"Dad!" They both fall into his open arms, hugging him together.

"I missed you so much!" Morgan says when she pulls back. She's beaming from ear to ear.

His son simply holds onto him and in his boy's arms, Brian feels a weight lift. Both his children have been through so much and right now, they're happy to see him. The memory of coming home to Rosa crying, of climbing the steps with the memory of being welcomed home by his children with love being a distant thing, comes to mind. It overwhelms him how long and overdue this welcome feels. The emotions drain out of him as he comes to terms with the fact that he is better and his family is okay.

Brian smiles for the first time since he arrived home, hugging back tightly. "I missed you both! What do you say—pizza night?"

Both exchange a grin and nod their heads. "Yes!"

With that, they get into the SUV and head home.

•••

That evening is a giant rewind button. Brian is thrown back in time to before everything went wrong. Things are normal. Pizza arrives and the family sits around the table, actually eating together; Ben, Morgan, and Rosa across from him. He tests the waters because it feels right to try to play their old game right now. It's been entirely too long.

"What was your favorite memory today?" Brian asks.

Rosa gives him a pearly white smile, and he sees her eyes sparkle with moisture. "Waking up with your dad by my side," she says.

The kids smile at this.

"My family," Brian shares. "This right now, with all of us together again."

"I got a singing role in the final school performance of the year," Morgan offers.

"What?" Rosa and Brian exclaim.

"It's called 'We Can Move The World,'" she beams

proudly.

"That's so great, honey," Brian tells her. He reaches for her hand and squeezes it. "I'm so proud of you."

"I guess pizza night," Ben says sheepishly.

When he laughs, everyone around the table does too. It's a perfect evening.

After dinner, the kids and Brian watch some TV together. There are no dishes to do thanks to the takeout and Rosa is upstairs, watching some crime shows in the bedroom. Brian is at ease with them, watching the peace between his kids and their childlike joy at simply being allowed to stay up late on a Friday night. When the double episode of their show finishes, the kids head upstairs and settle into their own bedrooms.

Kim seems to have given in to the screen time since the kids returned to her because Ben plays away on his handheld and Morgan is sending text messages back and forth to her friends, and Brian couldn't really blame his ex-wife. All he's done all evening is bask in the fact that he's home and things are good again, that they're smiling and neither of them are plagued with the fear of whatever the hell had been happening to them. There are no holes in Ben's bedroom wall and he gives a celebratory whoop. Switching out the hall light and leaving them to their devices, Brian heads into his and Rosa's room with a lightness in his step.

Rosa lies across the bed in silky shorts and a strappy camisole hemmed with lace, her smooth belly peeks out beneath it.

"Hey baby," he says. "You look so sexy."

Leaning over the bed, he gives her an intense kiss, stroking her cheek with his palm. Her lips smile against his.

"There is the man I remember," she says, reminding him how much he missed her beautiful accent. "My handsome chulo." She kisses him again and wraps her arms around his shoulders, holding him tight with a smile on her face.

"I missed you, baby," he says into her neck, holding her small body to his and willing his mind and feelings to return to normalcy and accept things the way Tamara told him to.

"Are the kids settled in?" Rosa asks when she pulls back from his embrace.

"Yes, they are ready for bed and hanging out in their rooms on their electronics."

"Good, my love…" She bites her lip, speaking softly to him. "I am so proud of you, Brian. You are such a great father. I was so scared for you and worried that something would happen to you when you were out there. I wasn't sure about the whole Vodou thing…" Looking away from him, Brian knows these are things that have been taking up her thoughts. "I looked some of it up. It's frightening. I prayed for you and God listened. He protected us from evil."

Brian strips down to his boxers and climbs into bed, gently pulling her into his arms. "I know… It *was* crazy and scary. I can't even explain… Finding out that all of these things are real, that evil is real…"

Rosa covers her eyes with her hands and then uncovers them rapidly. "Let's not talk about this ever again… ever."

That's great, because I can't seem to finish a sentence.

His girlfriend sits up in the bed. "God is good. He helped save our family." In a quick motion, she does the signs of the Holy Trinity: the Father, Son, and the Holy Spirit.

"Amen…"

Amen, he thinks but he says nothing.

"We have our family back and I have you back and that's all that matters!" Rosa pauses, a grin on her face. "I have something to tell you… And I'm gonna be honest with you, I am scared… But I'm really happy too!"

"What is it, love?" Brian furrows his brow. "It's okay… You can tell me."

Rosa glances down shyly and takes his hands. A smile plays on the corners of her mouth, the one he loves seeing, and she cries out, "I'm pregnant!"

At first, he doesn't believe his ears. His feelings quickly shift from shock to pleasure and he enthusiastically hugs her again. "Oh, my God, that's wonderful… That's wonderful!

"I was so worried you would be upset… I know you have been through a lot lately. I was scared this wouldn't be something you wanted."

Brian tightens his embrace. He can't believe that he's hearing tears in his girlfriend's voice right now. "No, my love, it's okay. It will be okay."

"I love you so much," she swipes at her eyes. "I was scared I could lose you, but I truly believe this is a gift. We are blessed to have our family back, to have survived this terrible ordeal."

He's smiling and she pulls back to find that there's moisture under his eyes.

"Oh, you're happy," she breathes. "You're going to be an amazing father to our baby!"

"Thank you," he mutters, hardly able to speak at all. "You will be an amazing mother. You *are* an amazing mother."

He excuses himself to go to the master bathroom to get ready for bed, starting with brushing his teeth. The mirror makes him self-conscious. He's not sure he's ready to face himself or what he did yet. The reality of everything that has happened begins to wash over him; from the secrets of PFC. Brennan, a man he no longer wishes to call his father, to the ordeal his son and family have been through, and finally the reality of being face to face with true evil, the kind he'd witnessed at the crossroads, and the evil of Tamara's deception. Tamara and his other unborn child come to mind before he can help himself from thinking of what she had done.

Spitting toothpaste into the basin, he pops his head out and asks in a casual tone, "How far along are you?"

She speaks to him even after he goes back into the bathroom, flossing his teeth next. "Not long. Maybe six weeks? I missed my last period and while you were gone, I took three different tests. They all came back positive!"

Brian looks himself in his eyes when he combs his hair and goes back to bed.

•••

The sound of a shovel, metal hitting solid earth, is distinct. This time, Brian's hands grip the handle and dig into it, creating the gravesite. It's another hole.

There's no doubt in his mind of where he is… the crossroads. It's as if he's walked through a portal and into a nightmare, one that feels far more real than he would like. Is this it? He's had a chance to check if his family are okay and now Papa Legba is coming to collect. Looking up, he sees the dark skies. Circling above, stars shine bright, appearing to swirl and swirl.

Brian squints into it, taking a second to see the black hole twisting in the sky behind the stars, absorbing the stars into it. In the background, he hears the faint sound of music. The song is a familiar one and he pauses to listen, waiting for the memory to come back to him.

"Soundgarden's 'Black Hole Sun?'"

This has to be a dream, right? A nightmare?

Brian covers his eyes, trying to drown out the music. If he can wake himself up, maybe this will go away. Without his hands on the shovel's handle, he slips off the edge of the hole he'd been digging and into the grave, the same place he'd been the first time he set his eyes on Papa Legba. Above the hole, Brian sees the granite headstone from before. This time, the name engraved into it is Rosa's.

Panicking, Brian climbs out from the hole. His eyes are drawn to the slope and down at the bottom of it, he sees Papa Legba at the crossroads with Tamara. They glance up at him and he spins away from the scene, turning back.

To his horror, he's faced with the sight of the holes, a thousand tiny black vortexes of empty lotus pods swell and roll as if alive and pulsing. Beneath them, Rosa's dead body is covered in blood. Her pregnant belly has been torn open and Brian's screams are blown away in the wind at the sight. He wants to run to her, but his feet won't take him there. The baby has ripped through her body... and the face of the Devil devours them both.

The heavy Creole accent of Papa Legba's voice calls out, coming from all around him, "A son for a sin cannot be undone."

•••

Brian wakes with a shock; a falling sensation leaves his heart racing. His forehead is sweaty and he's covered in goosebumps. Rosa sleeps soundly by his side.

"Thank God," he whispers to himself. "It was a nightmare... Only a nightmare..."

Now that he's awake, he calms down, sitting up and taking a sip of water. What did it mean that he'd seen Tamara on the crossroads with Papa Legba? The other day when he was in Tamara's house comes to mind, the day he confronted her and she admitted what happened. He springs out of bed, waking Rosa.

"What's wrong?" She asks him.

"I had a nightmare," Brian murmurs as he leaves the room, grabbing his cell phone off the nightstand on his way to the master bath, closing the door behind him.

It must be 4 or 5 a.m. in Haiti but Brian can't wait.

"Hello?" Tamara's voice comes through the phone's speaker.

"Tamara, it's Brian. I need to talk with you... It's important."

"It's still dark. Why have you called me?"

"I just had this horrible nightmare. Everything that has

happened… I don't know what is real anymore."

The Haitian woman is irritated. He can tell by the tone in her voice. "Brian, I cannot help you. After going to the crossroads and returning, you may never be the same again."

"I found out that Rosa is pregnant and, in my nightmare…" Brian pauses. His throat constricts and he's not sure he wants to repeat what he saw aloud. "I'm concerned that something bad is going to happen to her and our baby."

"You know not what you have done, Brian."

Blood rushes from Brian's face and his blood turns to ice. "What the fuck does that mean? I made my deal, a son for a sin! You are now carrying my baby. You told me to go…" Brian's voice breaks and he runs a hand over his face. "You told me to go back to my family and I have."

"You made your deal, a son for a sin. I made mine, to conceive a child," Tamara says firmly.

Brian interrupts. "Yes, my child. Papa Legba gave you a son by using me! A son for a sin!"

"No, Brian," Tamara's words are like bombs. "My trade was for a daughter."

Brian falls back against the side of the bath, dropping his phone to the floor with a clatter. The room around him spins and his vision blurs at the edges at the answer she's given him. He wanted answers, but not this…

From the speaker on the floor, Brian can hear Tamara speaking. "If Rosa is carrying a son… The child belongs to Papa Legba."

The call ends with a dead tone coming from the speaker,

a disembodied beep. Drained and emotional, Brian leaves the bathroom to enter the bedroom, only to find that Rosa is standing just inside the door. She heard everything.

"Explain," she whispers.

And Brian does. He comes clean about the events that occurred at the crossroads, of the confrontation in Tamara's house when he realized that it hadn't been a dream at all, and Rosa's face is flushed and her lips are pursed by the time he's done explaining himself.

"And... I also have the Vodou dolls here," he finally tells her. "Both mine and Ben's. We need to find someone more local who can help us because... I'm so sorry, baby, but I put my trust in the wrong people. Tamara told me all along that Papa Legba was a trickster but I never expected that she would be too."

At first, Rosa says nothing while Brian stares at her, practically willing her to speak, to say something—*anything*—that will put him out of his internal misery. He's afraid that anything he says or does at this moment will make things worse. *Hell, is that even possible?* To his horror, tears begin to spill down Rosa's delicate face. He takes one step forward, wanting to comfort her, and he's not sure if his movement is what triggers Rosa but in the next second, she turns around and swipes her arm across the bedside table, effectively knocking everything off it and onto the floor in one swift movement.

The lamp's wire snaps out of the plug outlet in the wall and lands with a loud crash. Out of the corner of his eye, Brian catches sight of the shattered bulb, but he dares not take another step. His heart is racing.

Is this the end of us? Have I fucked up that badly?

Rosa sits on the edge of the bed and looks down at the mess she's made, sniffling. Tears are no longer falling from her eyes, though her face remains wet. Brian can see the moisture shimmer in the reflection of the bathroom light behind him. Perhaps it's the fact that the bedroom light is off and they don't even have a single lamp to light the space, but something about her looks darker than usual, only a silhouette. She wraps her arms around herself, holding her elbows in her hands as if she's trying to pull what remains of herself together, as if she's trying to hold every broken part in place. Somehow, all at once, she's fragile, beautiful, and terrifying.

"I'm so sorry, baby," he whispers again, taking a slow step forward into their bedroom.

Rosa heaves a heavy, shaky sigh. "My heart is broken, Brian. I feel so betrayed and I'm so angry."

"I know," he says, hurrying closer. "You have every right to feel this way and I wish that I hadn't been the cause…"

He stops speaking as Rosa holds up her index finger. He notices her hand is shaking. "I wish things were different and this didn't happen, I do… But the most important thing to me is our baby. I know you're scared and I am too, but we have God and we will make it through this."

"How do you know?" Brian kneels in front of her, careful to avoid the bits of broken glass.

"Because we're going to fight to make it so," she answers simply, looking down at him with fearsome determination. "Family is everything."

"I'm scared."

"Me too."

25

THE HEALING HANDS OF LADY DARG

Researching the Haitian community in Tucson, Arizona yields almost no results. Still, hopeful that at least one leads somewhere, Brian calls every number that comes up in the search. Four of them are disconnected and the other two, he finds, are not able to help him with anything related to Vodou. Rather, they're a bowling club with roots in Haiti and a retirement home for immigrants with a few elderly Haitian men and women.

Despite the lack of a road to lead him, Brian doesn't give up. He finds himself back in the seat behind his computer, researching the Haitian community in nearby areas instead of Tucson. Maybe the key is to be a little less specific.

A result turns up an hour and a half's drive away, in Phoenix. Brian clicks on the link and he's redirected to a list of contacts within the parameters of his search. There are so many more than he found in Tucson and he's anxious with each number he dials to follow up on the inquiry.

"I was wondering if you possibly had someone with any experience in dealing with Vodou? I know it's a long—"

He didn't often get a chance to finish his sentence before the person on the other end of the line hung up the phone. The word *Vodou* is a deterrent apparently.

After days of looking and calling without a care for how high his phone bill got, Brian comes across something that could be tangible. An upcoming cultural fair will take place in Phoenix. All he can find is a flyer with the details printed across it in slanted text. Palm readers, card readers, and other related psychics are listed as the performers. One of the booths is operated by a local Haitian lady.

"Experience authentic culture," the flyer reads. The kids are going to be back with their mom when it takes place, the following weekend.

It may be their only chance.

•••

The weekend arrives and the kids are fetched from Brian's house by Kim, who is much kinder to Rosa than she has been before. It's clear that she's grieving, less put together than Brian's used to seeing her. The blonde hair curls in a way he hasn't seen since they first got together, before she started taking a straightener to it daily, and her skin is free of makeup. Although the circumstances are poor, Brian can't help thinking the look suits her.

At the end of the day, he's happy to see his kids get into Kim's car. It means that he and Rosa can go to the cultural fair, taking the long drive to Phoenix for their unborn baby.

The fair is unlike any they've visited before. There's a mix of cultures and it comes together in a kind of hodgepodge way, with no particular theme in mind. The people in the booths enthusiastically wave newcomers over but Brian and Rosa have one path in mind; they know the name of the booth they're looking for and they have no intention of straying from their goal.

"The Healing Hands of Lady Darg" shines in glowing letters above the booth. It has a violet theme, with a velvet cloth resting over the stall's surface.

Brian is in awe as he and Rosa sit across from her. Lady Darg is a heavyset Black woman, a Haitian in her mid-forties, if Brian had to hazard a guess. Her shoulders are broad, she's tall, and her most prominent and most attractive features are her plump cheeks. They give her a grandmotherly quality, making Brian feel safe. With everything that has happened, Brian reminds himself not to trust as easily as he has in the past.

"Hold out your hands," she says to him. He can hear the elusive trace of the Haitian Creole in her accent. He might have missed it were it not for his recent trip. "How can I heal you today?"

The booth is full of items that the woman sells for healing. Various colored and scented candles, oils, and herbs are laid out on the velvet surface before them. Each is carefully packaged and labeled with her booth's name. Brian and Rosa look at one another nervously and then around at the rest of the fair. Other people comfortably speak to the people behind booths and, mutually, they come to a silent agreement that they shouldn't dive into the subject at hand.

"Hi there," he says, unsure of where to go from here. "I'm Brian Brennan and this is my girlfriend, Rosa."

"Where are you from?" Rosa offers, starting with the most basic of questions. Building a rapport before they ask the big questions feels like the right way to go. "How did you get into this kind of thing?"

Lady Darg smiles and the apples of her cheeks stand out more. "My mother was once a priestess in Haiti. It's like a..." She waves her arm, and a collection of bangles rattle and clank together. "It's a type of medicine woman. She taught me all that I know, so I suppose my doing this kind of thing was always meant to be. That's the way it feels." She winks at them. "As for how I came to this country, my mother fled Haiti in 1984, bringing myself at age ten and my sister at age eight with her to the U.S."

"That's a very young age to come to a new country."

"The funniest thing is that it did not feel as if we'd left, in a way. Louisiana is where we found ourselves and we stayed with a friend of my mother's. The language and culture I grew up with were different in Louisiana, but the roots remained the same."

Vodou roots, Brian thinks to himself. He's fascinated, wanting to know everything about Lady Darg and knowing that it's not possible.

"Needless to say, I did not stay a ten-year-old girl forever and I later found my way to Phoenix. My ex... Well, what a mistake he was. I should have listened to the cards on that one," she laughs. It's a boisterous sound and Rosa giggles, some of the nervousness eases out of her. Lady Darg has a great outgoing personality, the size of which competes with her false lashes. "And now I'm here!"

The woman beams at the couple at the end of the story.

"What about you two? You're a cuuute couple."

"We're from Tucson," Rosa answers, looking over at her boyfriend. "Well, originally, I'm from El Paso. But we live in Tucson now."

Eyes sparkling mischievously, she gives Brian a conspiratory smile. "I can tell you're not from Tucson or El Paso." Another loud laugh, jiggling her belly. "You have an accent... Sounds like the East Coast?"

"Yes, actually. Boston."

"Ah, let me guess... You don't like the cold."

Brian nods.

"Seems like everyone I meet... hates the cold."

She receives a snicker from Brian. His palms are less sweaty than when he first took a seat at the booth.

"Pity, really. Hot chocolate, warm fires, and who could forget snow?" The woman gazes off mistily and pauses for dramatic effect. "But then, we all ended up in hot places, didn't we? The real question is what brought you *here* to my booth? Tarot reading, perhaps?"

"N—" Brian grunts in pain as Rosa's foot squashes his. He's anxious to get to the point but a look from Rosa silences him.

"Yes," she says. "That would be great."

"Great! I'll give you a discount because you're both so dang adorable. Only fifteen dollars today."

Lady Darg begins looking through a few decks of different Tarot cards from the collection of items she's selling. A special bag rests underneath and she shuffles through a set she pulls out of it.

"Do you have Tarot cards in Haiti?" Brian asks.

Intrigued by the interest, Lady Darg meets his eyes. "Actually, it's not as common in Haiti. There, you will find shamans and even the Vodou religion is used by some." She rolls her eyes back creepily, showing them the whites. "Oh… I do have a very old set of tarot cards that are considered a Haitian version. Want me to use those?"

Rosa and Brian agree.

Curiously, she pulls the cards out of the bag beneath the table. and begins to lay them out.

"Okay, let's do a past, present, and future read," she says.

Three cards are laid out before Rosa and Brian, face-down on the empty space. She flips the first card, the one indicating the past. An image of a child holding up the sun is revealed.

"Soley la, it means the sun. This is a card symbolizing positive energy, happiness, and joy. I see that in you," Lady Darg meets Rosa's eyes, pointing at her with a playful smile. "You seem like a happy person, one who celebrates life and loves to dance with a childlike innocence."

"Yes, I love to dance… and laugh," Rosa confirms.

"That card fits her so well," Brian adds. "She is full of

energy!"

Lady Darg flips the middle card around. Present. The image shows that of a pregnant woman, beautiful and radiant with a literal glow around her.

"Gwo Fanm... It means Big Woman, or Great Mother. It's represented by Venus, symbolizing love, beauty, fertility, and relationships. Do you have any children, Rosa?"

"No... Well, I have step-children?"

The healer doesn't miss the way she looks at Brian. "This could mean your current step-children... Or, perhaps you are pregnant?"

Another shared glance, wide eyes.

"Ahhh, congratulations," the Lady murmurs. "I can tell from that reaction that you are expecting!"

The two quietly thank her and she reveals the final card, the future. It's the image of the Devil, an image of a beast that's orange in color with horns coming out of its head and long black claws on its hands and feet.

"Dyab la. It means the Devil, as you can see. But don't assume the worst," she adds quickly, trying to lighten the mood. "... It's not the death card, which it's often perceived to be. This symbolizes greed or the dark side. Sometimes, it can be sexual in nature. Let's flip another card and see what else we get."

A cloud falls over the table as she flips the next one. It's the death card.

"Wow," she says. "That doesn't happen too often."

The energy at the booth has shifted and she can see that there's tension between the two people before her.

"Okay, so, don't worry about this," she waves her hands at the cards, giving Rosa a nervous smile. It's hard to justify though, and she flounders for words that will comfort the couple.

Rosa gasps at the sight.

"It's okay..." Brian tells Lady Darg. "You don't have to justify it or try to make us feel better about the card."

Tears begin to stream down Rosa's face.

"Oh, my dear... Please don't cry. These cards don't always mean what you think..."

Rosa interrupts, speaking between sobs, "But they do... We already know... Evil is coming for us, for our baby!"

The Lady of the booth looks on in shock.

"Lady Darg, we came here for a reason," Brian tells her. "We heard about you, found out about what you do online, and we came to seek your help."

From within his jacket pocket, the same one he wore to Titanyen, he pulls out two Vodou dolls. There's a lot of explaining to do to cover what has occurred to their family over the past several weeks and they're both nervous, fearful that she will not believe the story that they are spinning out for her. They don't know how long they sat at the booth, other people who are visiting the fair pass by the table without a glance at the three sitting with their heads together in such an intense story, but Brian doesn't leave out a single experience, though he skirts over some of the more graphic details for his girlfriend's sake.

But at the end of the tale, when Brian finally falls silent, Lady Darg tells them in a serious voice, "I will help you."

"You will?" Rosa asks, taking a tissue from her purse

and wiping her eyes.

"I have limited knowledge of the Vodou arts and black magic," Lady Darg admits to them. "But I have some books, old books from my mother, and I have witnessed rituals done in the past. The spell cast on Ben may indeed be broken, as you believed when you came back from the crossroads, Brian… But no matter what, the two dolls must be destroyed and this must be done in the right way. We must sever all ties to the crossroads and the spirit world. It is the only way to stop Papa Legba from coming through to take your baby from you."

"You have no idea what this means to us," Rosa says, her voice high with emotion. "Thank you so much for believing us. We were so terrified that you wouldn't. No one else has."

"I believe you because I have seen such things myself, especially as a child. The reality is that things like this happen, especially in places where Vodou is normal. When I was still a child living in Haiti, a local man raped a young girl in my village. Something similar was done…" She blinks and shakes her head. "A Vodou doll was created of the rapist, a ritual took place. The next day, the accused man was found hanged with his eyes cut out of his head, bloody holes where sockets once were. The villagers whispered that Papa Legba had taken his eyes out, removed them so that in the spirit world, he would only see what Papa Legba wanted him to see… Fear. Eternal fear for the rest of his existence, even after death."

Rosa's eyes brim over with tears.

"We won't let anything happen to your child," Lady

Darg promises. "We'll meet tomorrow evening to conduct the ritual. Do you know where we can do it?"

"Our house," Brian says without hesitating.

•••

The next evening when she arrives, Brian seeks a quiet word with Lady Darg.

"I'm worried, scared… What if Rosa isn't okay after everything?"

"I came here with a mission, Brian. I'm going to help you carry out the ritual to destroy the dolls. This is the most important thing to do."

"Lady Darg… Papa Legba, Tamara—they both told me that a son for a sin cannot be undone."

"The son would most likely be Rosa's child. You're not wrong about that. If we don't stop it, Papa Legba will take your child. There is no denying this."

The reality of it all sets in. As it happened in Haiti, Brian knows he needs to place his trust in someone else. Unlike the day he went to the crossroads, he doesn't feel left out of what's going to happen, doesn't feel as if he's placed his heart into the hands of someone who wants it to stop pulsing.

Heading into the house, the ritual begins. Lady Darg starts by ordering the couple to move the furniture in their living room out of the way, creating as much space as she can. She's brought with her a duffel bag filled with curious items and one of them is a bag of organic sea salt, which she takes out.

"Sit in the center of the room," she tells Brian and Rosa. She places the duffel beside them and drags the bag of sea salt, sliced open with a dagger, along the floor, creating a circle around them. They sit in the circle created to protect the three of them. In the center, they make a smaller circle out of an old cast iron pot surrounded by six small wax candles.

The pot receives some tobacco leaves, copper pennies, and rum. "These will be an offering," she tells the pair. "If all goes right, Papa Legba will take the offering and he will go away for good."

A memory of the Vodou priestess driving a sharp knife into the throat of a chicken pops into Brian's mind, unbidden. Blood spilling on the floor. The veve of Papa Legba.

This is different... Will it really be enough for him?

On the top of the selection of ingredients in the pot, Lady Darg places the two dolls.

"I will call upon Papa Legba and set fire to the contents of the pot. It will burn the offerings and the dolls, sending them to the spirit world. If Papa Legba takes and accepts the offering, he should see no reason to return to this world."

From the bottom of the bag, she pulls out a rumba, smaller than the ones the women in the temple at Titanyen had played. She begins to gently bang the drum in a rhythm similar to the song he'd heard then, lighting the six candles with her opposite hand.

"Stay inside the sea salt circle at all costs," she whispers to Brian and Rosa seriously, casting a suspicious glance around the room, looking into the corners for hidden figures and silhouettes. "Be careful of tricks... We are dealing with black magic and Papa Legba, a dangerous combination of tricks, and he could try to pull one over on you."

The couple nods slowly. For Rosa, this is an entirely new experience. Brian is simply relieved to know he won't suffocate.

"Also, this is dangerous, as I'm sure you both know," she tells them. "Once I open the door to the world between worlds, mind your thoughts… We do not want to draw the attention of dark forces."

Lady Darg begins chanting:

> *Papa Legba's offering is on the fire roasting.*
> *Oh, the service is going to begin.*
> *In front of the gate where I traced my veve this year, I can do the services of the Iwa.*
> *At the end of the gate in, where I traced my veve this year so I can do the services of the Iwa.*
> *Papa Legba… The table is ready, the table is ready, the table is ready.*

In one swift movement, the Lady flicks a lighter and drops it into the pot of gifts and the Vodou dolls. They set alight instantly and suddenly, the smell of sweet tobacco fills the air of their living room, a smell that Brian is all too familiar with. The flames in the pot grow hotter and higher, sparking and crackling.

"I love the smell of rum and tobacco," a heavy Creole accent with a deep voice rings out. Papa Legba materializes in the room from a dark corner on the outside of the salt circle, tilting his head in that eerie way that he had at the crossroads when Brian first laid eyes on him. "What is it you seek for such fine gifts?"

"We seek nothing," the Lady tells Papa. "The gifts are yours if you promise to take them and go, never to return."

Papa Legba laughs darkly. "Do you think tobacco, pennies, and rum will keep me from collecting my debt?"

"Brian and Rosa ask that no harm comes to their child."

"My dear lady, a son for a sin cannot be undone." Papa Legba looks down at the pot inside the sea salt circle with disdain, a sneer twisting his mouth. "Your gifts may have granted you my presence, but your unborn son is mine for the taking."

"Please," Brian says, resorting once more to begging Papa Legba for some form of mercy. "I offered you myself in return, I will do so again... You can have me."

"No, Brian, don't!" Rosa clutches at Brian's arm desperately.

Papa Legba laughs loudly. "Even your Rosa prefers you remain in the mortal world and don't think I don't remember the hesitance you showed at the crossroads when I almost took you up on that offer." He looks at Rosa and menacingly points to her belly. "I don't need your son fully baked; I will gladly remove him now so you have no memories of his human face."

The couple stand together, defiant.

"No!" Rosa shouts at the Loa. "I will not let you take my child!"

With his hands open in surrender, Brian adds, "Take me, please... Take my life for his."

"Papa Legba, you are the decider," the healer says. "You can bring good to Brian and Rosa. It is within your power.

I, too, beg you to spare their unborn child."

The Loa paces around the sea salt circle, tilting his head from side to side as he takes in the Haitian woman. "My fair lady, I see peace in your heart, but unlike you, I am not so willing to forget the past. Brian made a deal at the crossroads and a deal at the crossroads cannot be undone no matter how much you wish and will it. You on the other hand," he points a long slender finger with a yellowed, cracked nail at her. "You made your choice to forgive the man who once raped you as a child."

Lady Darg gasps, shocked, as Papa Legba opens his coat. Threaded through a necklace of assorted bones and body parts, ears and teeth, is a pair of bloody eyeballs.

"Shall I so easily forget what he did to you? Would you rather wear his eyes instead of your own?"

The Lady pulls back. "No... No, Papa Legba..."

"Good, then it is settled. I will take what is owed and leave your mortal world for now." Papa Legba steps closer, his hungry eyes on Rosa, but he does not cross the ring of sea salt. "Step closer, sweet Rosa... Give me my trade, a son for a sin..."

Brian grabs Rosa, pulling her form against his and stands in front of her in an effort to protect her. He's between her and Papa Legba, behind the salt protection. "Take me. I will not allow you to take our child."

Papa Legba laughs, holding an open palm out in the direction of Rosa's belly. As he does, she begins to cry out in pain, her hands move down to grip her abdomen, but the pain continues and she screams louder. Brian turns to her, pulling her into his arms in a helpless attempt to comfort her.

"Stop!" He yells at Papa Legba. "Please stop!"

Brian's mind wanders to the moment that he looked down upon the elderly man back at the crossroads in Titanyen, his father, standing in front of the Devil. He recalls the way he yelled at the Devil, asking to stop him as well.

"Stop," Brian hears another voice. It's familiar. His father's? "Let them be!"

At first, the voice sounds like it's coming from his own head, but Rosa and Lady Darg look on too. Their expressions are confused as they search for the source of the new voice. From behind Papa Legba, out of the darkness of the corner of the room, Paul Brennan walks into the dim candlelight. It flickers against his wrinkled skin. He's elderly and thin, his skin sticks to his bones the way it had before he died.

"The original sinner," Papa Legba says, looking at Paul. "What an unexpected surprise."

"Father?"

The elderly man stands upright, but not of his own strength. There are aspects of him that have certainly changed since he was alive. His body is burnt, skin melted and bubbly in some places, while his face is scorched. A hot molten cord of some kind wraps itself around his body, arms, and neck, as if he were a puppet and it was a string used to conduct his movements.

In pain and anguish, Paul struggles to speak to his son. "Brian, I am so sorry for all that I have done... for all the pain I have caused."

From the shadows of darkness filling the corner from

whence Paul came, a second figure emerges. This one is larger in stature, walking up behind Paul with thundering steps.

"Ahw, the Devil. Nice of you to join us. It seems my lady here has opened the door to the other side much too wide."

The Devil in all his horror reveals himself, taking the form of the final creature Brian remembers seeing down at the crossroads. He towers over Paul, who stands in front of him weakly, transforming into a winged beast with horns and red eyes. From his grip, like the leash of a dog, a sulfur cord runs to Paul, tethering the elderly man to his eternal grip, burning red hot.

"Father, what have you done?"

"I did what any father would do, my soul for the sins I put upon Little Paul."

"The fire in the pot is going out," Lady Darg says suddenly, panicking. "We don't have much more time."

"Time for me to go for now, but a son for a sin cannot be undone," he repeats with another laugh. He puffs a cigar Brian didn't see him take out, blowing sweet smoke into Brian's face. "I will see you soon, Brian and sweet Rosa!" He walks into the shadow of the opposite side of the room and fades into blackness.

Suddenly the Devil shapeshifts and huge wings open high and wide. They spread and flap once, twice, growing larger in size as they do. What appear to be dragon wings, scaly and massive, spread out across the room.

Paul looks straight at Brian and mouths silently before he's ripped away with the Devil, "I love you, my son!"

"Brian, forgive your father!" Rosa cries out as she grips the cross around her neck. "The Devil cannot take a soul forgiven. May the Lord have mercy on his soul!"

A lump as large as a rock in his throat, Brian shouts out his forgiveness before the two disappear. "I forgive you, father, I forgive you!"

Reaching for his father's hand, Brian is pulled forward by the wrath of the Devil as, angered, he rips Paul's body back from his son's touch with a snap of the sulfur cords. All at once, the two are ripped forward into the darkness, taking Brian with them, his hand still tightly wrapped around that of the old man's. Their screams of agony fill the room and then fade away, leaving Rosa and Lady Darg holding one another on the floor within the sea salt circle, helpless to stop the door to the other side from closing.

26

A SON FOR A SIN

The fall into oblivion is long and dark and on the way down, Brian can hear his father's screams fade away as he is taken further into the darkness than Brian can go. When he lands, it's as if he's waking from a dream. He finds himself lying on a bed, covered with a heavy blanket, and his breath is hot and wet against his own skin.

Brian senses movement in the darkness outside the blanket and he hears the sound of the door closing, followed by the fearful whimpering of a boy. Throwing the blanket off his body, Brian takes in the surroundings, surprised to find that he's in his childhood bedroom. There are neat shelves of wooden toys and smoke swirls through the air unpleasantly, making him cough.

On the other side of the room, curled up in bed, is his brother, Little Paul. The boy whimpers in his bed as Brian gets up and goes over to him.

"Little Paul?"

"Brian? Is that really you?"

Both men appear as they are: Brian is in his late-thirties, while Paul is twenty years old, exactly as he was when he died.

"Yes," Brian says sadly. "It's me."

Little Paul stands up from the bed and wraps his arms around his brother. "I missed you so much, brother," the boy whispers to Brian. "I'm so happy to see you."

The two unwittingly begin to walk, opening the door of their childhood room to a new place. Walking out of the bedroom, they find that they aren't in their childhood house. On the other side of the door, they appear on a bridge, walking over a body of water.

Brian blinks, confused.

"Remember this place?" Little Paul asks him.

The memories come back to him, but they leave him no less confused. How did they get from their childhood bedroom to Highbank Bridge? Ahead of him, Paul runs onward with a skip in his step.

"Try to catch up if you can! Remember this?" He calls back to Brian, who walks faster than before to catch up to his brother. "This is my favorite place!"

Feeling as though he's entered a long-forgotten memory, Brian watches as Paul reaches the center of the bridge. There are two brand-new fishing rods. Paul picks one up and hands it over to Brian. Wordlessly, the two stand side-by-side and begin to fish. The sky is dark, reminding him of a grainy old photo. Dust blows through, causing everything to fade away. They reach a certain point, where Paul excitedly starts reeling in the catch and then everything seems to fade away into a dreamy blur.

"This is my favorite memory," Paul says. He sounds far away but he's smiling from ear to ear and Brian enjoys the memory too. "My most favorite memory."

Why do you sound so far away from me? Brian wonders as he looks at his brother. The strange euphoria of the moment begins to fade away. *Something doesn't feel right… Where are we?*

Brian takes a closer look around, glancing up at Paul from where he stands on the bridge. Paul seems happy, but as Brian watches, a tear drops from the corner of his eye and glides down his face. On his forearm, Brian can see the heroin tracks.

"Paul… This isn't real… Our childhood bedroom, our fishing spot," he shakes his head and sets the rod down on the bridge. "None of this is real. You died. You died twenty years ago."

"I know, brother," Paul tells him. "I know this isn't real. But it was nice to see you again."

Paul sets his own rod down and hugs Brian before walking back in the direction that they came from. In the distance, Brian sees a doorway with a dim light shining through it. He knows exactly where it leads, back to their old bedroom again.

"Stop! What's happening?" Brian calls after his brother.

"Don't go!"

"I got to go, Brian." Paul stops and turns to face his brother. "Dad is waiting for me. I need to go back to my most horrible memory."

The memory of being pulled into the darkness with his father, when the Devil took him for his sins, returns to Brian.

"Purgatory," he yells from across the bridge.

"Yes, brother," Paul looks back toward the door again. "It's been twenty years." Tears drop like rain from his eyes and Brian can only watch helplessly. "Twenty years of reliving a moment of intense suffering, followed by my most joyous memory, again and again…"

A movement ahead of Paul catches Brian's eyes. His father walks out of the doorway, wearing no shirt and with his belt unbuckled.

"I'm coming, father!" Paul calls out.

"Stop, Paul! Stop! Father gave his soul to the Devil to be forgiven of his sins… all his sins."

His brother hasn't listened, continuing to walk toward the door until he arrives in front of his father.

"Son, I am sorry for my sins. I am sorry for what I did to you."

For the longest time, neither of them move and then, after glancing back at Brian, Paul nods slowly. "I forgive you, father," Paul tells the old man, burnt and scorched and unrecognizable compared to the one he's had to endure for the past twenty years.

This one, the broken man who's suffered for his sins, embraces Paul. Then, he points to a spot on a hill near the end of the bridge and says, "Go."

With that, his father turns around and walks back into the childhood bedroom of his sons, slamming it shut behind him.

Paul, seemingly unsurprised by what has transpired in only a few short moments, waves back at Brian and walks to the hill that his father pointed toward. When he approaches, a bright light appears and Paul waves again. Brian knows that this moment is the real goodbye.

"I love you, little brother, I'm allowed to leave this place now." Paul tells him before walking toward the light and fading into nonexistence amid the brightness.

Brian is left standing alone in his brother's purgatory, uncertain of what to do or where to go when he hears Rosa's voice calling out to him from across the bridge. He begins to walk toward the sound, but stops dead in his tracks as a familiar whiff of sweet tobacco hits his nose. It's the smell of Papa Legba. He can still hear Rosa calling out to him when he turns away from her voice and instead follows the smell of smoke into the darkness, taking neither the bridge nor the path to his childhood bedroom. He walks in blindly and, when he walks out of the darkness, he finds himself at the crossroads. Papa Legba stands there, as if he's been waiting for him. The Loa chuckles and exhales a puff of cigar smoke.

"Ah Brian, you have returned to the crossroads."

"I don't understand. How did I get here? I was in purgatory."

"Because here is where all roads lead," Papa Legba says with a tone that suggests this is the obvious answer to the question. "You and I have unfinished business!"

"A son for a sin?"

Papa Legba laughs again and Brian comes to terms with the idea that the trickster has been playing with him all this time. "Yes. Did you not find your Ben free of the spell?"

Brian recalls the way his son behaved. He certainly seemed better.

"Did you find a smile on his pretty face? Wasn't your Ben better? No more holes to run from."

"Yes," the father reluctantly admits.

"Ah yes, so you made a good deal… a son for a sin".

"No, I cannot trade one son for another. I cannot give you Rosa's child!"

Papa Legba reminds him for the millionth time, "What is done cannot be undone."

Rosa's voice has not disappeared. Brian can still hear her calling out to him in the distance. He looks hopefully down one of the roads toward the sound of her voice. Before him, Papa Legba reaches for a collection of keys that hang from a giant brass hoop on his gaudy belt. Fingering through them until one is chosen, Papa Legba tsks.

"It is time, Brian." He holds the key out in front of him. "The Metra key."

"What are you doing? What is the Metra key?"
An evil laugh, one that's deep and sinister. "The key into the womb of a woman, fully baked or not." His voice heightens, booming through the crossroads like the crack of lightning. "It's time to pay your debt. The soul of the unborn carries great value!"

From the other side, a ripping feeling builds in Rosa's

belly as her cries turn to pain. Papa Legba begins to turn the key. Brian is about to try and stop Papa Legba, to dive onto the powerful being hiding behind a frail facade when he hears a voice behind him. "Brian."

He turns and sees his brother Paul standing there and, despite the joy he felt at seeing his brother find salvation, he embraces him. He's relieved that he isn't alone. "Paul! I saw you go toward the light."

"I know what you have done and I couldn't leave you here."

They both turn to face Papa Legba in solidarity.

"Ah, big brother," the Loa puffs smoke their way. "Welcome to the crossroads." Papa lowers the Metra key for the moment. "Perhaps you would like to make a trade as well?"

"No Papa Legba," Paul responds. "I am not here to trade, but rather to pay a debt."

Papa Legba opens his coat and pulls out a small black book, flipping through the pages. A moment later, he looks up with narrowed eyes. "Paul Brennan Jr. has no debt upon me."

"A son for a sin! I, the son of Paul Howard Brennan, the murderer of Jonas Biassou, call upon Papa Legba to honor the trade made between himself and my brother. Take me, my father's son, for my father's sin."

"But Paul," Brian interjects.

Paul stares him down, taller and more confident than Brian's ever seen him. This is a man who has suffered endlessly and he's grown strong. "No," he tells his brother. "Let it be."

"I accept!" Papa Legba shouts, whipping through the crossroads.

"Brian!" Rosa's voice rings out again, this time teary.

"Go…" Paul turns to his brother. "Go back to your beautiful family."

"What will become of you?"

"It is my sin to bear, not yours." He holds his arm out, revealing the track lines of his heroin usage, of his sins. "What has already happened cannot be undone." Grabbing Brian by the shoulders, he tells his brother honestly, in a voice thick with emotion. "It was never an overdose. When I put that needle in my arm, I knew what I was doing, just like you thought I did all these years. I took my own life that day. I chose to carry our family's sins. Just like the Scare Game… When I told you to stay under the covers, to tuck in all the edges and not peek, I would stay awake, uncovered. I wanted to make sure father saw me, to make sure the beast always found me first." Paul shakes his head sadly. "Don't you see, Brian? It was always my burden to bear."

Brian doesn't know he's crying until his hands come up to brush the tears away. Paul spins him by his shoulders, pushing him back in the direction of his family, to the sound of Rosa's voice.

"Go… Return to your family."

As Brian turns to walk back into the darkness, he says one last thing to his brother, "Thank you, my brother. I will never stop loving you."

Slipping through the darkness in the next step, Brian opens his eyes and sees Rosa and Lady Darg leaning over him. He's on the floor within the sea salt circle. Both women, seeing that he's all right, lean in and wrap their arms around him in a hug, Rosa squealing with relief.

Their ordeal is finally over.

•••

Another Friday rolls around, bringing with it Ben and Morgan. When they arrive home, Brian walks into the kitchen to the most beautiful sight: his girlfriend making tacos for dinner. Aromas and colors of fresh vegetables make the table a happy space and he races up to her, hugging her from behind as she giggles and swats at his arms.

They eat together as a family, their game making another return. Brian thinks it will be a daily tradition moving forward as they go around the table from person to person.

"What's your favorite memory of the day?"

"Family being right here with us," Brian answers without thinking.

"I get to play a French girl in the school performance," Morgan says.

"Taco dinner," Ben laughs, choosing the food again.

"But last time you said pizza!" Morgan joins his laughter.

"I know, and now it's tacos," he says after a crunchy bite into the delicious meal.

The family laughs.

Rosa says, "Mine is that we are having a baby."

Everyone at the table's jaw drops.

ABOUT THE AUTHOR

A.G. SULLIVAN

Award winning author A.G. Sullivan grew up on Cape Cod in the small town of Dennis Port, Massachusetts. Since his youth he loved the art of story-telling. He studied at the Boston Architectural Center and later at the University of Phoenix, earning his degree in 1999. He lives with his two children in Arizona.

Known for his *Katzenstein Kids Trilogy* as well as his phycological thriller, *Trypophobia*. His work has earned him 5-STARS from READERS' FAVORITE, as well as a FIREBIRD BOOK AWARD.

CONNECT ONLINE

🌐 www.agsullivan.info
𝐟 facebook.com/agsullivanaz1
📷 instagram.com/AGSullivanaz
𝕏 x.com/agsullivanaz